Sin No More

Sin No More

KIMBERLA LAWSON ROBY

wm

WILLIAM MORROW

An Imprint of HarperCollinsPublishers

SIN NO MORE. Copyright © 2008 by Kimberla Lawson Roby. All rights reserved. Printed in the United States of America. No part of this book may be used or reproduced in any manner whatsoever without written permission except in the case of brief quotations embodied in critical articles and reviews. For information address HarperCollins Publishers, 10 East 53rd Street, New York, NY 10022.

HarperCollins books may be purchased for educational, business, or sales promotional use. For information please write: Special Markets Department, HarperCollins Publishers, 10 East 53rd Street, New York, NY 10022.

FIRST EDITION

Designed by Kara Strubel

Library of Congress Cataloging-in-Publication Data has been applied for.

ISBN 978-0-06-089250-0

08 09 10 11 12 OV/RRD 10 9 8 7 6 5 4 3 2 1

This novel is dedicated to my entire readership—
the people who make my career possible.
Thank you for such a joyous journey.

ACKNOWLEDGMENTS

The same as I've done with every single book I've written, I must begin by thanking God for everything. I thank Him for giving me blessings I never even imagined and for allowing me to celebrate the release of my tenth novel, *Sin No More*.

Will, for being my heart, my rock, my absolute joy; my mom, for being the best example in the world for me to follow—I never miss a day thinking of you and remembering all the happy times we shared together; my brothers, Willie and Michael Stapleton, for all the unconditional love and support any sister could ever hope for and for all the happy childhood memories, those that bring tears to my eyes and leave a smile on my face even as I write this—I am so proud of both of you; my stepson and daughter-in-law, Trenod and LaTasha Vines-Roby, for all your love and support. Of course, I can't say enough about your exceptional business acumen—so much so that I simply can't resist encouraging all of my Minneapolis and surrounding area readers to visit my stepson's fabulous barbershop, Twin City Cutz, in Crystal, Minnesota!

My aunts (Ada Tennin, Fannie Haley, Mary Lou Beasley, Vernell Tennin, Ollie Tennin, and Marie Tennin), my uncles (Clifton Tennin Jr., Ben Tennin, Luther Tennin, James Tennin, Charlie Beasley, Bob Thomas, and Earl Rome), all of my cousins (I have a ton of them, but I must mention Patricia Haley in particular, since we grew up more like sisters than we did first cousins. And hey to you, too, Jeffrey and little Tajanae!), and my nieces and nephews for all their love and support.

Kelli Tunson Bullard for nearly a lifetime of friendship, the kind I could never, ever imagine living without—thirty-six years and counting. You know I'll be the loudest person cheering at your graduation when you receive your RN degree, and Kel, I just couldn't be more happy for you and the straight As you've received every single semester, especially at this stage in our lives.

Lori Whitaker Thurman for more than two decades of extraordinary friendship and far too many other wonderful reasons to list here. Thank you for everything and know that life could certainly never the same without you.

Janell Francine Green for three decades of friendship, the sort of genuine friendship that words simply cannot explain and for never changing—not once since I've known you.

My friend and fellow author Victoria Christopher Murray, for always being so excited about my stories and for the closeness we share as friends in this amazing world of publishing. To my friend and fellow author, Trisha R. Thomas, for always being so kind and for being such a joy to talk to.

My agent, Elaine Koster, for ten of the most incredible years I could have ever prayed for—thank you for just being you; my editor, Carolyn Marino, for being the best in the business and for being one of the most pleasant people I know; my publisher, Lisa Gallagher, for genuinely caring about not just my work but about me as a person; my publicist, Pamela Spengler-Jaffee, for working so tirelessly at promoting my work and for keeping me so encouraged; to the entire sales force and all the other wonderful people at HarperCollins/William Morrow who work hard at getting my books out to the masses. What a blessing each of you is.

My website designer, Pamela Walker-Williams, at Pageturner.net and Lori Whitaker Thurman at Book Connections for all that both of you do to promote my work.

Dr. Betty Price at Crenshaw Christian Center for reading this novel a full year before its release date and for continuing to support me so unconditionally and with so much love. To Dr. Frederick K. C. Price, D.D., for all the wonderful sermons that Will and I continue to learn so much from every single time we hear you speak. What a blessing you are to millions of people worldwide.

Mrs. Eldora Davis for so willingly inviting Will and me into your home so we could finish our church orientation lessons—the one we should have finished a few years ago! Your spirit is so kind and we sincerely appreciate all that you are.

Kathy Vigna, my former boss at Sundstrand more than twenty years ago—the person I've always admired and who I aspired to be like professionally. Thank you for still being such a special person in my life.

To all of the remarkable book clubs who read my work as well as those that went out of their way to host such amazing events for me during the *Love and Lies* tour: Book Bunchers—WSFA-TV in Montgomery (Tonya Terry, Anchor), Euphoria Book Club in Miami (Patricia Nolan), Sisters That Love to Read in Raleigh (Stephanie Holloway), Sista Girl Book Club in Omaha (Sherri Culliver), and G.U.R.U. Book Club in Milwaukee (April Johnson).

To my local media supporters, Andy Gannon and Aaron Wilson at WIFR-TV; Jennie Pollock, Edith Lee Webster, and everyone else at the *Rockford Register Star;* Charlyne Blatcher Martin, host of Insight's *Something to Talk About* and to everyone at WREX-TV and WTVO-TV for being so gracious year after year.

To all of the bookstores, retailers, and salespeople who sell my books, every media person in all the other markets who publicizes them, and, most important, to all of my readers everywhere. I am indebted to all of you.

Much love and God bless,

Kimberla Lawson Roby

Prologue

SIX MONTHS EARLIER

The phone rang and when Curtis saw the words *Mitchell Memorial* on the Caller ID screen, his stomach immediately started to churn. He felt a nervousness that he hadn't felt in a very long while and the fact that his wife, Charlotte, was sitting right next to him and had clearly seen where the call was coming from wasn't helping.

He knew with everything in him that Tabitha was calling to announce the baby's arrival.

He answered after the third ring. "Hello."

"Baby, I've got the best news," she said, clearly ecstatic. "You've got the most beautiful little girl in the whole wide world!"

"Is she healthy?" was all Curtis could think to say.

"She's wonderful. She's the most precious little thing I've ever seen and, baby . . . she looks just like you. I mean, she's only been here for less than an hour but I can already see so many of your features. Baby, she's everything you could possibly ever hope for and you just have to come see her. You have to come see what a beautiful child you and I have created together."

Curtis was speechless. Literally speechless. Not because he didn't have a ton of questions for Tabitha, because he did. But it was just that Charlotte was now standing across the room, looking as though she were ready to pounce on him at any moment. She was outraged and he knew he needed to choose his words very carefully and end this conversation with Tabitha as soon as possible. Not to mention, Charlotte would become even more irate if she knew Tabitha was referring to him as "baby."

"Did you hear me, baby?" Tabitha continued. "I said, you need to come see your daughter."

"You know I can't do that," Curtis finally told her. "You know we have an agreement, and once you send me a certified copy of the birth certificate, I'll be transferring the last half of the fifty thousand dollars into your account."

"And then what?" she asked, and Curtis could tell her happy attitude was changing.

"You and I won't contact each other again. I'll continue to send you fifteen hundred dollars every month for child support until the child turns eighteen, and I'll also pay for all health care. Then, when she's out of high school, I'll cover all college expenses, and I'll give her a monthly allowance until she graduates. But other than that, this will be our last conversation."

"How can you be so cold? I mean, how can you sit over there and just pretend you don't have a new baby to worry about?"

"I'm really sorry, Tabitha. More than you know. But this is the way it has to be. You and I made a terrible mistake, and I regret that the baby will have to suffer certain consequences, but this really is best for everyone."

"What you mean is that this is what's best for that crazy wife you're married to."

"Like I said, I'm sorry."

"Don't you even want to know her name?" Tabitha asked, and at the same time, Charlotte said, "Curtis, why are you apologizing to that witch? Hunh? I mean, do you even see me standing here?"

Curtis sighed and wished he could run and hide the way he had done as a child whenever he'd done something he shouldn't have. He wished he could vanish and never have to deal with this fiasco ever again. Better, he wished he could turn back time, because if he could, he would surely do things a whole lot differently. He would be faithful to Charlotte and he would never get mixed up with Tabitha under any circumstances.

But it was too late for that. Too late and no way to send his baby girl back into her mother's womb.

"Tabitha, please try to understand. I can't change the past but know that I pray only great things for you and the baby. I pray for all the blessings I know God already has in store for you."

Tabitha laughed out loud, and Curtis wondered what was so funny.

"At this point, your prayers don't mean one thing to me. And just for the record, I'm not asking you to change the past. I'm asking you to do right by your daughter or else."

"Or else what?"

"Keep blowing off our baby like she's some unwanted little orphan, and you'll see exactly what I'm talking about."

"You know what, Tabitha," he said. "I think it's time we end this conversation."

"Do whatever you want but just know that I'm not going anywhere and neither is Curtina. She's here to stay and you can either do right by her voluntarily or involuntarily. Makes no difference to me. But understand that if I have to force you, it won't be pretty."

A second later, Curtis heard the phone click.

She'd hung up but her words were still lingering midair and making him more uncomfortable than he wanted to be. Uncomfortable because her tone had sounded vindictive and like some sort of guarantee.

Curtis pressed the Off button and set the cordless on the kitchen island.

Charlotte folded her arms and leaned against the refrigerator. "She was threatening you, wasn't she?"

"If you want to call it that."

"What did she say?"

"It's not even worth going into. You heard what I told her and whether she likes it or not, she's going to have to accept it."

"And you're naive enough to think it's going to be that simple?"

"Why wouldn't it be?" he said, although he knew Charlotte had a more than valid point. Especially after just hearing Tabitha speak to him the way she had.

"Curtis, are you that blind? Are you so blind that you can't see that this woman is going to be a serious problem?"

"What can she do? Because it's not like I want anything to do with her. When I said I was committed to you and that I was finished with Tabitha, I meant it."

"But now there's a baby in the picture. It was one thing when she was pregnant but now that she's actually had it, she's thinking she has another chance with you."

"I don't think so."

"Oh, really?"

"Yes. Really."

"And why is that?" Charlotte asked, now tapping her foot against the floor with her arms still folded. She could be so sarcastic when she wanted to be, and Curtis could hardly stand it.

"Because she knows my decision."

"What did she say to you exactly?"

"That she just had the baby and that it's a girl."

"I hate that whore," Charlotte said, moving toward the counter and slamming a crystal glass into the sink.

Curtis could no longer see the gold-trimmed goblet, but he'd heard it shatter into what seemed a million pieces. He knew Charlotte was thinking of their daughter, Marissa, and how she'd tumbled down the stairs, hit her head, and died almost instantly. He knew Charlotte despised the fact that she no longer had a daughter of her own but now Tabitha proudly did.

"Baby, please," he said moving closer to where she was standing and pulling her into his arms once again. "I love you with everything in me, so please don't let this come between us. Not now."

This time, to Curtis's surprise, Charlotte didn't pull away from him. She hugged him tightly and wept in a way that said her pain was deep within her soul. She wept over the loss of her own child and now Curtis was feeling sorrier than he had been.

What a huge mess all of this had turned out to be, and he had no idea what he was going to do about it. If he didn't go see his new daughter, there was no telling what Tabitha might actually do. But on the other hand, if he did, Charlotte would spin into an uproar and the peace they'd shared between them over the last year would quickly cease to exist.

So his hands were tied. Tied because he loved his wife and even though he hadn't seen her yet, he loved his baby girl. Curtina. His youngest and the one Tabitha had decided to name after him. His own flesh and blood.

Curtis continued holding Charlotte closely against his chest but he couldn't help trying to picture what his daughter looked like. He tried and tried and without warning, tears slowly streamed down his face.

He and Charlotte cried while still holding each other.

They cried, but sadly, for very different reasons.

Chapter 1

Charlotte couldn't imagine life being any better than it was currently. She and Curtis were closer than they'd ever been and, best of all, they hadn't heard from Tabitha. Not once. Which was a wonderful surprise because Charlotte had been sure Tabitha was going to become the intrusion of a lifetime. Especially since she'd called the day the baby was born and tried to get Curtis to come see it. Or actually, come see her, because whether Curtis wanted to admit it or not, Charlotte knew Tabitha still wanted him. She knew because she'd never heard of any mistress who didn't have high hopes that the man she was sleeping with would somehow miraculously leave his wife for her. She knew because to be honest, she'd felt the same way herself when Curtis had still been married to Tanya. Her desire had been as wrong as wrong could be, however, she had still wanted what she wanted and hadn't cared a whole lot about who might be hurt in the end.

But right now, none of that mattered. What mattered was that she and Curtis had just finished making exceptional love to each other and they were lying in bed, snuggled closely, enjoying a beautiful moment.

"Woman, what in the world are you trying to do to me?" Curtis asked, breathing more easily than he had been five minutes ago.

Charlotte chuckled. "Are you saying you can't handle it?"

"Me? *The* Curtis Black? Not able to handle my wife when it comes to making love? Please."

"Well, that's what it sounds like."

"As Matthew would say, 'Girl, don't get it twisted.'"

They both laughed.

"You're right," she said. "That's exactly what he would say. Although now he doesn't have much of anything to say at all."

"I know. He's been on the quiet side ever since we told him the truth but I still say we did the right thing. He needed to know that I'm not his biological father."

Charlotte heard what Curtis was saying but if she'd had it her way, she would have left well enough alone and worried about telling Matthew the truth at a later date. When Marissa had died, she'd begun feeling as though it wasn't a good idea to keep secrets of any kind from anyone, including Matthew. She'd kept secrets most of her adult life and far too many people had been hurt because of them, so she'd decided she didn't want Matthew learning about his paternity from anyone other than Curtis and her.

But now he was basically moping around the house, not saying any more than he had to to either of them, and Charlotte was starting to regret telling him anything. She'd wanted him to know the truth but she hadn't wanted him to feel the amount of pain she could tell he was feeling and she certainly hadn't wanted to create any tension or distance.

"He'll be okay," Curtis finally said. "It's just that this is all very new to him and it's going to take some getting used to."

"I guess. But I hope he's okay sooner rather than later."

"He will be. He'll be fine."

Charlotte nestled closer to Curtis and laid her head on his chest but as soon as she did, the phone rang.

"Who could that be?" she said. "It has to be at least eleven o'clock."

"Something must be wrong," Curtis added.

Charlotte picked up the cordless from the nightstand and sighed deeply. It was Tabitha.

"Hello?"

"Could I speak to Curtis, please?"

"Tabitha, do you realize what time it is?"

"No, and to be honest, I really don't care."

Charlotte sat up and swung her legs over the side of the bed.

"You don't care?"

"That's what I said, didn't I?"

"I don't believe you. You're actually calling here this late at night to speak to my husband, and you've got the nerve to be getting smart with me? You've got to be kidding."

"Look, Charlotte, will you just get over yourself and put Curtis on the phone? I need to discuss something with him about Curtina."

The whole idea of the name Curtina was enough to make Charlotte cringe. She was annoyed by the fact that Tabitha had chosen to give the baby a name as close to Curtis as she could. Not to mention, Curtina had to be the ugliest name she'd ever heard.

"First of all," Charlotte began, "you've been told more than once not to call this house and not to contact Curtis in any way, so why can't you just leave us alone? Why can't you just move on and forget about him?"

"Because whether you want to accept it or not, Curtis and I have a baby together. We have a gorgeous little daughter and you're just upset because you don't have any children with him. I mean, I know you claimed Matthew was his and then you lied and schemed about Marissa for as long as you could, but in the end, neither of those children was his."

Charlotte felt her breathing accelerate a few notches and was thankful she wasn't in the same room with Tabitha. If she had been, she would have beaten her unmercifully. She would have done whatever necessary to make sure Tabitha never bothered her and Curtis ever again.

"Will you just put him on the phone?!" she yelled.

"No. And the only way you'll speak to my husband is over my dead body."

"Oh, and you think that can't be arranged?"

"Are you threatening my life?"

"Give me the phone," Curtis interrupted, and reached for it.

But Charlotte snatched it away from him, turned on the lamp, and stood up.

"You look here, you crazy heifer," Charlotte said matter-of-factly. "Just because you were stupid enough to mess around with a married man, stupid enough to get pregnant by him, and then stupid enough to think he was going to leave me once that baby was born, well, that's simply not my fault. You hear me?"

"Oh, I hear you very well, but which do you think is worse, Charlotte? My getting pregnant by Curtis or your getting pregnant by your cousin's husband? And let's not forget about how you got pregnant by that schizophrenic, Aaron, who tried to burn down your house while you were still inside it. So, no matter which way you look at any of this, you're as loose as Mary Magdalene. Actually, you're much lower because even Mary Magdalene had the decency to take Jesus's advice to go and sin no more. And those are not my words, sweetheart, they're Curtis's."

Charlotte pressed the off button and threw the phone at Curtis as hard as she could. It landed against his chest.

"What did you do that for?"

"You actually had the audacity to say I was worse than Mary Magdalene?"

"What are you talking about?"

"That tramp just told me you compared me to her. So, is it true?"

"Charlotte, why are you listening to anything Tabitha tells you?"

"No, just answer my question. Did you ever say that about me?"

Curtis leaned his head against the headboard and covered his face, and Charlotte knew Tabitha wasn't lying.

"Is that what you really think of me?" she asked.

"No. No."

"Then why did you tell her that?"

"You know how hurt and angry I was after that whole Aaron situation, and I said a lot of things I didn't mean."

"Still. How could you be low enough to talk about me that way to some woman you were sleeping with?"

"Baby, you know Matthew is in the other room, so please don't speak that way."

"I'll speak any way I feel like speaking. And for the record, which do you think is worse? Words or committing adultery?"

"I don't know. You tell me."

Charlotte knew he was referring to her own infidelity, but she ignored him. She pretended he hadn't said a word and kept on her mission.

"I'm telling you right now, Curtis. You'd better stop Tabitha from calling here or else."

"You know I've already told her not to contact me, and she hasn't until now."

"I knew when we didn't hear from her over the last six months, it was all too good to be true. I always knew it was just a matter of time before she started thinking she still had a chance with you."

"Tabitha knows what we had is over. She knows it's over for good, so I don't know why she called here."

"You really piss me off when you do that."

"Do what?"

"Pretend like you're so naive about everything."

"I'm not pretending anything. I'm just saying that Tabitha knows how I feel about you and that there's not one chance of her and me being together."

"Well, all I know is that you'd better handle this. You'd better handle it before it causes some serious problems between you and me. I told you I would stay with you but I only agreed to forgive you because you claimed that your only involvement with that woman would be through child support payments."

"And that's the only involvement I've had."

"All of this makes me sick. It makes me wish I had divorced you right when you told me she was pregnant."

"You don't mean that."

"Oh . . . yes . . . I . . . do. Because if I had, I wouldn't be receiving phone calls like the one I just answered."

"I can't believe you're saying this. Not after all this time."

"You thought just because I never brought up this pathetic situation that it doesn't bother me?"

"No, that's not what I'm saying."

"Then what are you saying?"

"That I thought we made a pact. I thought we agreed to forgive each other and move on with our lives."

"We did. And I was fine. That is, until a few minutes ago."

"If it will make you feel any better, I'll call Tabitha and explain to her that if she contacts me again, she'll be violating our contract."

"From the way she sounded on the phone, she probably couldn't care less. As a matter of fact, I'll bet it's only a matter of time before she does something even worse."

"What else could she do?"

"Go public. Demand more money. Drop the baby on our doorstep. You tell me."

"When we agreed to pay her that fifty-thousand-dollar lump sum and she signed on the dotted line, she knew that meant complete silence."

"Yeah right."

"All I can do is call her."

"No."

"Then what do you want me to do?"

"I don't know, but I don't want you talking to her."

Curtis shook his head in frustration and Charlotte gave him a dirty look. Then she stormed out of the bedroom.

She felt like screaming and the only reason she didn't was because Matthew's room was just down the hallway. If only Curtis hadn't started that affair with Tabitha and gotten her pregnant. Life would be so much easier. So much happier. So much more bearable.

But no matter how she fantasized about the way things could have been, reality struck her straight across her face. To be honest, it struck her so forcibly that she wondered how she would ever be able to live with it. She did love Curtis and of course she wanted the best for Matthew, but after hearing Tabitha's indignant tone, she didn't know if she could deal with this for years to come. Not to mention, the idea that Tabitha had a baby with Curtis and she didn't made her ill. It made her wish for certain tragedies. Tragedies that would free them from Tabitha for good. The kind of tragedy that would allow her and Curtis to live happily ever after the way they'd planned.

The kind of tragedy that might happen by accident.

Or intentionally.

Chapter 2

Curtis strolled across the bedroom to the window and gazed toward the brightly lit sky. The moon was only half the size it would be by the end of this month but the stars shone luminously. The evening had started out beautiful and peaceful, and he couldn't help wondering how it had turned into such a nightmare.

Although who was he kidding? He knew it had gone sour because of that phone call from Tabitha. And the thing was, he didn't know exactly how he truly felt about it. Sure, Charlotte had made it clear that she didn't want him communicating with Tabitha—ever—but deep down he really wanted to see his daughter. His daughter who was now six months old, yet he still hadn't laid eyes on her. That is with the exception of a photo Tabitha had sent to the church that Charlotte didn't know about.

He could still remember the warm and loving feeling he'd felt as soon as he'd pulled it from the envelope, especially when he'd seen that she really did look like him. Although, to be honest, he'd never once doubted that he was the father and the only reason he'd basically forced Tabitha to have the DNA test was that Charlotte refused to accept anything different. Then, once the results had confirmed what he'd already known, he'd decided to do whatever it took to satisfy his wife.

That was then. Because now he not only wanted to see Curtina, he needed to see her. He needed to see and hold the newest addition to his offspring, and he didn't know how much longer he'd be able to live without her. As a matter of fact, at this very moment, he had a mind to tell Charlotte that he needed to run over to the church to pick up something for tomorrow's sermon; that way he could slip by Tabitha's to see his baby girl. But he knew she'd never believe him, not with it being almost midnight. Not to mention, he was trying terribly hard not to start up his old habits—habits such as lying and sneaking around. He was trying his best not to do anything that Charlotte didn't approve of. Because even with the devastation of Tabitha's pregnancy and their mourning over Marissa, they were now happier than ever and his priority was to keep Charlotte content. He'd made a commitment to her and their marriage and he would just have to forget about having a relationship with his daughter.

Curtis left the bedroom, headed down the hallway and stopped at the guest bedroom he knew Charlotte was holed up in. He reached toward the knob, preparing to turn it, but decided it was probably best to let her cool off a bit more. So, instead, he walked toward Matthew's room and eased open the door. He expected him to be asleep but the glare of the television screen against his face showed that he wasn't.

"Son, I thought you'd be completely knocked out by now."

Curtis waited for him to say something but he didn't.

"Anything good on?"

"Not really."

"You know tomorrow is your Sunday to help the trustees with the morning collection, right?"

"Yes."

"I know you don't love doing it, but now that you're thirteen, you're old enough to start learning more of the business aspects of the church. Plus, it's not like I can trust anyone more than I can trust you."

Matthew just looked at him. Then back at the television.

"Son, I promise you'll eventually feel a whole lot better about what we told you last month. Your mother and I can't apologize enough but telling you the truth really was the best thing to do. You understand that, right?"

"I guess."

"I know you're hurt but please don't ever forget that I love you. I love you with all my heart, and I would give my life for you if it was necessary."

This time Matthew averted his eyes from the TV and looked at Curtis.

"Matt, you have my word that nothing will ever change between you and me. Not ever."

"But, Dad, why did Mom do what she did? Why did she have to be with cousin Anise's husband?"

"Unfortunately, we all make mistakes. We all fall short and that's just the way it is."

"I'm so mad at her, Dad," he finally said, sitting up and breaking into tears. "I don't want to be, but I can't help it."

"I know," Curtis said, sitting down on the side of the bed. "But you have to forgive her. She's your mother, and she loves you so much. And she's worried sick about you."

Matthew hugged his father and sobbed the way he had when he was only five and Curtis could no longer maintain his composure. Before long, he felt tears welling up in his own eyes and he had no other words to say.

But Matthew eventually did.

"No matter who my other father is, you'll always be the most important person in my life. I'll always love you more, okay?"

"Of course. And it's like I just told you, nothing will ever change. You'll always be my son, regardless."

They held each other for a minute or so longer and then Curtis said, "Why don't you turn off the television and try to get some rest."

"I love you, Dad."

"I love you, too, son."

Once Curtis walked back into the hallway, he rethought his decision to leave Charlotte alone and went into the room she was lying in.

"What is it that you want?" She spoke quickly and in a nasty tone.

"Baby, please. Let's not do this, okay?"

"Well, Curtis, what do you expect? Do you think I'm going to just pretend that I like having Tabitha call here, disrespecting me and trying to get you to come be with her?"

"No, but I've already told you that I'm not going to have anything to do with her. I've told you multiple times and that's all I can do."

"I know you have, but this whole thing still upsets me in more ways than one."

"Look," he said, sitting down next to her the way he had with Matthew. "I'm sorry and I'll always be sorry. But the truth is, I can't change what happened. I wish I could, but it's just not possible. It's not possible and all that should matter now anyway is that I love you and no one else."

"I know," she finally relented. "And I'm sorry for flying off the handle the way I did earlier."

"Let's just forget the whole thing and move on. That's all I want."

"Me, too, but you know what? I'm still worried about Matthew."

"I just looked in on him and we had a nice conversation."

"He actually talked to you?"

"Not at first, but eventually he said a lot and he was crying."

Charlotte sighed. "This is all my fault and I don't know how I'll ever be able to forgive myself for hurting him like this. Because it almost seems like he's more upset with me than he is with you."

Curtis wanted to tell her how right she was but he didn't want her to feel any worse or any more guilty. He certainly would never tell her that Matthew had wanted to know why she'd slept with another man and then pretended Curtis was his father. Matthew hadn't asked about it with those exact words but it was pretty obvious that this was what he'd meant.

"What you need to do is spend as much time with him as possible and apologize as much as you can," Curtis advised.

"I just hope he doesn't stop loving me."

"What?" he said, lifting Charlotte's chin with his finger. "Baby, you're his mother. So, trust me, he'll never stop loving you."

"If I have to spend the rest of my life making this up to him, I will. Because it's not like he should have to suffer just because his biological father and I chose to do the wrong thing. No child should ever have to suffer because of some horrible decision two adults made."

Curtis didn't respond, but he agreed with Charlotte completely.

He agreed because he felt the same way about his own baby, Curtina.

Chapter 3

T his is the day the Lord hath made, let us rejoice and be glad in it," Curtis said out loud, even though no one was with him. This was one of his all-time favorite scriptures and after last night, he was hoping it would give him a certain sense of peace.

For the last hour, he'd been sitting in his study at the church, praying and reviewing the sermon he would be delivering this morning, but no matter how hard he tried, he just couldn't seem to stay focused. He couldn't stop thinking about the call from Tabitha and how he really wanted to see Curtina.

Curtis sighed, leaned back in his chair, and closed his eyes. Then he shook his head in disappointment. He was so sorry for all the problems he'd caused for so many people and sorry that year after year, he'd continued to disobey God's Word repeatedly. He was sorry because God had certainly given him more chances than he'd deserved. Specifically, like the time he'd been ousted from his first Chicago church but had eventually found a second. Then there was the time he'd been kicked out of his second church, but had been blessed enough to found his very own right here in Mitchell.

Or even more was the way he'd hurt his first wife, Tanya, the mother of his firstborn child, yet she'd still found it in her heart to forgive him. Or how about when he'd totally misused his second wife, Mariah, but had still been blessed with his third and current wife, Charlotte.

And Lord knows, the most memorable chance God had given him was the time He'd been gracious enough to spare his life. The time his former mistress, Adrienne, had decided she couldn't live without him and had walked into the sanctuary and shot him down from the pulpit. Just thinking about that entire incident sent chills rushing through his body and he regretted the day he'd begun messing around with her.

As a matter of fact, he was tired of regretting anything. He was tired of doing wrong, repenting, and then doing wrong again. His motto had always seemed to be, "It's okay to sin as long as you remember to pray about it later—it's okay as long as you ask God to forgive you."

But deep down, Curtis had always known this wasn't the way God wanted him or anyone else to live. Yes, it was true that God was a forgiving God but Curtis knew God didn't mean for people to abuse His mercy. He knew this more than anything else, and he also knew he would have a lot of questions to answer on Judgment Day.

Just as Curtis opened his eyes and leaned forward, he heard a knock at his door.

"Come in."

"If you have a few minutes, I need to speak with you about a couple of items," Reverend Tolson said, entering the office.

"No problem. Have a seat."

Reverend Tolson sat in one of the seats directly in front of Curtis's mahogany desk but didn't seem too happy. Reverend Tolson had been the interim pastor ever since Curtis had begun traveling around the country, doing book signings and speaking engagements, but now that Curtis was home on a regular basis, Curtis had been delivering the Sunday morning messages himself, at least two to three every month, and he wondered if Tolson was finding issue with it. Especially since Curtis had noticed that, as of late, Tolson had been somewhat short with him. At first, Curtis had thought maybe it was his imagination, but the more he thought about it, Tolson's tone on last Sunday had sounded almost sarcastic and when Curtis had asked him to direct the morning's praise and worship service, he'd seemed sort of rebellious.

"Just quickly before you begin," Curtis said, "I have a couple of things to request of you. First, I need you to go visit and pray with two of our elderly, shut-in members. Here are their names and addresses, and if you could see them this afternoon or tomorrow that would be good. The other thing is that I need you to oversee this Wednesday's Bible study session."

"Again?" Tolson blurted out.

"Yes. Unless there's some reason you can't."

"See, this is why I needed to talk to you. Ever since you came off the road, I've felt like nothing more than some lowly assistant and you and I both know that this isn't what I signed up for."

Curtis leaned back in his chair and locked his fingers together. There was a whole lot he already wanted to say but instead he said, "Go on."

"My contract states that I'm supposed to be the interim pastor for at least another two years, so with all due respect, I think you need to step back and let me do my job."

Curtis stared at Tolson and then wondered if the man knew who he was dealing with. It was true that Curtis had changed for the better and was trying to live in a more God-like way, but he would never be told what he should or shouldn't do at his own church.

"I guess what I'm trying to say," Tolson continued, "is that I'm not happy with the current arrangement and something needs to be done about it."

"Is that right?"

"Yes."

"Well, I'm sorry to hear that because the bottom line is that

I'm the senior pastor and founder of this church and that means my elder board and I decide who does what and when."

"Maybe. But you just renewed my contract one year ago, and I don't see how you can simply ignore it."

"I'm not ignoring it. And that's why you're still being compensated what we promised."

"Nonetheless, you're not allowing me to do what I'm being paid for and I can't continue like this."

"Well, if that's the case, then you know what to do."

"Meaning?"

"Pack up and leave this church in the same amount of speed you rushed here in."

"To be honest, Pastor, I would like nothing more. But only if you buy me out. Only if you pay me for the two years I have left in my contract plus an additional year's worth of salary for my trouble."

See, it was people like Tolson who made life so difficult, Curtis thought. It was people like him that made men like Curtis say and do things they didn't want to. From the time this discussion had begun, Curtis had tried to keep an open mind and a friendly demeanor. But now Tolson was pushing too many buttons. He was acting too boldly, and it was time Curtis told him just the way things were going to be.

"You can either take the two years we owe you or nothing at all."

Tolson smiled at Curtis. "Then I guess you've decided to take the high road. Which is too bad because now I want more than what I was originally asking for."

"Man, you must be on crack or something if you think you can waltz in here, making all these outrageous demands. Now get out of my office before I put you out."

"If you know what's good for you, you'll do what I tell you."

"No, if you know what's good for you, you'll leave while you're still able," Curtis said and stood up.

Tolson stood as well. "Fine. I'm leaving. But just for the record, I do have ammunition. I have more than you could possibly ever imagine, and I certainly won't hesitate to use it if I have to. I'll do whatever I need to in order to get what's mine."

"I'm only going to say this one last time. Get out."

Tolson turned toward the door, opened it and then looked back at Curtis. "I'm not afraid of you or anyone else, Mr. World-Renowned Reverend Curtis Black, so if I were you, I'd consider myself warned."

After Tolson practically slammed the door, Curtis called Elder Jamison on his two-way pager. Elder Jamison was his right-hand man and confidant and he wanted to fill him in on the Tolson state of affairs as soon as possible. They didn't use two-way communication all the time, but always on Sunday mornings, just in case Curtis needed to locate him immediately.

"Where are you?" Curtis asked.

"Actually, I'm on my way up to your office right now. We have a situation."

"I'll see you in a minute."

Now what? And as Curtis strolled back around his desk, he hoped it wasn't Leroy again, out in the parking lot, flirting with all the women who stepped out of their vehicles, those that didn't have a man riding with them. They'd had a problem with him a couple of weeks ago and now Curtis was almost sorry they'd fed and clothed him a few months back. Of course, the church was in the business of helping anyone in need, especially the homeless, but Leroy was turning into a nuisance. Curtis liked him, but sometimes he was a bit much to take.

"Pastor, man," Elder Jamison said as soon as he entered. "There's a woman named Tabitha standing inside the back entrance, saying that if you won't see her, she and her baby are staying for service and then she's going to tell the congregation some very interesting news."

Curtis was floored. He couldn't believe Tabitha would go to such extremes, and he was already praying that Charlotte wouldn't find out about this.

"Pastor, are you listening to me?"

"Yes. I heard you. Bring her in."

"Who is this woman?"

"Elder Jamison, it's a long story."

"Are you in some sort of trouble? Because if you are, we can call the police."

"No. That won't be necessary."

"Well, then, I'm not leaving you alone with her."

"I'll be fine. Just go get her and bring her up the back way."

Elder Jamison looked dumbfounded and Curtis knew he was going to have to tell him everything. This had always been one of his greatest fears, that Tabitha would show up at the church. He'd feared it because with every scandal he'd gotten himself caught up in, the church was where they'd all been exposed.

When Tabitha and the baby arrived, Curtis asked Elder Jamison to wait outside and Elder Jamison closed the door.

"Tabitha, why are you here? We just went over this last night and you know we have an agreement. You know you're not supposed to come near me. You know you're not supposed to go public with any information regarding our past relationship or the baby."

"Well, Curtis," she said looking as radiant and as confident as ever. "I hate to ruin your little plan, but I've changed my mind. The contract doesn't stipulate anything about public places so the church is definitely not off limits to Curtina and me. We're just as welcome as anyone else who attends here."

"I can't believe you're doing this. Not now. Not when I paid you all that money up front and then I've been sending you child support payments without fail."

"But it's not enough."

"Why?"

"Because I want more."

"How much more money could you possibly need?"

"I'm not talking about money. I'm talking about your time."

"Charlotte will never stand for that and if you keep breaching our contract, she'll have you in court with a lawsuit. Now do you really want that?"

Tabitha laughed louder than Reverend Tolson had. "Your wife can do whatever she wants, but you'd better make sure she knows I'm ready for anything she throws my way. I'm ready for any and every court battle she wants to take me through because my daughter deserves to see her father the same as Matthew and Alicia. My daughter deserves better than the circumstances she's been forced into, and she deserves having not one, but both her parents in her life. And on a full-time basis."

Curtis was more than troubled by what he was hearing but he couldn't help noticing the gurgling sound coming from the baby carrier. He couldn't help watching the kicking of Curtina's tiny little feet even though they were covered with a blanket.

Tabitha must have sensed where his attention was now focused, because she quickly picked up Curtina and walked closer to where Curtis was standing. Curtis was amazed to see that she was even more beautiful in person than she was in her photo. Her eyes were so stunningly dark that if there were such a thing as black eyes, he would surely have to call them that. His daughter was a perfect little doll and when Tabitha placed her in his arms he never resisted. He was completely mesmerized by her being and tears slid down his face and onto Curtina's.

He held her in total silence and wished he never had to let her go.

He wished he could see her every day for the rest of his life and prayed that Charlotte would accept her. He prayed that Charlotte would be more reasonable and understanding than she had been because at this very moment, he knew he could no longer neglect his child. He loved Charlotte and he wanted them to be happy but he could not and would not allow Curtina to grow up not knowing or spending time with him. It just wasn't right and Charlotte would have to be okay with his decision.

Either that or he was prepared to deal with whatever issues he had to.

Chapter 4

Is everything okay?" Charlotte asked Curtis. They were on their way home from church and Matthew was sitting all the way back in the third row of the Cadillac SUV, watching some DVD.

"Curtis, did you hear me?" she said when he didn't respond.

"What . . . did you say something?"

"What's wrong with you?"

"Nothing. Why do you ask?"

"I'm asking because you're so quiet and you seem like you're in deep thought."

"I'm just thinking about what I have to do over the next few days. I have meetings every day this week."

"Even tomorrow? Because tomorrow is your day off."

"I know, and I'm sorry, but I have a meeting with Pastor Reynolds and Pastor Jones. We've been trying to get together for the longest and this was the only day we all were available."

Charlotte looked away from him and back toward the road.

"What?" Curtis asked.

"You know what."

"No. I don't. So tell me."

"You promised me that you wouldn't do any church business on Mondays. You promised me that this would be our day to spend together."

"I know and this is a one-time deal. I'll only be gone for maybe two or three hours at the most."

First it was the call from Tabitha last night and now this. Charlotte was trying to stay positive but she couldn't help being suspicious of Curtis and his sudden desire to meet with two of his minister friends. She hadn't heard him talk about them much at all lately and for the last year, it had been automatic that she and he would spend time together on his days off. They'd made a pact but now he was breaking it. She couldn't help but wonder why.

When they arrived home, Matthew darted up to his bedroom and Charlotte and Curtis followed behind to theirs. Once inside, Charlotte removed her St. John outfit and thought about her mother, who loved nice clothing but thought the idea of spending well over a thousand dollars on anything to wear was just plain ridiculous. Charlotte, of course, didn't see what the problem was, especially since she and Curtis could afford it. Not to mention, after all that Curtis had put her through, she deserved to have anything she wanted.

"Why are you acting so distant?" she asked.

"I'm not."

"Yes, you are. And now that we're on the subject, why were you doing all that crying in the pulpit this morning?"

"Charlotte, please. You've seen me filled with the Holy Spirit hundreds of times, so why was today so different?"

"Because it was. You seemed almost sad and like something was really wrong with you."

"You're just being paranoid."

"I hope so."

"You are."

Charlotte covered her head and face with a silk scarf so she wouldn't get makeup on the cashmere sweater she was getting ready to pull down over her head. She even did this when she tried on clothing at the mall because she didn't think it was fair to soil items that she might not end up purchasing in the first place.

"So where are we going for dinner?" she asked.

"It's up to you. Matthew mentioned pizza."

"Matthew always wants pizza, but today I was thinking we could go to a good steak house. Actually, we should have just gone directly there after church."

"It would have been nice," Curtis said, straightening the collar on the turtleneck he'd just slipped on. "But remember you were the one who promised Matthew we could come home first to change out of our dress clothes."

"I know, but only because I'm trying so hard to do whatever he wants."

"And there's nothing wrong with that, because right now, we both need to do everything we can to make him happy."

Charlotte watched Curtis's expression and no matter how well he was attempting to hide what he was thinking, she knew something was wrong. He was conversing with her like normal, but something was very different in comparison to when they'd left for church this morning.

"Curtis, did Tabitha try to call you again today?"

"No." He frowned. "Why do you ask?"

"Because something isn't right. I know you keep saying everything is okay, but I know you better than that."

"Okay, look. I'm bothered by this whole thing with Tabitha and Curtina. It bothers me because even though I agreed not to see Curtina, I know it's not the right thing to do."

"Of course, it's the right thing to do. That is, if you want to stay married to me."

"See, that's why I didn't want to say anything. You keep asking me what the problem is and now that I'm telling you, you're already getting upset."

"I'm upset because I thought I'd made myself clear. Before the baby was born, while that whore was carrying it and then once she'd had it. Actually, I thought I'd explained myself pretty well but apparently not, because you're still whining about this whole thing."

"You're impossible."

"No. You are. Because now all of a sudden you're thinking I'm going to just forget everything that happened and that I'm somehow going to say, 'Sure, Curtis, go see Tabitha and Curtina. Shoot, even spend the night with them if you want to.'"

Curtis looked at Charlotte and then went inside his closet.

Charlotte walked over and stood in front of it.

"What is it going to take for you to get what I'm saying?" she said, raising her voice.

"Look, I don't want to argue about this."

"Well, I do, because we need to get this straight once and for all."

"Let's just go to dinner."

"No. Not until we settle this."

"I don't see how it *can* be settled. Not with you being so dead set against me seeing my daughter."

Charlotte didn't like the way he'd referred to Curtina. Thus far, he'd called her by her name or had simply said "the baby" but now he was calling her his daughter. He was allowing himself to use a more personal and familylike term and this bothered her.

"Curtis, did you or did you not tell me that if I stayed with you, you would do whatever I wanted?"

"Yes."

"And did you or did you not tell me that once this baby was born you would never have any contact with the baby or Tabitha?"

"Yeah, I did."

"Then why are we having this conversation? Why do you keep bringing this up and now you're even moping around here like someone just died."

"Why? Because Curtina is innocent in all of this. She's just as innocent as Matthew and Marissa were when they were born, even though you lied about who their father was. You lied but I still loved and treated them as if they were my own."

"Oh please, please, please just stop it! Stop bringing our children into this because they have absolutely nothing to do with it."

"They have everything to do with it, because if it was okay for me to be their father, how in the world could you possibly decide it's not okay for me to be a father to my own flesh and blood?"

Charlotte didn't know what to say but no matter how Curtis tried to make his case, she would never change her opinion. She would never, ever welcome that baby into her household. She would never allow Curtis to go anywhere near her.

"Why can't you just leave well enough alone?" she asked him. "Why can't you just move on and leave the past behind?"

"Because Curtina isn't the past."

"As far as I'm concerned, she is."

"Charlotte, look, let's just leave this alone, okay?"

"Not until you agree to forget this whole thing."

"I can't do that."

"Then you and I are headed for a lot of turmoil."

"If you would just try to be more understanding, it wouldn't have to be that way."

"I've told you how I feel and either you're going to respect that or you're not."

When Charlotte turned to walk away from Curtis, she heard a knock at the door. Then she heard Matthew's voice.

"Mom. Dad. Can I come in?"

"Of course, honey," Charlotte told him.

"What is it, son?" Curtis moved closer to him.

"I wanna meet my other father."

Charlotte's heart was already beating faster than normal and without warning, she dropped onto the bed. She was mortified.

"I'm sorry," Matthew apologized. "But I really want to see him."

Charlotte looked at Curtis, who didn't seem bothered by any of what he was hearing and she couldn't understand why.

"Are you sure?" Curtis finally said.

"Yes. I mean, I'm sort of afraid, but I want to see who he is."

"I don't know if that's such a good idea," Charlotte added.

"Why not?"

"Because Curtis is your father. He's always been your father and he loves you more than David ever could."

"I know and I love Dad," he said, glancing at Curtis. "But, Mom, I still want to see my other father. My friend at school just got a chance to meet his and he said it helped him stop being so sad. It helped him a whole lot."

"Then we'll make it happen," Curtis assured him.

Charlotte wanted to scream. She couldn't believe Curtis was being so understanding and so willing to send their son off to meet with some stranger. It was true that she knew David, but she hadn't seen him in over thirteen years and she just couldn't see how Matthew's meeting him was going to make any difference in the way he felt about everything.

"Can you call him for me, Mom?"

"I'll have to see if I can get his number. I'm not even sure where he lives."

"Can't you call Cousin Anise?"

Charlotte had been hoping he wouldn't think of that. Hoping he wouldn't realize that Anise probably had David's number memorized. They were divorced and had had a terrible marriage, but from what she'd heard from Aunt Emma, Anise and David sometimes spoke by phone and had become friends.

"I'll try to call her this week," Charlotte finally answered.

"Can you call her now?"

Matthew was being persistent and he was making Charlotte uncomfortable. And she wanted to kill Curtis, who was standing by practically waiting to see what she was going to do about this.

Then he said, "If Matthew feels this strongly about meeting his father, then I think he should be able to."

"Mom, please. Can you call her?"

"Fine," she said and picked up the phone.

She dialed the number and Anise answered almost immediately. "Hello?"

"Hi, Anise. This is Charlotte."

"Uh-huh."

"How are you?"

"I'm well."

Charlotte waited for her to return the question, but she didn't and Charlotte was already regretting having to make the call. Yes, it was true that she'd slept with David while her first cousin was still married to him but how long was Anise actually planning to hold a grudge against her? Charlotte had apologized more times than she cared to remember and it was high time for Anise to get over it. It was time she dropped her petty pride, forgave Charlotte, and moved on with her life.

"I'm calling because Matthew asked me to."

"And?"

"He wants to meet his father."

"I don't blame him."

That witch. Charlotte couldn't stand her and if she'd been standing side by side with her, she probably would have slapped her. At the least, she wanted to give her a piece of her mind.

But since Matthew was staring and listening to her every word, she said, "Do you have his number?"

"Actually, I do, but it's probably best if I have him call you and Curtis instead."

"If you don't mind doing that."

"I don't mind at all. Especially since this is for Matthew." Anise spoke in a short tone, letting Charlotte know she wasn't doing her any favors at all.

Still, Charlotte ignored her. She wanted to slam the phone down, but she acted as though she wasn't bothered by Anise in the slightest bit.

"Can you call him today?" Charlotte asked.

"He's in New York, but he'll be back tomorrow."

"Fine. Can you try him then?"

"Sure. Like I said, anything for Matthew."

"Well, I guess that's it. And thanks for all your help."

Anise hung up the phone without even saying good-bye and, for some reason, that really hurt Charlotte. It hurt because there had been a time when they'd been as close as sisters. A time when they'd laughed so hard they'd begun crying. They'd always enjoyed each other's company, but not since Anise had learned of Charlotte and David's affair.

"He's out of town, honey, but Anise is going to call him as soon as he gets back."

"I love you, Mom," Matthew said and hugged her. "I love you, too, Dad," he said, glancing over at Curtis.

"We love you, too, son," Curtis told him.

"We love you more than anything or anybody else in this world," Charlotte added.

"Can we go to Giordano's?" Matthew asked, and interestingly enough he was sounding happier than he had in weeks.

"I guess so," Charlotte answered. She'd already decided that she wanted steak but at this point, she was willing to do whatever she had to in order to keep Matthew content.

When he left the room, Charlotte looked at Curtis and got angry all over again.

"Why didn't you try to discourage him from wanting to see David?"

"Because he has every right to see his father."

"And what if David doesn't want to see him? Hunh? Then what, Curtis?"

"I don't see that happening."

"You don't even know him, so how can you say that?"

"I think he'll want to see his only son. I mean, didn't you say he doesn't have any other children?"

"That's my whole point exactly. Because maybe that means he never wanted any, period."

"You're blowing this way out of proportion. And what I think we need to do is support Matthew any way we can."

"Why are you doing this? Don't you love him?"

"What kind of crazy question is that? You know I do. Plus, how can I be hesitant toward helping him when I'm basically in the same predicament myself?"

"Oh, so that's what this is all about? You and that baby of yours?"

"All I'm saying is that Matthew has a right to spend time with David and Curtina has a right to spend time with me."

"She may have a right, but it's like I keep telling you, it's not going to happen. You're not having anything to do with her or her lunatic mother and that's all there is to it."

Charlotte left the room and headed down the stairway. She walked down each step, slowly but surely, and wondered how she could get rid of Tabitha.

How she could do it and legally get away with it.

Chapter 5

Curtis turned the corner and headed out of the subdivision. It was late Monday morning, eleven thirty to be exact, and while Charlotte thought he was on his way to meet two of his friends for lunch, he was actually on his way to nowhere in particular and, for the most part, just needed some time away from her so he could think. He needed to think about everything that was happening in his life at this very moment, specifically the baby, Matthew's wanting to meet his "real" father, and Reverend Tolson's idiotic demands.

The last thing he wanted to do was keep secrets from Charlotte or go behind her back doing things she wouldn't be happy about, but after seeing Curtina in person for the very first time, he hadn't been able to take his mind off her. He'd tried to weigh the good with the bad but no matter how he figured any of what he was dealing with, the bottom line was that he was in fact Curtina's father and not having anything to do with her just wasn't right.

But on the other hand, he'd made a solemn promise to Charlotte and was trying at all costs not to cause an uproar in their marriage. Worse, he knew any trouble between Charlotte and him wouldn't be good for Matthew either. Not with him preparing to meet David. Curtis had given Matthew his blessing but deep down it did sort of bother him because he couldn't help wondering if Matthew might end up wanting to be with David more than he did him. Curtis had never thought any man was a better man than he was but this whole thing with Matthew and David was taking a slight toll on his ego.

Although he would never let Charlotte know about his reservations because if she learned how he truly felt, she would do everything in her power to keep Matthew and David apart and that wouldn't be fair to either one of them. The same as it wasn't fair for him and Curtina to live separate lives. This was another reason Curtis had no choice but to support Matthew in what he wanted to do.

Curtis drove clear to the other side of town, stopped at a very well-known, old-fashioned, drive-in restaurant, and ordered the most fattening meal on the menu.

"I'll have a bacon double-cheeseburger, large fries, and a large root beer."

"Would you like your root beer in a frozen mug?" the woman said from the speaker he'd pulled up to.

"Yes. That'll be fine."

"Sir, if I could repeat your order back to you, you'd like a bacon double-cheese, large fries, and root beer in a mug. Is that correct?"

"Yes, that's correct."

"Will that be all?"

"Yes."

"We'll bring that out to you shortly."

"Thank you."

Curtis switched his XM-Radio channel from one of the talk stations to XM-33, The Spirit. For as long as he could remember, he'd loved gospel music and what he liked about this station was that they played both modern and traditional. They played anyone from Shirley Caesar to Mary Mary, from James Cleveland to Kirk Franklin, and Curtis enjoyed them all. Right now, Shirley Caesar was belting out words from her song "Church Is in Mourning," and he couldn't help thinking of his beloved mother and how she'd passed away just over six years ago. He still missed her terribly and he still felt a load of regret for not seeing or talking to her for so many years. He'd made the terrible decision to distance himself from her and his sister and no matter how hard he tried, he never felt better about it. Not to mention, his sister still wanted nothing to do with him and whenever he tried to call her, she either didn't answer or she had her husband or one of the children say she wasn't home. He was sorry for the way he'd cut her off but he would never give up on trying to win her forgiveness.

When the carhop brought out his food, he rolled his window down and she placed the tray on the top edge of his window. Thankfully, it was an unseasonably warm, early-October day and the sun was shining, so leaving the window halfway open wouldn't be uncomfortable.

"That'll be seven dollars and fifty-eight cents, please," the young woman announced. Curtis laid a ten in her hand and told her to keep the change.

When he'd finished eating, he flipped what they called the "pickup" switch and the young girl came back out and removed the tray. Then he backed out of the stall and left. He wasn't sure where he wanted to go next, but then it dawned on him that he was maybe only a mile from the park where the church always had their annual picnics. It was his favorite in all the surrounding areas, and he'd always been able to think very clearly when he spent time there.

It didn't take him more than a couple of minutes to find a nice quiet space, park, and step out of his vehicle. The area was quiet and the tiny breeze was refreshing, so he decided to take a stroll through the grass.

He walked for more than an hour, trying to gather his thoughts, and when he returned to his SUV his decision had been made. He'd decided that the best thing to do was tell Charlotte the truth.

He would tell her about Tabitha showing up at church yesterday with the baby and how if Elder Jamison hadn't allowed her to see him, she had threatened to go public. He would tell Charlotte the truth because just maybe if they talked this thing out, she would realize that Curtina was not at fault and that she was simply just an innocent little child. He didn't know what the outcome was going to be, but he was going to take his chances and pray for the best.

When Curtis closed his door and turned on the ignition, his cell phone rang. He smiled when he saw that it was Alicia.

"Hi, baby girl."

"Hey, Daddy. How are you?"

"I'm well. What about you?"

"I'm good. I just left one of my writing classes, and I don't have another until an hour from now."

"I'm really glad you decided to stick with English. It's a great major with more options than most people realize."

"I know. I really want to write a book, and I still haven't ruled out going to law school next year."

"Why don't you just do both?"

"I don't know."

"Well, you're more than capable. No doubt about it."

Curtis was so proud of Alicia. She wrote short stories about as quickly and as efficiently as someone who'd been writing professionally for the last twenty years. It came just that naturally to her, and Curtis had always encouraged her to keep at it until she was published. Which is exactly what had happened last year when she'd entered a national magazine contest and had taken first place. She'd beaten out thousands of other aspiring writers and the prize had been five thousand dollars and having her story published in one of the upcoming issues. After that, she'd been submitting one manuscript after another and had continued to win other competitions as well.

"So how're Matthew and Charlotte?" she asked.

"They're doing fine. Although Matthew told me he wants to meet his real father."

"Wow. I'm really sorry, Daddy."

"No, honey, there's nothing to be sorry about. Of course I want my relationship with him to change, but he has every right to see and know the man he came from."

"What did Charlotte say?"

"Not much, but she's definitely not happy about it."

"Matthew must be really nervous because I know I would be."

"Yeah, it's all going to be very interesting, but, baby girl, that's not the biggest news I have to tell you."

"Why? What else is going on?"

"I shouldn't have kept this from you for as long as I have, but I guess I didn't know how to tell you."

"Tell me what, Daddy?"

"That you have a baby sister."

"A what?"

"A baby sister. She's six months old, and she lives right here in Mitchell."

Alicia didn't say anything and now Curtis wasn't sure what he should say either.

"Wow. Wow. Wow. A baby? At your age?" she said, and to Curtis's surprise, she laughed.

"Now come on. I'm not that old."

"You're over forty."

"And you think that's over the hill, I guess?"

"Well . . . yeah! Because it is."

"Young people," Curtis said and laughed with her.

"So who is the mother and why didn't you tell me?"

"Her name is Tabitha, and I didn't tell you because I was ashamed. I've done a lot of things in my life that I'm not proud of, and I certainly haven't always been the best example for you."

"You're still my father, though, Daddy, and I'll love you no matter what."

"I appreciate that, baby girl, but still, I've made some pretty bad choices and this is proving to be the most troubling one yet."

"Have you seen her? What's her name?"

"I saw her yesterday and her name is Curtina."

"She was at the house?"

"No, it's a long story, but her mother brought her to the church."

"So other people know?"

"Not exactly. I mean, Charlotte knows and now Elder Jamison sort of knows but I haven't told anyone else. We're trying to keep Tabitha from telling anyone, but now she's wanting me to spend time with the baby."

"And you're not going to?"

"Like I said, baby girl, it's a long story. I would love to see her, but Charlotte doesn't want that. She doesn't want me to have anything to do with Curtina ever."

"Maybe she'll eventually change her mind."

"That's what I'm hoping, but we'll see."

"Do you think I can see her next time I come home?"

"I'll ask Tabitha, but I'm sure it'll be fine."

"Can I tell Mom?"

"Well, I kind of wanted to tell her myself."

"Oh, that's fine."

"I'll call her when I hang up with you."

"Well, I guess I should get going, but, Daddy, you call me if you need to, okay?"

"I will, and, baby girl, I love you so much."

"I love you, too, Daddy. Bye."

Curtis ended the call with his daughter, adjusted his Bluetooth earpiece, and dialed her mother's office number. She answered on the first ring.

"This is Tanya."

"Hey."

"Hey yourself."

Amazingly, after hearing his first wife's voice, he was already feeling a lot more at ease. After all these years, them being divorced, he still sometimes felt more comfortable talking to her than he did anyone else—including Charlotte. Tanya had been his first real love and the woman who'd understood him from the beginning and he had to admit that there were still many days when he couldn't help regretting the fact that he'd lost her long ago to someone else. James was a good man, and he treated her and Alicia well enough, but still, Curtis couldn't help being a bit envious.

"Did I catch you at a bad time?" he asked.

"Not really. I'm working but I have a few minutes. What's up?"

"What isn't, is what you should be asking."

"Well, that doesn't sound good."

"For one thing, Matthew wants to meet his biological father."

"Really?"

"Yes. But the other thing is that I have a six-month-old little girl."

"Curtis. Please tell me you're kidding."

"No. I'm not."

"With whom?"

"A woman I met a few years back and was having an affair with."

"Does Charlotte know about this?"

"Yes. And I don't have to tell you how upset she is. She's basically beside herself."

"Can you blame her?"

"No. Not really. But at the same time, I truly feel that I have an obligation to my child."

Tanya didn't comment one way or the other, so Curtis went on to tell her about the arrangement he had made with Tabitha and how he wasn't supposed to have anything to do with her or Curtina. He spilled his guts about everything and felt almost relieved. He felt better because he was tired of walking around, not being able to talk about his troubles. He and Charlotte were now frequently arguing about this whole ordeal, but Tanya was the first person he'd finally been able to discuss it with in a cordial manner.

"I guess I don't know what to say."

"Most of the time, I don't either."

"After all that happened last year with Marissa passing away, I really thought you and Charlotte had worked things out and that you were now closer than ever."

"We were. But then the baby was born and ever since then, our marriage has become a lot more strained."

"I'm sure."

"But hey, can I ask you something?"

"What's that?"

"How would you feel? I mean, if you were Charlotte would you try to keep me from seeing my own daughter?"

"You want the truth?"

"Yes."

"Of all the terrible things you did to me, in the end, my divorcing you wasn't as much about your affair with Adrienne as it was about Charlotte being pregnant with your child. I know it eventually turned out that Matthew wasn't your son, but back then, we were sure he was. So, for me, an affair was one thing, but a lifetime reminder was a whole other story. It was just too much for me to bear and that's why there was no way I could stay married to you."

Curtis wanted to respond but he was too saddened by what Tanya had just explained to him. He knew he'd hurt her in a major way, but somehow hearing her talk about it with so much emotion made him feel worse.

"I'm really sorry, Tanya. I know I've apologized over and over, but I'm really sorry for all the pain I caused you back then."

"You know I forgave you a long time ago so don't worry about it."

"It just seems that no matter what I do, I keep messing up. I keep trying my hardest to do the right thing but somehow I always end up doing just the opposite."

"That may be true, but Curtis, you can't deny the fact that you simply don't make the right choices. You've got a serious problem with temptation and until you get control of it, you're always going to have consequences to deal with."

"But that's just it. I do have control. And ever since I told Charlotte a year or so ago that Tabitha was pregnant, I've been completely faithful to her. And I want to stay faithful to her."

"Then I suggest you work out this situation regarding the baby."

"But how, when Charlotte doesn't want to hear anything about it?"

Tanya fell silent again and Curtis wondered why.

"Do you agree with Charlotte?" he asked. "Do you really think it's right for me to turn my back on Curtina?"

"No. But my theory has always been that if a woman can't accept a baby born outside of her marriage then she should leave the situation and let the husband be a father to his child. However, if she chooses to stay with her husband, then she should accept the child and love it as her own."

"I don't think Charlotte will ever accept Curtina. Which, to a certain extent, really angers me because I accepted Matthew and Marissa."

"I hear what you're saying, but you still need to try to come to some sort of understanding with Charlotte. Maybe all you need to do is give her a little more time to digest all that's going on. Maybe you just need to be a little more patient with her."

Curtis sighed. "Thanks, Tanya. Thank you for always being there for me when I need you to be. Because you definitely don't owe me anything."

"You're right," she said, teasing him. "But seriously, our issues are way in the past and you're still Alicia's father."

"That I am, and I'm so proud of her. She's doing so well at U of I, and I'm also very proud of the way you've raised her. You've done an excellent job, and I will always be indebted to you for that."

"I'll be praying for you and Charlotte and the baby. And Matthew, too."

"I appreciate that. And I'll let you go, okay?"

"Take care now."

Curtis placed the gear in drive and headed out of the park area. He wasn't sure what the future held for Charlotte and him, but what he did know was that they could no longer continue as they had been. Constantly at each other's throats. It just wasn't working for either of them and as Tanya had suggested, maybe he just needed to be more patient with her. Maybe he really did need to give Charlotte a bit more time to understand where he was coming from.

If he did, maybe there would be a fighting chance for them after all.

Chapter 6

If it wasn't one thing it was another, Charlotte thought, driving past the health club where she sometimes went to work out. Only months ago, her life had seemed better than ever, yet now, it was leaning toward uncontrollable disaster. That is, thanks to Tabitha Charles.

Naively enough, Charlotte had tried to believe that the signing of the contract, the huge checks, and the monthly child support payments would be enough, but at this very moment, she knew she'd simply been fooling herself. She'd been relaxing in fantasy land, refusing to acknowledge or deal with reality, and today she was suffering the consequences. Today, she was being forced to accept the unfortunate possibility that Curtis was not going to go much longer without seeing his child. She'd been threatening him in every way she knew how and thus far he'd been obliging her requests, but she couldn't help wondering how long his hesitation and obedience would last. Especially since he still hadn't laid eyes on the baby.

But whether he longed to see her or not, there was one thing Charlotte was certain of. There would be no baby invited into their household, not Curtina or otherwise, and that was that.

Charlotte drove down the lengthy two-lane road and saw rows and rows of vehicles lining the college campus parking lot. She was on her way to meet her best friend, Janine, for lunch and she could already tell all the close spots were taken. So, after entering and driving up and down a few aisles, she gave up and parked what seemed like a mile away from the building Janine taught in.

When she exited her vehicle and locked it, she headed toward her destination and had to smile at the three handsome-looking young men she was approaching.

"Mm, mm, mm," one of them said, and Charlotte ignored him.

"Do you go here?" the taller one asked. "Can I get your number?"

"So you're not speaking?" the third and most obnoxious one said when Charlotte didn't respond.

"Hi. How are you boys today?"

"Boys?" Mr. Obnoxious mimicked.

"Oh, I'm sorry," she said, correcting herself. "How are you gentlemen today?"

"We're good," the first one answered.

"I'm glad to hear it," she said. "Now you all take care."

"Man, wouldn't you like to rock that all . . . night . . . long?" Mr. Obnoxious blurted out and Charlotte turned to look at him.

The others snickered but seemed almost embarrassed by their friend's outrageous comment.

Charlotte wanted to tell him how ridiculous he sounded and how disrespectful he was but decided it wasn't worth it. Mainly because deep down, she was flattered to know she still had it. Which had to be the case if boys who appeared to be nineteen or twenty were trying to come on to her. She knew it was silly and she would never tell a soul what she was thinking, but with her being thirty-one and pushing thirty-two, every compliment was good for her ego.

When she arrived inside the building, she took the elevator up to the third floor and walked down to Janine's office. Her door was slightly ajar, so Charlotte knocked while opening it the rest of the way.

"Hey, girl," Janine said, standing and hugging Charlotte.

"Hey, J. It's so good to see you."

"It's been almost a week since we had lunch and you know that's pretty unusual."

"That it is. But I've had a lot going on emotionally, and I was to the point where if I didn't see you today, I was going to explode."

Janine closed the door and they both took a seat.

"What's wrong?"

"Everything. You name it, and I'm probably going through it."

"Like what?" Janine was noticeably concerned.

Charlotte sighed. "Well, first, that tramp, Tabitha, is all of a sudden calling our house again."

"For what?"

"Guess."

"For Curtis?"

"Exactly. And she's got the nerve to think Curtis is going to start seeing Curtina. Actually, she's just using the baby as a lure because I know with everything in me, that what she really wants is to sleep with Curtis again."

"You think? After all this time?"

"I know she does."

"Gosh, girl, I'm really sorry to hear that."

"I'm sorry, too, but I'm not having it. I'm not putting up with Tabitha, her baby, or any more unnecessary phone calls."

"Have you and Curtis talked about this?"

"If that's what you want to call it, but mostly all we've done is argue. He claims he's not going near them, but if you could see the look in his eyes whenever the subject comes up, you'd think otherwise."

"I can only imagine how you must be feeling."

"With the exception of Marissa falling to her death, I haven't felt worse. I feel like my whole life is being ripped away from me and Tabitha and that baby are enough to make me commit murder."

Charlotte watched Janine's body language and saw a horrified look on her face.

"I know you're not going to like what I'm about to say, but, Charlotte, you're going to have to find some way to accept this situation. You're going to have to pray for strength and understanding because if you don't, things are going to get worse."

Janine was right. Charlotte *didn't* like what she was saying in the least, and if Janine hadn't been her best friend, she would tell her in no uncertain terms what she thought of her ludicrous advice.

So instead she offered her the cordial version.

"Not under any circumstances will I ever accept what happened. I'll never accept any outside baby and, truth be told, I haven't fully forgiven Curtis either. We've been happy, but there's always been that small part inside me that I can't seem to get past. He keeps throwing up the fact that Marissa and Matthew weren't his and how he loved them anyway, but I don't care about any of that. All I care is that Tabitha and that baby stay as far away from us as possible."

"It's your call, but I just don't want to see you and Curtis at each other's throats over this. You've had a great relationship for more than a year and sometimes we have to accept things we don't want to just to have peace."

"You mean like the way you let Antonio lay up on you with no job and deal drugs out of a house you were paying for?"

A sadness consumed Janine's demeanor and Charlotte immediately regretted the harsh words she'd just spoken. She was beyond remorseful because she would never purposely try to hurt Janine in any way.

"I didn't mean that," she finally said, resting her hand on top of Janine's. "I'm so, so sorry. I had no right saying that to you, and even though I disagree with the way you feel, I know you're just trying to help."

"Don't worry about it. I know you're frustrated and that you're feeling a lot of pain."

"I am. And I don't know what I'm going to do if this doesn't go away. Because not only am I worried about her trying to lure Curtis back into bed, I'm worried that she'll take her story to the tabloids and everywhere else."

"But you and Curtis handled that legally, right?"

"I thought we did, but who's to say what that hooker will end up doing. Desperate people do desperate things. I'm living proof of it."

"Well, if she hasn't said anything so far, maybe she won't."

"She hadn't been calling him either, but now all of a sudden she is."

"I understand what you're saying, but the fact that Curtis still refuses to see her probably means she'll eventually give up."

"If only I could count on that. If only she would pack her bags and take that baby to a whole different state, we could get on with our lives. We could be happy and never have to think about her ever again."

"Everything will work out. It did for me and I just believe good things can happen for anyone."

"So how is that wonderful husband of yours? I've been so busy burdening you with my problems that I didn't even think to ask about him."

"He's fine. Working hard, though, opening another locksmith location."

"J, you are so blessed. You couldn't have found a better man to marry even if you'd tried."

"I know. I thank God every single day. For giving me such a loving and caring husband and for saving my life. It's so hard to believe that Antonio used me the way he did and then tried to stab me to death. I mean, it's just unimaginable but at the same time a harsh reality I had to experience."

"It was the worst, J. There are times when I still picture you lying in that hospital bed, fighting for your life. I was so afraid we were going to lose you and then the very next day, Marissa died. At one point, I remember wishing I could just die. Anything to make the pain go away."

"That was a terrible time, but look at us now. Life is so much better and we have a lot to be thankful for."

Charlotte heard what Janine was saying, but she couldn't agree with much of her sentiments. It was true that Janine and Carl were doing great and that life probably couldn't be more perfect for them, but Charlotte didn't feel this way at all. As a matter of fact, there was only one word to describe her current state. Miserable.

"I'm really happy for you and Carl, J," she finally said. "Both of you are good people and you deserve to be together."

"Thanks, girl. And hey," Janine said, glancing at her watch. "We'd better get down to the dining area before it gets too full. In about thirty minutes, all the students who are out of class for the day will be lining up in droves."

"Let's go."

"I wish we could have met at a restaurant, but my schedule is pretty tight today."

"This is fine. I just needed to see you as soon as I could."

"I'm glad you came by."

When they arrived downstairs, there were only five people in line waiting for food and two others at the two checkout locations. Charlotte ordered the enchilada entrée and Janine chose the Caesar salad and chicken noodle soup. Next, they took seats over in a far corner, near the windows.

"What an amazing view of the campus grounds," Charlotte commented.

"I know. And now that it's fall, it's more beautiful than ever."

They each took bites of their food and then Janine asked, "So how's Matthew doing?"

"He's doing okay, but that's the other dilemma we're dealing with."

"Meaning?"

"He wants to meet his real father."

"Really?"

"Yes, and I'm just sick over it. I'm totally against him seeing

David, but there's not much I can do to stop it. Not to mention, Curtis is acting like he's pretty much in love with the whole idea of it."

"Have you tried to contact David?"

Charlotte took a sip of her lemonade. "I called Anise yesterday and asked her to call him."

"Wow. How was that?"

"She was her same evil self. But she did agree to call David and then have him call us."

"Does he know about Matthew?"

"I don't think so. I mean, I asked Anise not to say anything so hopefully she never did."

"Well, even though you're not happy about them meeting, maybe this will allow Matthew to be more at peace. Because you've been saying how quiet he's been and not like himself."

"He did seem happier yesterday, but my worry is that David will reject him or disappoint him in some other crazy way."

"Let's hope not. Let's just pray that this will be good for every-one involved."

"We'll see. But if you want to know the truth, I'm hoping David doesn't call at all. Matthew will probably be hurt, but he'll eventually get over it."

"Well, either way, I think you and Curtis have done the right thing by not denying him his right to meet his father."

Charlotte disagreed with Janine on this issue the same as she disagreed with her about Curtina, but again, she decided to keep her feelings to herself. She loved Janine, but because Janine always tried to see the positive side of even the most haphazard situations, she sometimes unnerved Charlotte. Her good-side-of-life mentality was sometimes too much for Charlotte to take but Charlotte knew she had no choice but to tolerate it. Especially since Janine loved her unconditionally and never judged her for her wrongdoings, past or present. Which was certainly far more than she could say for that cousin of hers, Anise.

"Hey, I wasn't going to tell you this until I was sure, but guess what?" Janine said.

Charlotte smiled. "No. Are you serious?"

"Yes, I think I'm pregnant."

"Oh my God, J. That's truly wonderful news."

"I haven't told Carl yet, but I'm planning to pick up a pregnancy test after work."

Charlotte grabbed both of Janine's hands. "You'll make the best mother in the world."

"You think so? And, of course, I'll be depending on you to teach me everything you know."

"I'll always be here for you. Always, and I know I get to be the godmother."

"You should never even question that. You and Curtis are the only godparent choices for any children we have."

"I'm so excited, and I can't wait to head to the baby section of every department store."

"You crack me up. But first I have to confirm it."

"You have to call me as soon as you know."

"I will. That is, after I tell Carl."

"Of course. He'll be so excited."

"We've talked about children a lot lately, so I really hope I am. We both want them, and that's why we decided not to use any birth control from the very beginning."

Charlotte truly was elated for her friend, but there was still a tiny smidgen of envy she was feeling. Partly because she so missed Marissa and still couldn't believe her little girl had died when she was only five, and partly because she sort of wanted her and Curtis to have a child together. She wanted them to have a child genetically of their own, but when she'd stressed her desire to Curtis, he hadn't had a lot to say. He'd basically changed the conversation and hinted that he was too old.

Although now Charlotte wondered if his lack of interest wasn't about age at all but had everything to do with the fact that he already had a newborn baby. He already had a daughter with another woman and didn't see a reason to conceive another.

Charlotte became angrier by the second and while she was thrilled for Janine, she couldn't stop thinking about that problem of hers that needed to be disposed of. She'd tried to push such unthinkable thoughts from her mind, she'd tried real hard, but she just couldn't seem to do it. At least not for long, and she feared what the inevitable might have to be.

She feared that of all the underhanded, conniving, vicious things she'd done in her thirty-one years on this earth, they would never compare to what she was planning to do now.

When she was finished, her past actions would resemble nothing more than child's play.

They would resemble no more than what an infant was capable of accomplishing.

Chapter 7

It had been six years since Curtis and Charlotte had moved into their current residence, but no matter how much time passed, Charlotte still got excited every time she drove up to it. It had been a dream come true and just looking at their three-level, all-brick estate and the five acres on which it sat gave her a warm feeling. She knew material wealth wasn't the most important gift in life, but she was glad she'd been blessed with it. Glad she'd chosen to marry a man who knew how to make money and lots of it. Glad she didn't have to look at price tags when she shopped. Glad she didn't have to cook or do housework the way so many other women had to. Glad she was considered, by most, very well off.

Charlotte pressed one of three buttons on the overhead console of her car and waited for one of the two-car garage doors to open. When it did, she drove in, turned off the radio, and left the vehicle. Once inside the back hallway, she slipped off her black stiletto boots and entered the kitchen. Curtis and their housekeeper, Tracy, were laughing loudly.

"What's so funny?" Charlotte asked, removing her sunglasses.

"Hey, baby," Curtis greeted her. "Tracy was just telling me about her father and how when she was little, he used to be so afraid of mice that one day when he saw one run across the living room, he ran out of the house, yelling and screaming with just his underwear on. And it was only ten degrees with snow on the ground. But even though he was freezing, it took her mother almost an hour to beg him back inside."

Curtis and Tracy laughed again and acted as though the story had just been told for the first time. Charlotte guessed it could be considered humorous, but she didn't see anything all that funny. Not because she didn't like Tracy, but because, lately, she hadn't been in a laughing mood. She had way more important issues on her agenda that needed to be worked out and, as far as she was concerned, joking around was the least of her worries. As a matter of fact, Curtis should have felt the same way.

Charlotte flipped through the mail and tossed all of the junk in the garbage can. There were still a ton of catalogs and magazines and she definitely wanted to see what Bloomingdale's and Neiman's had on sale, but she was glad they no longer had to worry about bills coming in and then having to pay them. Curtis had hired an accountant to handle the check writing for all their liabilities and it was well worth the fee the accountant charged them to do it. It was one less responsibility Charlotte had to worry about and somehow, not ever really having to see how much money she charged on her American Express card, well, that worked for her. Curtis wasn't always happy when he received the quarterly expense reports, but she never paid him any attention. She'd always felt she had the right to spend as much money as she wanted as long as it was breaking them.

"So how was Ms. Janine, Ms. Charlotte?"

"She was fine. It was good seeing her this afternoon."

"Glad to hear it. And tell her I'm going to make her that Cajun seafood dish of mine she likes so much. I'll make a real big helping of it for her and Mr. Carl."

"She'll love that. And, speaking of which, what mouthwatering dish are you making for us today, Tracy?"

"Actually, Ms. Charlotte, I was planning on making one of my nice little Jamaican concoctions, but Mr. Curtis told me to take the afternoon off."

Charlotte smiled because she loved Tracy's accent and because she knew Curtis must have been planning a romantic interlude between the two of them before Matthew made it home from school and practice. It was the only reason he usually gave Tracy sudden vacation time with pay.

"Is that right?" Charlotte finally responded. "Well, I hope you get some time to relax."

"I'll try, but I have so much to do around my own house."

Charlotte understood exactly what she was talking about because she'd been to Tracy's house on several occasions. Tracy definitely wasn't the most tidy person in the world. Which was interesting because she kept Charlotte and Curtis's house spick-and-span. She kept every single room immaculate, but maybe it was only because this was her job and she was well compensated for her duties.

"You should take a rest and worry about cleaning another day," Charlotte told her. "You're always so busy and everyone needs some time to do nothing. I know I do."

Tracy laughed and removed the rest of the dishes from the drying rack in the sink and placed them in the cupboard. Charlotte had noticed early on that Tracy seemed to prefer washing them by hand and rarely used the dishwasher. The whole idea of doing more work than one had to was totally beyond Charlotte's thinking but whatever worked for Tracy was fine with her.

Before Tracy left, she wiped down the double ovens, wiped around the burners, and even went over the steel refrigerator, all of which didn't need it. They were as clean as could be, but Tracy was just that thorough.

When she was finally in her car and on her way down the street, Charlotte stared at Curtis. He was sitting across from her, reading the current issue of *Men's Health*.

"So I take it that you're ready to call some sort of truce?" Charlotte began.

"I guess you could say that, but mostly I want us to talk things out."

"Talk?"

"Yes. Why do you think I told Tracy she could go home early?"

"I don't know, you tell me." Charlotte didn't like the sound of what she was hearing.

"There's something I really need to tell you."

"What?"

"I had a couple of visitors yesterday before service."

"Who?"

Charlotte was already on edge and hoped it wasn't who she thought it was.

"Who?" she yelled when Curtis didn't answer.

"Tabitha and Curtina."

"What? And you're just now telling me?" Charlotte stood in a fury.

"Look, baby, I wanted to tell you yesterday, but I didn't know how. I knew you were going to be upset."

"So instead of telling me the truth, you decided to hide this crap from me?"

"No. I wasn't trying to keep anything from you and that's why I'm telling you now."

"Whatever, Curtis."

"I'm serious. Baby, I always want to be on the up and up with you, but you're making it very hard for me to talk to you about anything anymore."

"I know you called the police to file a restraining order, right?"

Curtis stared at her with dismay, and she knew he hadn't called anyone.

"Why didn't you?" she continued.

"Because it just wouldn't have been right calling the police to the church to arrest my daughter's mother."

"Oh, so now you're defending Tabitha?"

"No. It's nothing like that."

"So what did she want? I mean, what was so urgent that she had to come traipsing all the way over to the church? On a Sunday morning, no less."

"She just wanted me to see Curtina. She wants me to be a father to her the way I'm supposed to be."

"And when you told her it was never going to happen, what did she say?"

"Baby, you have got to find it in your heart to be more reasonable about this."

"Curtis, what part of 'no, I'm never accepting any baby' don't you understand? Hunh? Because I think I've explained myself rather well. As a matter of fact, I've explained myself so much, even I'm sick of hearing me say the same old thing over and over again."

"So that's your final answer. I can't see my daughter."

"Did you or did you not hear me the other night when I was on the phone and I told Tabitha that her seeing you would be over my dead body?"

"And?"

"Well, I'm telling you the same thing."

"Look, baby, I understand how you feel, but at the same time, I'm really struggling with what God would want me to do. I mean, do you honestly think He would want me to deny a child I helped conceive?"

"Actually, I don't care about any of that, and you'd just better be concerned with what *I* want you to do."

"I don't believe you said that."

"Well, believe it, sweetheart, because I meant every word."

"I can't believe you're standing here saying you don't care what God wants."

Charlotte rolled her eyes at Curtis and took a few steps toward the family room but the phone rang. Curtis didn't bother moving, so she went back across the kitchen to answer it. The number showed private, but she picked it up anyway.

"Hello?"

"Charlotte?"

"Yes?"

"This is David."

Now she truly knew what it felt like to feel weak in the knees. She'd had other similar experiences, but this feeling topped them all.

"Charlotte, are you there?" he asked.

"Yes. How are you?"

"Not good. Anise just called me a few minutes ago about Matthew and I have to tell you, I'm stunned. Literally stunned in disbelief."

Charlotte stood holding the phone, with no words to speak, and Curtis stared at her, obviously not sure who she was talking to.

But David continued.

"What right did you have not telling me I had a son?"

"Look, David, I know you're upset, but I didn't want to cause even more problems for you and Anise. You were still married, and I also did what I thought was best for Matthew."

"No, what you mean is that you did what was best for you."

Charlotte didn't know what else to say and she wished Curtis would find something else to look at. He was staring fixedly, and she didn't like it one bit. It was almost as if he were enjoying her discomfort.

"Can you just put Matthew on?" David said impatiently.

"He's at football practice."

"Then I'll call back later."

"No."

"What do you mean, no?"

"It's just that I think it would be better if the four of us, you, Matthew, my husband, and me, were all together when you and Matthew talk for the first time."

"Don't you think the fact that I've had to wait thirteen years to speak to a son I didn't even know I had should take precedence over what you want?"

"Yes, but I just feel that getting us all together will make things easier for Matthew."

"I disagree, but I'm not going to argue with you about it. So when?"

"Can you come this Saturday?"

"Fine. What time?"

David was very short and Charlotte knew it had been a mistake to contact him.

"Three o'clock?"

"Fine. I'll call later in the week for the address and directions."

"Then I guess we'll see you this weekend."

"I guess so. Good-bye."

He hadn't even waited to see if she had anything else to say. He'd hung up like she didn't matter and she had a feeling he was going to be trouble.

"I know you're not happy about David meeting Matthew, but we really are doing the right thing," Curtis finally said when Charlotte hadn't spoken. "And while I know you're probably tired of hearing me say this, every child has a right to spend time with his or her biological father."

"Curtis, you know what? You go to hell. Go straight to hell and don't look back."

Chapter 8

It was Tuesday morning and Curtis watched Charlotte enter the kitchen, purposely not looking in his direction. He and Matthew were sitting at the table, waiting for Tracy to serve breakfast, and Curtis was reading the business section the way he did every morning. He and Charlotte hadn't said two words to each other, not since she'd told him where he could go, and for the time being that suited him just fine. It was true they had problems—serious problems—they needed to work out, but he had to admit, hearing her tell him to go straight to hell wasn't sitting well with him. Her words were totally uncalled for and not at all the sort of words a pastor's wife should be using when speaking to her husband. He knew she was upset about a number of issues, but his patience was slowly but surely beginning to wear thin. He was slowly but surely getting to the point where he would have to do what was right, regardless of whether Charlotte liked it or not. He'd begged and pleaded with her long enough, and he was tired of it. He was tired, and if she didn't soon hear what he was trying to tell her, then that would be her dilemma and her dilemma alone.

"Dad, you should've been at practice yesterday when I made that bomb touchdown," Matthew said and was more excited than he'd been in a while.

"I wish I could have seen it. But you'll get a couple more in during the games."

"We only have two more, this Thursday and next Thursday and then the championship if we make it."

"You've had a great season and if you keep playing like you have been, you'll be prime for a starting position in high school next year. And then, if you do well there, the top universities will be practically throwing scholarships at you."

"I hope so."

"Has your coach found any more football camps for us to check out? Because I really think it would be good for you to go next summer. Even if it's just for a couple of weeks or so."

"No, but he said he'll have some more brochures by the end of the month."

"That's good, and once we decide on which one, we'll get you registered."

"Thanks, Dad. I love football more than anything."

"I can tell," Curtis said, laughing. "Everyone can tell."

Charlotte finally took a seat next to Matthew but still didn't look at Curtis.

"So, sweetie, did you get all your homework finished last night?"

"Yes. All I had was something from English and math."

"Just as long as you finished it, I'm good."

"Mom, I always do my homework. And I'm getting A's in every class except art and that's only because art is crazy."

"It's not crazy," Curtis said. "You just don't like it."

"You're right. And I wish I'd taken another elective."

"It'll be over in a few months, so you just hang in there," Charlotte encouraged him.

"I will, and I'm still getting a B, anyway. Journalism is my favorite class, though. I could write articles for the school newspaper every day and never get tired of it. And as soon as football season ends, I'll be taking over as editor. Ms. Lundvall promised it to me last year and she has someone filling in for me right now."

"That was really nice of her to do that," Charlotte told him.

"Yep."

"You must be as good as you say you are then, hunh?" Curtis teased.

"Must be," Matthew said and bumped knuckles with his dad.

Once Tracy had brought breakfast to the table, whole wheat toast, scrambled eggs, turkey sausage, and grits, Curtis said grace and they all dug in. Curtis moaned slightly when he bit into his helping of eggs because no one made eggs like Tracy. He consistently asked her what she used to season them, but she would never say. Said it was some historical family secret and that if she told him, she'd have to kill him, and she didn't want to do that.

She joked with Curtis about her eggs all the time and even Charlotte had tried to steal a few looks from time to time whenever Tracy made them, but to this day, neither of them had a clue in terms of what spices she used.

Matthew's car-pool ride honked and he quickly finished off his freshly squeezed orange juice, grabbed his book bag, bumped knuckles with his father again, and hugged his mother.

"Bye, Mom. Bye, Dad. Bye, Tracy."

"See you, son," Curtis said.

"Have a good day, sweetheart."

"Yes, have a good day," Tracy told him. "And don't forget the check for your lunch. It should cover you all the way through December. That is, if you don't eat too many extra snacks."

"I won't," he said.

Curtis was so proud of Matthew. He was so talented and so intelligent and it was interesting how he had such a gift and love for writing the same as Alicia did, even though, technically, they weren't related. Alicia loved him the way any sister loved her little brother and Matthew loved her the way little brothers love their big sisters, but they didn't have the same mother or father. Of course, this was all because of Charlotte's great desire to sleep with her cousin's husband, right in their own home like it was nothing.

Which is why, more and more, Curtis was having a difficult time understanding her objection to his having a relationship with Curtina. Her standards were beyond double and she had no justifiable claim for what she was demanding.

As soon as Tracy closed the door behind Matthew, Charlotte told Tracy how good everything tasted and headed back upstairs. She still wasn't speaking to Curtis, and while he had a mind to follow behind her, he decided against it. Instead, he struck up a conversation with his housekeeper.

"So, tell me, Tracy, are we paying you enough? Because if we're not, I wanna know."

"Yes. Yes, Mr. Curtis. You and Ms. Charlotte are very good to me. You're more than generous, and I couldn't be happier. I'm always bragging to my friends about how well you treat me."

"Well, good. That's what I want to hear. But you will tell me if something changes, right?"

"Yes, Mr. Curtis. But I tell you, I'm fine. I have no complaints and no requests. That is, unless you can find me a nice Christian man. Not one of those jokers that don't mean a woman any good, but a decent one."

"I'll have to see what I can do. There has to be someone out there dying to meet a great catch like you."

Curtis smiled and flipped through another section of the newspaper. He felt bad for Tracy because even though she was the sweetest woman and would certainly make some man a very good wife, she wasn't too attractive. And that was putting it mildly. In fact, her homeliness was the reason Charlotte had not one ounce of worry when it came to Tracy and Curtis being in the house together when no one else was around. Charlotte never felt threatened even slightly.

After maybe another half hour passed, Tracy started washing clothes and Curtis went up to the bedroom to let Charlotte know he was leaving for the church. When he walked in, she was sitting in bed with her knees bent, watching what must have been an old episode of *Girlfriends*.

"So you still don't have anything to say, I guess?" he asked.

"Actually, I think I've said it all. I've made my point, and frankly I don't see a reason to keep discussing it."

"Are you coming to the board meeting this morning?"

"Since when do we meet on Tuesdays during the day?"

"With everything that's been going on, I forgot to tell you about the Tolson situation. He's not happy, and he's making financial demands. Wants us to buy him out of his contract and then some."

"Well, I won't be there."

"Charlotte, this is serious. It's an emergency meeting and you need to be in attendance."

"Did you hear me?" she said, raising her voice. "I said no."

"Fine. Do what you want to do."

"I will."

"And so will I," Curtis said, turning to leave.

"And what is that supposed to mean?"

"Just what I said."

"For the last time, Curtis, I'm warning you."

"No, I'm warning you. Because I've had enough of your whining and ultimatums. I'm sick of it, and I'm getting to the point where I'm sick of you. I've been babying you and trying to get you to see where I'm coming from but you just won't listen. I've forgiven you for every single thing you've ever done to me but now you're acting as if you can't do the same."

"I can't and I won't."

"Then don't. But understand this. I'm through tap dancing around you like you're some queen."

"I don't have to understand anything. I've told you how things are going to be and that's the end of it."

"Well, it certainly wasn't the end when you slept with crazy Aaron and then had his baby. And don't get me started on all the pain you've caused Matthew with all your lying. You're the reason Marissa turned out the way she did, because if you hadn't slept around with Aaron while you were still married to me, she wouldn't have ended up with his psycho traits. And if you'd kept your legs shut that weekend you spent time at Anise's, Matthew would be my son and not David's."

"Curtis, I was only seventeen when I got pregnant and you were married. Remember? So just shut up. Just shut up and leave me alone."

"You know, there were a lot of people at the church who said I should have dumped you when I found out about Aaron, and now I'm wondering if I should have listened to them."

"Pleeeaase. You, the so-called man of God who's had affairs on every woman you've been married to? Huh! And I'll tell you something else, your publisher should be shot for paying you all the money they do. You've got so many people fooled, but you and I both know that you're the last person on earth who should be writing spiritual books that give advice on relationships. Not to mention the ones you've written on how people should live their lives. You're the worst example I've ever seen."

"I'm done with this."

"I don't care how done you are. All I know is that if you see Tabitha and that baby again, you'll be sorry."

"Charlotte. Dear. Sweetheart. By now, you must know that your threats don't mean a thing to me. And don't get me wrong, I really wanted us to work this thing out, but since you keep refusing to even try, there's nothing I can do about it. So, from this point on, whatever happens, happens."

"That sounds like a threat."

"No. I'm just telling you the way things are."

"So you're going against everything I've asked you not to do?"

"I'm out of here."

"Just answer the question. Have you decided that you are going to see that tramp that almost ruined our marriage?"

"I haven't decided what I'm going to do but for the record, I have no desire to see Tabitha. I just want to see my daughter."

"It's all the same thing. If you see Curtina, you'll have to see Tabitha and that's what Tabitha has been planning all along."

"But why can't you just trust me? Your husband who you say you love?"

"Because for five years you slept with that woman behind my back, added your name to her mortgage, and the list goes on."

"And I've apologized to you for that for what seems a thousand times. I've done things I'm not proud of, but, Charlotte, so have you."

"Don't you dare keep trying to turn this on me. This is about you and that home wrecker you committed adultery with."

"I need to get to the church," he said.

"Whatever."

Curtis looked at her, frustrated, and left.

He headed out to the SUV and wondered how this whole scenario would play out in the end.

He wondered if he and Charlotte would still be husband and wife one year from now.

Chapter 9

Curtis relaxed his body in the one-month-old, executive-style chair, folded his arms, and took a long deep breath. His life was in such shambles right now that he could barely even think straight. He knew he was supposed to be focusing on the Tolson meeting, which would take place in an hour, but he was hugely consumed by the massive blowup he and Charlotte had just had only a short while ago. He was trying so hard to see things her way but the more attempts he made at doing so, the more he thought about his own position and how he had some very valid points himself.

Yes, it was wrong to have slept with Tabitha, yes, it was wrong to have gotten her pregnant, but no matter what Charlotte claimed, it wasn't wrong for him to be the father he should be to Curtina. The situation was uncomfortable for Charlotte and it was clearly causing a major strain on their marriage, but none of this was Curtina's fault. Not one small bit of it.

Curtis opened his top right drawer, reached all the way toward the back, beneath one of his many Bibles, and pulled out an envelope. He closed the drawer and wasted no time removing the contents, two photos of Curtina. He didn't know which of them he liked the most, but he stared from one to the other for several minutes. Tabitha had left the latest one on his desk on Sunday morning, but he purposely hadn't told Charlotte because he knew she would never allow him to keep it. She would tear it to shreds, as she would the other photo that Tabitha had sent when Curtina had been born.

He knew it wasn't right, his receiving and hiding photos behind Charlotte's back, but he just couldn't make himself discard them. He wanted and needed to look at them on a regular basis and couldn't help it. Truthfully, he felt no different from a child who wanted something so badly, he was willing to disobey his parents and take whatever punishment he had coming. Of course, he didn't like the consequences he was having to deal with but, somehow, having at least this small photo connection to his daughter was well worth anything Charlotte brought his way.

As Curtis slipped the pictures back inside the envelope, Lana, his administrative assistant, entered his office dressed as jazzily as ever.

"Pastor, here's the agenda, but just let me know if you have any changes you'd like me to make."

Curtis took his copy from her. "I'm sure it's fine."

Lana was one of the best people Curtis knew. She'd been with him ever since he and Charlotte had founded Deliverance Outreach six years ago, and he couldn't imagine having anyone else in her place. She was a good woman with strong Christian values and Curtis was very close to her. She was fifty-six and only ten years his senior, but still, she treated him like a son. She gave him advice and sometimes it felt as though she were ministering to him the way he sometimes ministered to others. She had no thoughts of being a minister, but she had this very special way of telling people what they needed to be told, regardless of what they had going on in their lives.

Which is why Curtis had no idea why he hadn't confided to her what he was dealing with at the moment. He'd wanted to tell her but whenever he'd thought about doing it, his shame overtook him. She knew his history, but he wasn't sure how she would feel knowing that after all this time, he still had skeletons to contend with.

"I know you've been back a few months now, Pastor, but I just wanted to say again how wonderful it is to have you here on a regular basis. We all missed you when you were on the road."

"It's good to be home. And good to be back involved with our church family."

"Now, don't get me wrong, I like Reverend Tolson well enough, but I missed you being our on-site leader. Everyone got along fine, but it wasn't quite the same. I think it was because even though we all have many talents and gifts, some of us excel in certain areas so much more than we do in others."

"Well, I appreciate hearing that. And thank you for the compliment. I just wish Reverend Tolson had turned out a whole lot happier than he is."

"It's so unfortunate. But some people feel the need to be chief and don't know how to be team players."

"That's very true, so I guess it is what it is."

"I have a couple of meetings to schedule, but again, let me know if the agenda needs some revisions."

"Thanks again for putting this together so quickly."

As soon as Lana closed the door, Curtis placed Curtina's photos back inside the drawer and started thinking about Charlotte again. He wasn't happy about her not attending the meeting. She knew she was an important member of the elder board and was needed at all impromptu, mandatory gatherings. Especially one where they were having to discuss financial and staff issues. It would have been one thing if she'd been sick or had some other legitimate reason why she couldn't be there, but Curtis knew her rebellion was personal. She hadn't come because she was angry with him, and it was hard for him to respect anyone who couldn't separate business and personal matters.

But then that was simply who Charlotte was. It was the way

she'd always been and if he'd been a betting man, he'd quickly gamble on the fact that she was never going to change. She would never make any sacrifices that didn't directly benefit her.

He was reviewing the agenda when there was a knock on his door. It was Anise.

"Hey, Ms. Miller."

"Curtis."

"So how are you?" They hugged at the side of his desk and then took seats.

"I'm good."

"And Aunt Emma?"

"Mom's fine. Couldn't be better."

"I'm glad to hear it."

"So what's up with the emergency meeting?"

"It's Tolson," Curtis answered and gave her a short synopsis of what was going on.

"Some people really amaze me," she said. "I mean, he's always known you wouldn't be gone forever, and what exactly did he think interim meant anyhow?"

"Oh, he knows, he's just not happy about having me back here so soon."

"That's ridiculous. And ungrateful if you ask me."

"I think so, too, but since he's so unsatisfied, we have to do what we have to do."

"He always seemed like such a nice man, he and his wife, so I never would have expected him to make these kinds of demands."

"It just goes to show that you can't trust everyone. As human beings, we always want to, but the truth is, we can't."

"Don't I know it."

Curtis knew Anise was referring to the way Charlotte had betrayed her with David, and he wasn't sure if he should comment. When he didn't, Anise continued.

"Sometimes, it's the people you care about the most. Sometimes, it's the people you would least expect for all eternity."

"I hate what happened, and whether you know this or not, Charlotte is truly sorry. And she really misses you."

"She should have thought about that before she slept with my husband."

"I hear what you're saying, and I'm not trying to defend what she did in any way, but you have to try to forgive her."

"I have forgiven her, but I'm just not ready to be friends with her again. She's my cousin and deep down, I love her, but whenever I think about her and David, well . . ." Her voice trailed off in a sullen way.

"I understand, but don't be like me. After that Aaron fiasco, I held a grudge against Charlotte so severely that I ended up doing more harm than good. I caused the kind of trouble that I'll never be able to take back."

"Such as?"

Curtis immediately regretted what he'd just said. As far as he knew, neither Anise nor Aunt Emma knew about Tabitha, his affair with her, or about the baby. He trusted Anise but now he wrestled with the idea of telling her.

"It's a long story."

Anise checked the time on her watch. "We've got time, so tell me."

Curtis paused for a few seconds and then disclosed practically every detail. He even pulled out the photos again and showed them to her. He was so relieved to share his story with yet another person, the same as he had with Tanya.

"How old is she?"

"Six months."

"She's beautiful, Curtis."

"A perfect little doll."

"I had no idea."

"That's a good thing, because that means it's probably safe to assume that no one else in the congregation knows either."

"Do Aunt Noreen and Uncle Joe know?"

"They do. There was no way Charlotte wasn't going to tell her mother and father."

"Well, I can guarantee you Aunt Noreen has never said a word to Mom because Mom definitely would have told me. Although you know Aunt Noreen and Mom still don't have much to do with each other."

"Which is very sad. Sisters and brothers should never let anything come between them, and I know all too well because I allowed my resentment toward my father to keep me away from my sister and mother for years. I'll always regret that, especially now that Mom is gone and even today, my sister still wants nothing to do with me."

Anise looked down at the photos again and Curtis knew she was avoiding any further conversation about family, forgiveness, and making amends. He could tell she had no plans of reconciling with Charlotte.

"So what are you going to do?" she asked.

"About Curtina?"

"That's her name?"

"Yes."

"Are you going to see her?"

"I want to. Desperately. But like I just told you, Charlotte is completely against it."

"I know it's not my place to tell you what to do, but I do know this. Mothers and fathers have a responsibility to their children. Regardless of how those children got here."

"I agree, but I also love my wife."

"I guess."

"It's not as easy as it seems because let's just say you'd still been married to David when you found out Matthew was his. Would you have stayed with David and accepted Matthew as your stepson?"

"Probably not. But the thing is, Charlotte did stay with you. And when she made that decision, she was all but saying she was fine with your daughter."

Anise had the same theory as Tanya, and he just wished Charlotte could feel this way, too. If only Charlotte could look at the bigger picture and realize she was the only woman he wanted. If only she could realize he didn't love Tabitha and had no desire to be with her.

"All I can do is keep praying," he said when Anise passed him back the pictures.

"I'll be praying for you as well."

"I appreciate that, and while I know you don't want to hear this, I hope you'll pray to end this separation between you and Charlotte."

Anise respectfully ignored his statement. "So David told me he's going to be meeting Matthew this weekend."

"He is. He called yesterday, and Matthew is pretty excited about it."

"And what about you? Because I know this must be a little difficult."

"I have some mixed feelings, but it's mainly because I know Matthew will now have another father to turn to. Still, though, I'm happy for him, and, in the end, I want whatever he wants."

"You're a good man, Curtis, and Matthew will always love you for being okay with this."

"I love him to death. You know that."

"I do, and so does Matthew. And that's why you'll never have to worry about anyone taking your place in his life. He knows who raised him and who's been there for him without fail."

"I just hope Charlotte can eventually come to terms with this, too."

"It would definitely make things easier for Matthew. That's for sure."

Curtis and Anise chatted a while longer and then left for the conference room. When they arrived, the other nine members were already seated, and of course Charlotte's chair was empty. There were twelve elders in total, more than enough to vote on the matter at hand, so in reality Charlotte's absence wouldn't make that much of a difference.

As soon as Curtis sat down, he called the meeting to order and asked Lana to review the minutes from last month's meeting. After she finished, they discussed a couple of minor topics and then moved on to the real reason they were there.

"As some of you probably know by now, Reverend Tolson came to me this past Sunday morning and asked that we buy out his contract."

The late-sixties, oldest, and most outspoken member, Elder Dixon, jumped right in. "For what?"

"In his words, he's not happy with the current arrangement."

"Not happy? Ain't that somethin'? We bring his nonpreachin' jackleg behind in here with top pay and he got the nerve to be makin' demands?"

Everyone in the room cracked up laughing.

"Well, sir," Elder Dixon continued, "I guess I've heard it all then."

"I don't get it either, Elder Dixon, but since he wants out, and if you're all in agreement, I move that we pay him the remainder of his contract. He has two years left on it, and that's what I think we should write the check for."

"I'm surprised he didn't ask for more," Elder Dixon joked.

"Actually, he did, but I let him know right away that we weren't paying him a dime more than we owed him."

"I'll bet that went over well," Elder Richardson commented. Which made Curtis smile because usually she was the quietest person in the room.

"He was pretty defensive and basically stormed out of my office."

"You know, the more I think about it, I never liked him all that much anyhow," Elder Dixon admitted. "Was always just a little too highfalutin for my taste. Wannabe-preachin', fake . . ."

"Puddin'! . . . I mean, Elder Dixon," Lana said, trying to tone him down and then trying to gracefully correct what she'd called him. Curtis and Anise smiled at each other, as did Elder Jamison and one of the other members, because after all these years, Lana was still trying to keep her relationship with Elder Dixon a secret. It was common knowledge that they were significant others and the reason Curtis knew this for sure was that Elder Dixon had told him so a long time ago.

Elder Dixon couldn't help smiling either, but he didn't look at Lana.

"I should also tell you that Tolson was making threats," Curtis remembered. "Something about how he didn't want to be forced to use certain ammunition."

"Please." Elder Jamison dismissed the entire notion. "I doubt it."

"I have no idea what he's talking about, but that's what he said." Curtis spoke genuinely but couldn't help wondering if maybe Tolson had somehow learned about Tabitha and Curtina. What a disaster that would be.

Elder Dixon jumped in again. "Just bluffin'. That's all that fool is doin'."

"Let's hope. But in the meantime, I say we move forward with ending his time here at Deliverance Outreach. I asked Elder Jamison to have our attorney draw up a separation letter yesterday afternoon and copies of it are attached to your agendas."

Each of the elders read through it, but as soon as they finished, Reverend Tolson barged in.

"Well, isn't this just perfect. I'm casually driving by the church, minding my own business, and suddenly I see all these elders' cars in the parking lot, this early on a Tuesday morning. And then I think, I wonder if they're trying to sneak and have a secret meeting about me."

Elder Jamison stood up. "Reverend Tolson, this is a closed session and only for the board members. Not to mention, you weren't invited."

"I don't care whether I was invited or not. I'm here now, and I have a few things I need to get off my chest."

Curtis was stunned by Tolson's continued audacity but was curious to hear what he had to say.

"First of all, I want every person in here to know that I don't play games when it comes to my livelihood. I take my position as a minister very seriously and I feel the same when it comes to my business. So, having said that, I want four years of pay and I expect to have my check in hand by the end of this week."

Dumfounded stares consumed the entire room, but Elder Dixon couldn't keep quiet.

"Boy, you must not know who you dealin' with. And if you know what's good for you, you'll take what we give you and leave here runnin'."

Tolson laughed out loud. "Old men should know their places and should speak only when spoken to."

Elder Dixon left his seat and rushed toward Tolson. But Curtis interceded. The women in the room gasped and the rest of the men moved closer to Tolson, letting him know that if he wanted one, a fight was clearly not a problem.

"Reverend Tolson, I think it would be in your best interest to leave," Curtis told him, and surprisingly, Tolson backed down. But not without delivering more threats.

"If I don't get what I want, every person in this room is going to be sorry. Every person in here will wish they'd voted to give me ten times what I'm asking for."

Next, Tolson walked out and Elder Jamison followed behind him, making sure Tolson left the building. When Elder Jamison returned, the board voted unanimously to pay Tolson two years of salary and nothing more and Curtis adjourned the meeting.

Still, though, Curtis had a feeling this wouldn't be the end. His feeling was as strong as oak.

Chapter 10

Charlotte was glad Curtis had decided to pick up Matthew from practice so the two could spend some quality time together because she'd decided she needed to talk to at least one more person about the troubles she was struggling with. She'd shared her story with Janine, but at the same time, she still felt the need to confide in someone else. Of course, that someone was none other than her Aunt Emma, the woman she loved and admired but who was estranged from her sister, Charlotte's mother. They did speak to each other whenever they were in each other's presence, but they never said more than a few words. Sadly, this was all because Charlotte's mother had betrayed Aunt Emma many years ago.

Still, regardless of the distance her mother and aunt kept between them, Charlotte still looked up to Aunt Emma. She loved her mother more than anyone, but Aunt Emma had always polled in as a close second.

Now she and Aunt Emma were sitting at the dining room table, eating her delicious casserole. It was tuna and no one made it as well as Aunt Emma did. As a matter of fact, she would never tell her mother, but Aunt Emma's casserole tasted even better than hers.

"Honey, I'm so glad you came by to see me."

"I am, too. I know it's been a few weeks."

"I wish you'd brought Matthew."

"He would have loved seeing you and he definitely would have loved having dinner over here."

Aunt Emma laughed. "That he would have."

"Curtis wanted to spend some time alone with him."

"Because of David?"

"Yes. And I have to tell you, Aunt Emma, I'm so afraid I don't know what to do."

"Why? What are you afraid of?"

"I don't know. I guess, I'm worried that David will cause problems for Matthew."

"Honey, I really doubt that. I mean, David and Anise had their issues, but I can't imagine him doing anything to harm his own son."

"Maybe not. But I still don't like it. And I never would have called him if Matthew hadn't asked me to."

"It'll all work out the way it's supposed to. Matthew and David will get along just fine, and you'll eventually be at ease about it."

"Do you know if he's in a serious relationship? Because I even worry about what strange women he might end up subjecting Matthew to. Not every woman is overly receptive toward another woman's child," Charlotte said and couldn't help thinking about her own feelings toward Curtina.

"I'm not sure. He got married only a few months after he and Anise divorced, but that lasted only a little over a year."

"I remember that."

"Like I said, I'm sure everything will be okay."

"I hope you're right."

"I am. You'll see."

Charlotte lifted her fork to take another bite of food, paused, and set the fork onto her plate.

Aunt Emma noticed. "Are you okay?"

Charlotte broke into tears. "No. I'm not."

"What's wrong?"

"Everything."

"Like what?"

"Curtis has a six-month-old baby girl, and now the mother is calling our house."

"Honey, no." Aunt Emma set her fork down and placed her elbows onto the table.

"It's true, and I feel like I'm losing my mind."

"How long have you known about this?"

"Before Marissa died."

"My Lord. I just can't believe what you're telling me."

"We paid her off and we made her agree to leave us alone, but now she's hounding Curtis. She even showed up with the baby at church on Sunday morning."

"Why?"

"Because she thinks she has the right to, I guess."

"What is Curtis saying about all this?"

"Not much, but he definitely wants to see the baby."

"Then why hasn't he?"

"Because I told him not to." Charlotte spoke matter-of-factly and didn't like her aunt's question. Aunt Emma was sounding as though she didn't see any problem with what Curtis wanted to do. If that was the case, Charlotte wasn't going to be happy.

"I know this has to be the worst time for you, but, honey, you're wrong."

"Wrong how?"

"Charlotte, please try to settle down. I'm not taking sides or trying to disregard what you're feeling, but right is right and I would be less than an aunt to tell you differently."

"How can you say that? How can you actually think it's okay for Curtis to see some illegitimate child he conceived behind my back?"

"I know he was wrong for what he did. He was way wrong."

"Then why would you expect me to just welcome her into our lives like everything is normal?"

"Look. Two adults may have made a terrible, terrible mistake but no matter what, that little baby is as innocent as innocent can be."

Charlotte gazed down at her plate and picked up her fork. She was so furious with Aunt Emma that she didn't know what to do. So angry that it was best she didn't even look at her.

"I know you don't want to hear what I'm saying, but it's the truth."

Charlotte dropped her fork, not caring where it fell. "Aunt Emma, I love you and you know I respect you, but I will never allow Curtis to have any kind of relationship with Tabitha or that baby, period."

"Then, honey, I'm sorry to tell you this, but you and Curtis are in for a very rough ride. If you don't find some sort of common ground, your marriage is going to suffer. It's going to suffer in a way you can't even imagine."

It was all Charlotte could do not to tell her aunt where she could go—the same place she'd advised Curtis he could go just yesterday. What was with everybody? First it was Janine and her far-fetched opinion and now Aunt Emma was being just plain out tactless. They were so quick to offer inappropriate advice, but she wondered just how well they'd be willing to take that advice themselves. There was no way they would be able to handle what she was dealing with and she was sorry she'd confided in either one of them. Next to her mother, they were her two favorite women, but after this, maybe she needed to reevaluate her choices. She'd never been at odds with Aunt Emma, particularly the way she was now, so she didn't see any other alternative except to leave. It was best that she went ahead and thanked her for dinner, told her good-bye, and went to her car.

Charlotte left her aunt's subdivision in a noticeable hurry, but about a mile into her drive, she dialed her parents and quickly told her mother what had happened.

"Mom, can you believe Aunt Emma?"

"Actually, I do. Emma tries to see good in everyone, and she's always had this crazy idea that God wants us to do whatever we have to when it comes to forgiving people. She thinks we should all let bygones be bygones in every situation."

"Well, that's just too bad because I'm not doing it."

"I don't blame you. Everyone you talk to about this is going to have a different opinion, but under no circumstances should you allow Curtis to communicate with that woman. I love my son-in-law, but he's wrong for even asking you to see his ex-mistress. Baby or not."

"I'm glad you understand, Mom, and that you support my position on this."

"Of course I do. I support you because no matter what that Tabitha says, deep down, her reasons for contacting Curtis are less about the baby and more about her wanting to be with him the way she used to. I'm telling you that woman can't be trusted, and I hope you never forget that."

"I won't. I know what she's up to, and she's not taking my husband from me."

"Ever since you told us that baby was born, your daddy and I have been worried sick about you and Curtis."

"I'm sorry to place such a heavy burden on you."

"No. Don't apologize, because this isn't your fault."

"Where is Daddy, anyway?"

"He had a library board meeting tonight."

"Then maybe I'll call him later."

"He'll be glad to hear your voice."

"Oh and hey, Mom, I almost forgot to tell you. Janine is pregnant."

"Really? Well, good for her."

"She took two home pregnancy tests last night, and they were both positive. She's still going to her doctor to get final confirmation, but she's very sure that she is."

"That's wonderful, and tell her I said congratulations."

Just then, Charlotte heard a beep from her Palm Treo and moved it away from her ear. She frowned when she saw Curtis's cell number. She had a mind not to answer but relented and told her mother she had another call.

"What?" she answered tersely.

"I just wanted to say how sorry I am for blowing up the way I did this morning."

Charlotte continued driving but didn't respond.

"I know I upset you, and I didn't mean it."

"Is there something important you needed to speak to me about? Because if not, I really don't want to talk to you."

"I just want to make things right. That's all I'm saying."

"Does that mean you're going to forget about Tabitha and that baby?"

Curtis paused. "Charlotte, I love you with all my heart, but I can't forget about Curtina."

Charlotte blasted XM-Radio and dropped her phone on the seat without ending the call so Curtis could hear it. She'd been listening to Suite 62, a wonderful R&B channel, but she purposely changed it to XL RAW, the channel that played uncut, hardcore rap, something she knew Curtis couldn't stand. She'd hoped they'd be playing the kind of rap with lyrics capable of telling Curtis exactly what she thought of him and right now 50 Cent was doing a fabulous job of it.

Charlotte pulled Matthew's comforter up to his shoulders and smiled when she saw the squirrelly look on his face.

"What? You think you're too old to be tucked in?"

"I am, Mom. And you stopped doing that a long time ago, remember?"

Charlotte sat on the side of the bed. "I know. But you're my baby, and I can't help myself. Especially not now."

"It's because I want to see my father, isn't it?"

"I love you more than anything or anyone in this world, Matthew, and I'm scared."

"But you don't have to be. You'll always be my mom and Dad will always be my dad."

"Yeah, but things might change after this weekend."

"No they won't. I promise."

Charlotte smiled and kissed him on the forehead.

"Did you say your prayers?"

"I always do."

Charlotte was glad he did, but admittedly, she rarely prayed herself at all. Just didn't see a reason to.

"Sleep tight."

"I love you, Mom."

"I love you, too, sweetie."

When Charlotte left Matthew's room, she went to hers and Curtis's but when she entered, she made no eye contact with him. In her peripheral vision, she could see that he was in bed, leaning against a stack of pillows and looking her way, but she proceeded through to her bathroom, which was adjacent to his. Inside, she opened the glass door, turned on the shower, and closed the door leading to the bedroom. She didn't even want to think about Curtis and once she finished showering, she would go to her favorite guest bedroom until morning.

After removing her V-cut, flare-leg jeans, waist-length sweater, panty hose, and underwear, she washed her face and slipped into the shower. The water was hot and soothing and she stood there longer than usual, enjoying it. She was tired, more mentally than physically, and she just wished her life could go back to the way it used to be. She was beyond miserable, and if Tabitha didn't leave them alone soon, Charlotte would be forced to take matters into her own hands, something she was trying so hard not to do. She was trying her best to wait this whole thing out, hoping Curtis would finally come to his senses, but after hearing what he'd said in terms of not forgetting about Curtina, well, that wasn't good.

He was sounding more and more like he'd made his mind up to see her. He'd sounded pretty adamant about it and unwilling to change his decision and this wasn't working for Charlotte.

When she finished drying off, she wrapped the Egyptian cotton towel around her body and opened the door. The mirror above her vanity was completely fogged, so she went to her closet to get her nightgown. That way, she could give the mirror some time to clear up before she came back to tone her face and moisturize it. She hadn't done so prior to showering because the steam always did such an excellent job of opening her pores.

But after finishing her skin-care regimen, she turned off the light and went over to her nightstand to grab the latest issues of *Essence* and *O* magazines.

"Charlotte, you know I love you, right?"

"Curtis, all I want to do is get something to read and then I'm gone. So please save whatever it is you have to say."

"I know you're hurting really bad over this, but, baby, I really do love you. I love you from the bottom of my soul, and I can't bear the thought of living my life without you. I know I said some horrible things to you today, but I'm truly sorry."

Curtis reached across to where she was standing, attempting to pull her into bed with him, but she jerked away.

"Baby, please don't do this," he said. "You're my heart and joy, and we've been through way too much not to be together. And regardless of what problems you and I have, I love that young man down the hallway. I don't care that David is his real father. All I care is that he loves me, and I love him . . . and I guess what I'm trying to say is that we owe Matthew. We have an obligation to him and we need to set aside our differences so we can be there for him on Saturday. It's bad enough that us arguing was the reason Marissa fell down those stairs and died the way she did, so do you want our bickering to cause pain and tragedy for Matthew, too? I mean, is being angry with me really worth causing a ton of heartache for him? I know you're upset, but there comes a time when we all have to start thinking about other people. We can't just think about ourselves, Charlotte," he said, pausing, but then continued.

"I've turned my life completely around so that I can honor God the way I'm supposed to as a minister and so that I can honor you as my wife, so do you think it's right for you to act the way you're acting? Do you think it's fair for you to have expected me to forgive you for every one of your mistakes but yet you don't see a reason to forgive me for mine? I mean, are you really that ready to end our marriage? Because that's where we're headed if we don't get control of this situation. Which would be a shame because I love you so much. It took me losing two other wives to finally be in a place where I want to be faithful to one woman for the rest of my life. And, baby, that someone is you."

Tears streamed down Charlotte's face, and Curtis slid his body to the side of the bed and sat up. He pulled her into his lap, and she rested the side of her face against his. Charlotte cried until her body shook, and Curtis consoled her the way he had so many times before. He held her and caressed the back of her head, and for the first time in three days, since Tabitha had dialed their number, Charlotte felt somewhat relieved.

Chances were, this cease-fire might only be temporary, but a small break from rage and anguish was certainly better than no break at all.

Better because she hadn't been sure how much more she could take.

Chapter 11

The day for Matthew to meet David had finally arrived and Charlotte still didn't feel much better about it. Her nerves were running rampant and a part of her was counting on the fact that David might cancel at the last minute. He was supposed to arrive in a half hour, so there was still more than enough time for him to back out and she hoped he would. She knew Matthew would be crushed and she certainly didn't want that, but for all their sakes, she just wished the subject of David would go away.

On the other hand, Curtis was clearly ready to meet him and while Matthew seemed a little nervous, he was also excited. Charlotte knew this because Matthew had already been to the dining room window three times, checking to see if David had driven up.

"Honey, why don't you sit down?" Charlotte advised.

Matthew pulled the drape back again. "I'm fine, Mom."

"He should be here shortly," Curtis added.

Matthew finally walked over to the family room and sat on the edge of the sofa. "I wonder what kind of car he drives? Because at least then I'd know what to look for."

Charlotte wanted to say something, anything, but she didn't. Then the phone rang.

Curtis went into the kitchen to answer it and Charlotte could tell from the conversation that it was David calling to request more directions. It sounded as though he was only a few miles away and now Charlotte knew he was really going to show up.

When the doorbell rang, Charlotte looked at Curtis and then at Matthew and then Curtis opened the door. "Please come in," he said, shaking his hand. "I'm Curtis."

"Good to meet you and thanks for having me over."

David still looked as gorgeous as ever and still dressed immaculately, and it was interesting how he and Curtis had those two qualities in common. They were also both tall, toned, and had the smoothest skin.

"Charlotte, how are you?" he asked.

"I'm well, David. And you?"

"Fine." David turned toward his son and placed his arm around his shoulders. "So you must be Matthew."

"Yes. Nice to meet you."

"It's wonderful to meet you, too."

Curtis started toward the family room. "Why don't we all have a seat?"

Matthew and David sat on the sofa, but at opposite ends, and Charlotte and Curtis sat together on one of the short sectionals.

"Wow," David said, smiling in awe. "You're such a handsome kid, and it really is good to meet you. I know I've already said that, but I really mean it."

Matthew blushed.

"So what grade are you in?"

"Eighth, and I can't wait to get to high school next year."

"I'll bet. And I hear you play football, too."

"Yep. I mean, yes. I've been playing since sixth grade but I really didn't take it seriously until last year and now this year."

"I'll have to make it to one of your games."

"We only have one left before the championship, and that's next week. Do you think you can come to it?"

"Definitely. If it's okay with your parents."

Charlotte wanted to scream. She felt ill and she hated how he was suddenly trying to invade their space any way he wanted.

"Mom?" Matthew looked at her with begging eyes. "Dad?"

"It's okay with me," Curtis answered.

"I don't see why not," she finally said.

"Then it's set. What day is it and what time?"

"Thursday at four."

"I'll be there."

Everyone sat in silence for a few minutes and then David asked another question.

"So what's your favorite subject?"

"Journalism. I like English and math a lot, too, but I love journalism."

"So do you want to be a writer?"

"Uh-huh. And I already write for the school newspaper. I'm the editor."

"So you're athletic and smart. Charlotte and Curtis, you must be very proud of him."

"We are," Curtis assured him and smiled.

Charlotte said nothing and how dare he care one way or the other about how proud she and Curtis were. They were his parents. They were the ones who'd raised him up to where he was now. They would also be the ones who'd be there to love him long after David was gone.

"So what else do you like? Fishing? Camping?"

"I love both. My dad and I went last year with some other fathers and sons and we had the best time."

"Maybe you and I will go sometime, too."

Matthew shook his head in agreement, but Charlotte would never let that happen. Matthew spending the weekend with some stranger? She didn't think so.

David and Matthew chatted for at least another thirty minutes, discussing one topic after another. They really seemed to connect with each other and that worried Charlotte. She'd been hoping the whole meeting wouldn't work out and that David's visit with Matthew would be his first and last. But she could tell David had gotten rather comfortable and wasn't planning to leave anytime soon.

"Baby," Curtis began. "Why don't we leave David and Matthew alone for a while?"

It was the last thing Charlotte wanted to do, but she didn't argue. She knew it wouldn't make a difference.

When they went upstairs, Charlotte told Curtis how she felt.

"I hate this. It's a bad idea and I just can't stand David waltzing in here like he's been Matthew's father all his life."

"Actually, he has been."

"Curtis, you know what I mean."

"Well, at least he seems like a decent man, and he definitely seems taken with Matthew."

"But that's what I don't like. I just don't want him thinking he can be with Matthew anytime he wants. I don't want David interfering in our lives this way."

"Still, we have to remember that Matthew was the one who wanted to see him. David didn't come to us, we called him. Plus, for Matthew's sake, we have to be okay with this. You know that."

Charlotte dropped down onto the bed and flipped on the television. She searched through a number of channels and called Janine to pass the time. Curtis sat reading through one of Rick Warren's new Bible study guides and seemed basically content.

Charlotte sat for another few minutes and then stood up. She debated whether she should go check on Matthew, but just then he knocked on the door.

"Mom? Dad? Can you come downstairs for a minute?"

"Of course," Curtis said.

When they went back into the family room, David said, "Matthew and I were talking and I wanted to see if you were okay with me taking him to dinner and then to a movie."

"Please, Mom." Matthew was practically begging. "Please, Dad."

"I'm fine with it, but it's up to your mother."

"Mom?"

Charlotte could kill Curtis for agreeing to this because now she had no choice but to say yes. If she didn't, she would be seen in Matthew's eyes as the bad guy.

"What time will you have him back?"

"It's three-thirty now, so probably no later than eight or nine. "We'll pick up something quick to eat and then try to make a five or six o'clock show."

Matthew didn't bother waiting to hear his mother officially say yes or no; instead, he dashed up to his room to get his leather jacket and was back down there before they knew it.

"Thanks, Mom." He hugged her and started toward the front door.

"I'll take good care of him, Charlotte, so don't worry. And again, Curtis, it was great meeting you."

"Same here. You two have a good time."

Curtis opened the refrigerator, pulled out a bottle of Perrier, and shook his head. He could hear Charlotte walking through the house, talking on the phone with Janine and going on and on about the fact that she didn't like Matthew being out with David. She'd even gone as far as saying that for all they knew, David might try to kidnap Matthew. Then she'd switched her theory and had told Janine that maybe David had only been pretending to like Matthew but now that they were alone he might be treating Matthew horribly. Curtis couldn't hear Janine's responses, but he could only guess that Janine was doing more listening than anything else. He couldn't imagine anyone agreeing with Charlotte and her irrational thinking. He knew she was uncomfortable with the whole idea of Matthew having a relationship with David, but she was taking this too far. Yes, Curtis would have loved nothing more than to not have to share Matthew, but still, he understood how David must be feeling.

He understood all too well because he knew how he felt about Curtina, his beautiful, beautiful baby girl, the one Charlotte was still forbidding him to see. But deep down, he was dying inside. Dying because what he wanted was to hug Curtina with all his might, letting her know how much he loved her. Because regardless of the fact that he'd seen her only once, he did love his child. He loved her, the same as he loved Alicia and Matthew, and he wanted her to be a part of his life. He wanted her to get to know her sister and brother so she would never feel left out.

But for now, his dream of being with Curtina had been placed on hold, and he and Charlotte hadn't spoken one word about her since four nights ago when he'd said everything he could, trying to get Charlotte to see how much he loved and wanted to stay married to her. Then, once Charlotte had relented, they'd shared the kind of intimacy every man and wife should experience on a regular basis. He'd felt a closeness to her that he hadn't felt in a long time, and he could tell her feelings had been mutual. Tuesday night had reminded him of the time when he and Charlotte had first fallen in love.

Curtis took a seat at the island and for the next twenty minutes, he tried reviewing pages of the sermon he'd written for tomorrow morning, but mostly he found himself daydreaming—actually fantasizing about Curtina. He'd tried to stay focused but no matter what, he couldn't seem to do it.

But then he jumped when he heard Charlotte yelling his name and realized she must have been calling out to him for quite a while.

"Didn't you hear me?"

"No."

"What were you thinking about?"

"Nothing."

"Nothing, hunh?"

Curtis could tell Charlotte had an idea of where his thoughts were, so he glanced back down at his sermon and flipped through the pages, trying to look busy.

"Did you know it was almost eight thirty?"

"And?"

"Matthew's not home yet, and I think we should call David to see where they are."

"He said eight or nine, so let's give him at least until then."

Charlotte looked at him disagreeably and walked over to the sink. She wet the dish towel and added a little detergent to it and started cleaning the countertops. She did it in an almost nervous fashion and just the idea that she'd found the need to clean anything at all was proof that she was on edge. She was truly worried about David and Matthew, and Curtis wondered how she was ever going to accept their relationship.

At eight forty-five, Curtis heard Matthew unlocking the door and Curtis could already see how relieved Charlotte was. First Matthew walked in and then David followed behind him.

"You're back," she said to Matthew.

"We had so much fun, Mom."

"Good."

"You guys have a wonderful boy. You've done an excellent job with raising him."

"Thanks for the compliment." Curtis thought it was a nice thing to say, but Charlotte said nothing.

"We really did have a great time."

"You're definitely coming to my game on Thursday, right?"

"I'll be there. Ready to root for you."

"Don't you have to work?" Charlotte asked. "Not to mention you live all the way over in Chicago."

Curtis almost laughed at his wife, and he wished she wouldn't act this way.

"I do, but I'm going to take the day off and drive down well before the game begins."

Charlotte was definitely disappointed but she smiled a fake smile and folded her arms.

"Oh, and Mom, is it okay if we go to dinner and to the movies next Saturday again?"

Curtis watched Charlotte's body language, which said "No, absolutely not!" and he couldn't wait to hear her response.

"If that's what you want."

"I do."

David patted Matthew's back. "Then it's settled, Matt. I'll pick you up around the same time I did today."

Wow, he was already calling him by a nickname. Curtis wasn't feeling the kind of insecurities Charlotte was experiencing, but he had to admit, David was awfully comfortable for just having spent a few hours with Matthew for the first time in his life. There was nothing wrong with it, but Curtis couldn't deny feeling a bit protective.

"Well, I'd better get going, and I'll see all of you on Thursday."

As soon as Curtis closed the door behind him, Charlotte hugged Matthew tightly. "Are you okay?"

"Yes. We had the best time. David is a top sales executive at this pharmaceutical company and, Dad, he loves football just as much as you and me do."

"That's great, son."

"I'm going upstairs to call Jonathan and Elijah to tell them everything," he said, referring to his two best friends. "Good night."

"Good night, honey," Charlotte spoke sadly.

Curtis watched Matthew disappear from the room. "It sounds like they really hit it off, doesn't it?"

Charlotte frowned. "Actually, I'm a little surprised at David's unselfish attitude because the David I remember used to be completely full of himself. And anyway, how can you be so nonchalant about all of this?"

"Because Matthew and David have every right to spend time together."

"You know what? Let's not talk about this anymore, because if we do, we'll only end up arguing."

"Fine."

Charlotte went upstairs, and Curtis went back into the kitchen. As he sat back down at the island, his phone vibrated. He pulled it from his jeans pocket and saw that he had a text message, which was strange because rarely did anyone send those to him.

He wasn't sure what to think when he saw that it was from Tabitha.

Curtis,
I really need to speak to you tonight, and if you don't call me, I can't be responsible for what might happen.
T

Curtis looked up when he thought he heard someone coming down the stairway but realized it was only his paranoia. He reread the message and then quickly deleted it. But Tabitha wasn't finished. Another message came through, but this time when he opened it, there was a photo of baby Curtina looking as cute as ever.

He knew he wasn't supposed to be calling Tabitha, but since her message sounded pretty desperate, he went outside to the garage and phoned her. He hated doing this because he knew Charlotte was probably already checking their cell phone statements, trying to see if he'd been calling Tabitha or vice versa. But it was just a chance he would have to take.

"Tabitha, I got your message. So what's so urgent?"

"Curtis, I can't take this anymore."

"You can't take what?"

"You and the way you're neglecting our daughter. I'm tired of it and the more I think about the way you used me and then just dumped me when you found out I was pregnant, well, it makes me sick. It makes me sick to know how badly you treated me but yet I've still faithfully kept our little secret to myself."

"Tabitha, you always knew I was married. And not once did I tell you I was going to leave Charlotte. I'm not making excuses for the way things turned out, but still, you always knew I had a wife."

"I don't care, you still dumped me. And then the other reason I'm hurt is because I know you really want to spend time with Curtina. I could tell how happy you were to be holding her when I brought her to the church last week."

"That's neither here nor there, and you know my situation here at home isn't that simple. You know how Charlotte feels about all of this."

"Regardless, I need you to come see Curtina. Not tomorrow, not next week, but tonight. You owe her, Curtis, and that's the least you could do."

Curtis sighed and felt guilty because he truly didn't want to continue disowning his daughter, but his hands were tied.

"All I need is a little more time to work everything out with Charlotte."

"No! What I need is for you to get in your car right now and come see your baby. Our baby, Curtis."

"You know I can't do that."

"That's really too bad. And just for the record, this was my last try."

Curtis didn't like the sound of what she was saying or the tone of her voice, which was definitely threatening.

"If you'll just be patient—" he tried to explain.

But Tabitha hung up abruptly.

Now Curtis didn't know what to do. He had a mind to do as she'd asked, head over to her house, but he knew he couldn't take the chance of Charlotte finding out. On the other hand, he really wanted to see Curtina, and why shouldn't he be able to? At some point, Charlotte would simply have to understand.

She would have to understand because he didn't know how much longer he could keep this charade circulating in his own mind let alone with other people. He didn't know how much longer he'd be able to claim to the world that he didn't have a daughter with his ex-mistress, one who lived right there in Mitchell. It just wasn't logical to believe he could keep this lie going.

Worse, he could tell Tabitha was ready to disclose everything she knew to anyone who would listen.

He could tell it was only a matter of time.

Chapter 12

Curtis slipped his sermon notes inside the pad folio on his desk and closed his eyes for a word of prayer.

"Father, as I prepare to deliver today's message, I just want to thank You for giving me yet another opportunity to minister to such a wonderful congregation. Thank You for the words You have given me, and as I speak those words, I ask that You guide me completely from beginning to end. And then, Lord, thank You for my family. Thank You for my wife, my son, and both my daughters. I thank You for watching over them and for protecting them in every situation. These and many other blessings I ask in Your son's, Jesus's, name. Amen."

Next, Curtis picked up his Bible and turned to the first scripture he would be reciting, and then there was a knock at his door.

"Come in?"

"You ready, Pastor?" Elder Jamison asked as he and Elder Dixon walked in.

"As ready as I'll be. And hey, did you all have a check cut for Tolson?"

"Yes," Elder Jamison said. "We cut it on Friday, but we can't get him to answer his phone. Attorney Hallstrom has left messages and so have we, but he hasn't returned any of them. So we don't know what's going on."

"Then maybe what we should do is just go ahead and ask Attorney Hallstrom to send him the termination agreement by certified mail. Maybe he'll sign it and we can get the check sent out afterward."

Elder Dixon had other words of wisdom to speak.

"He made all that noise and now he's got the nerve to be ignorin' us? I say we void that check and pretend like Tolson never even existed. Then, if he wants to make somethin' of it, let him."

"But you know he made threats," Elder Jamison reminded him.

"All that joker is doin' is sellin' a bunch of wolf tickets. I mean, what could he possibly have on any of us or the church as a whole? Nothin'."

Curtis still hadn't told Elder Jamison about Tabitha, but now that Elder Dixon was sounding so sure that there was absolutely no incriminating information Tolson could have, he knew it was time to tell them about his affair and the baby that had resulted from it.

"Men, please have a seat. There's something I need to tell you."

Both elders looked confused but also curious.

"There's no easy way to say this, but about six years ago, I started seeing a woman named Tabitha Charles, and six months ago she had a baby."

Elder Dixon raised his eyebrows in shock. Elder Jamison seemed numb.

"I wanted to tell you when it first happened but Charlotte and I agreed that it would be best if we said nothing at all."

"So that was the woman who demanded to see you last Sunday?" Elder Jamison asked.

"Yes. And when you came to me about it, I wanted to tell you everything, but I was too ashamed."

Elder Dixon said, "And you think Tolson has information about this?"

"I'm not sure. But just the idea that he's threatening us was enough for me to tell you the one thing he might be referring to.

I wanted you to be aware so there won't be any surprises. I'm still going to ask that you not share this with anyone else, though."

"Pastor, son, I don't wanna judge you, but what were you thinking?"

"Elder Dixon, I really can't say. Back then, I was so upset about all the problems Charlotte and I were having that the next thing I knew, I was seeing Tabitha and taking her on road trips with me."

"I'm surprised she hasn't told everyone she knows," Elder Jamison commented.

"We had her sign an agreement, stating that she wouldn't. And we also paid her money. And we're still paying her monthly child support payments."

"Well, I'm glad you told us," Elder Jamison said. "Because this gives us a heads-up and a chance to start preparing damage control."

"I agree," said Elder Dixon. "And I know you might not want to do this, but I think it might be best if you went forward with tellin' the congregation. You need to tell them and apologize. We'll still have some angry folks here and there, but it'll be worse if rumors start floatin' around and they find out from other sources."

"But it's not just the church that I have to worry about. It's also everyone nationwide. My readers and the thousands of people who have come to hear me speak in their respective cities."

"I hear what you're saying, but, Pastor, I have to admit, I tend to agree with Elder Dixon."

Curtis wasn't sure how to proceed. "I don't know."

"Well, let me ask you this," Elder Dixon said. "Are you still seeing this woman?"

"No. I haven't since she was three months pregnant."

"Are you spending time with the baby?"

"No, but Tabitha is pressuring me more and more about doing that."

"Uh-oh," Elder Dixon said, and Elder Jamison sighed.

"I'm so sorry about all of this. I'm sorry for the sin I committed and sorry for causing such potential disgrace to the church."

"What I think you need to do is talk to Charlotte and let her know what we're advisin' you to do," Elder Dixon suggested. "Then we need to call another emergency elder board meeting, so you can tell them what's goin' on. Then next Sunday, you need to speak to the congregation directly."

"Charlotte will never go for that. She's already more outraged and humiliated than I've ever seen her, and I don't have to tell you what it's doing to our marriage. Especially now that Tabitha keeps trying to contact me."

"I don't see where you have any other choice," Elder Dixon told him. "I know it'll be hard, but if that woman was bold enough to show up here last week, it's just a matter of time before she does something else."

"She was definitely the persistent type," Elder Jamison remembered. "I tried to tell her you weren't available and she made it clear that she wasn't taking no for an answer."

Curtis looked away from both of them. He'd been in trouble many times before but this was the most shameful he'd ever felt. Probably because this was the first time he'd gotten caught in a scandal after he had truly changed for the better. He wasn't the sinful man he used to be, and he was working hard to remain the good person he'd become. But whether he agreed with the elders or not, he knew they were right. He knew it was time to talk to Charlotte and move forward with revealing all that they'd been hiding.

"I'll talk to her after service."

"Good," Elder Dixon said. "You're doin' the right thing, and just so you know, I'm behind you all the way. We all make mistakes but, Pastor, I hope you've learned a valuable lesson. I hope you've learned that these harlots out here don't mean you any good and that they're not hardly worth messin' with."

"I have learned. And that's why I've been faithful to Charlotte ever since."

Elder Jamison stood up. "Let's talk after service, and then I'll contact the rest of the board this evening to get them in here tomorrow morning. And it goes without saying that I'm behind you as well."

"I appreciate that. I appreciate both of you."

Curtis picked up his Bible and notes and the three of them headed over to the sanctuary. When they entered, praise and worship service was in full progress. The Spirit was moving in an amazing way and Curtis was glad to know that God was still blessing his congregation, in spite of the terrible thing he'd done.

After Curtis stepped up to the pulpit, he shook hands with the young associate minister standing there and then set his possessions on the glass podium. Next, he reached behind his back and under his blazer, flipping on his microphone switch.

"When we all get to heaven, what a day of rejoicing there will be," he sang, joining in as the lead singer. It was one of the older songs they sang from time to time, but Curtis always loved hearing it, especially today when heaven was the one place he wished he could be. He wasn't ready to die, but he didn't know if that would be any worse than what he would have to face in the coming days. Confessing everything to everyone would be a task of a lifetime, but he knew there were no other options available.

When the members settled into their seats Curtis began his pastoral observations.

"Isn't God good?"

"Amen," most everyone responded.

"He's the best of the best, but sometimes we don't always appreciate that. Sometimes we don't do what He tells us to do and we go against His Word. Then, of course, when we do that, there are always going to be serious consequences to pay. And sometimes, they are so serious we don't know how we'll ever live them down."

"Say that," a woman agreed.

"Speak today," one of the elder gentlemen of the church offered.

"But the good news is," Curtis continued, "God is a forgiving God. He's the only one we can count on to forgive us, even when others don't."

Curtis glanced at Charlotte but he could tell she basically couldn't care less about what he was saying.

"I know I've found myself in a great many situations over the years, many that I'm not proud of, but God still allowed me a chance to turn my life around. He allowed me a chance to make things right with Him along with everyone that I hurt. So I'm thankful today. Thankful to know Him, love Him, and have unwavering faith in Him."

Curtis spoke a few more words and then took his seat. The male chorus rendered a couple of selections, the associate minister led altar prayer, and Curtis preached his sermon, which was entitled "Forgiving and Forgetting."

When he finished, he stepped back down from the pulpit.

"The doors of the church are open, and I ask you to come right now. Whether you're coming to Christ for the very first time or you're simply looking for a new church home, we welcome you with open arms."

Curtis watched two young men leave their seats and head toward him.

The congregation applauded and Curtis smiled. "Praise God. This is what we want to see."

But his smile disappeared completely when he saw Tabitha entering the sanctuary with Curtina in a baby carrier and walking down the center aisle. Curtis couldn't believe what he was seeing, and when he looked over at Charlotte he saw absolute fury written across her face and thought he would pass out.

The congregation applauded the same as they did for every soul that wanted to be saved and of course they had no clue that this particular woman and child had a connection to their pastor.

But now Curtis wondered if he should go ahead and tell his congregation everything since there was a chance Tabitha was planning to beat him to it.

Although the more he played possible scenarios back and forth and back and forth again, he decided that he couldn't. He knew what Elder Dixon and Elder Jamison had suggested but he was willing to take his chances.

He decided he would depend on prayer instead. He did so because he had nothing else going for him at the moment.

Curtis asked the two young men who'd come forward to stand again. When they did, Curtis announced that they were candidates for baptism and the church applauded and yelled many words of praise.

When they were seated, Curtis asked Tabitha to stand. But before he could say anything, she reached for the mike. And that's when Curtis knew his cover was blown.

"Good morning."

"Good morning," everyone responded.

"First and foremost, I want to thank God for allowing me to be here this morning."

"Amen," a group of people said.

"I also want to thank Him for loving me no matter what. Because, you see, I committed a horrible sin. I slept with a married man and ended up getting pregnant. Now, don't get me wrong, I know what a blessing my baby is, but I still know that I didn't have her in the way God would have wanted me to. I was wrong and so was the man I had a five-year affair with. And to make bad matters worse, this man wasted no time dumping me when I was barely in my first trimester. He dumped me almost as soon as I told him and then quickly reconciled with his wife. And I have to tell you, I've never been more hurt in my entire life. I was so hurt that on many nights, I cried myself to sleep and there were days when I contemplated committing suicide. But thank God, He kept me from it. He kept me in His care and He continued to love me just the same. So today I'm here to repent and to ask God to forgive me."

The congregation roared with approval and the majority stood on their feet. They were happy to know a sinner had found the courage to confess her wrongdoings.

"I'm also asking each of you to forgive me and to accept my daughter and me as new members. Actually, I attended service here a few times some years ago, but when I took up with the father of my child, I stopped coming and never officially joined. But now I want to serve God and I want to do it at Deliverance Outreach."

Amens resonated throughout the building, but when they quieted down, Lana stood and walked forward. "Sweetheart, whomever this man is you're talking about, the father of your child, you just let God handle him. This man will get what's coming to him. Make no mistake about it. He'll either do right by that baby of yours or like Pastor Black was just preaching earlier, this man will have some truly terrible consequences to pay. So, yes, honey, we welcome you and this beautiful little doll you have," Lana said, pulling the baby from the carrier and holding her so everyone could see her.

The women in the church acted as though the baby was their own, smiling and making sounds that said they thought Curtina was the cutest baby they'd seen in a while. Curtis had a mind to see what Charlotte's reaction was, but he didn't have the nerve to look her way. He did, however, look toward the back and saw Tracy and he couldn't have felt more ashamed. They'd never had a lot of discussion with Tracy about Tabitha, but because Tracy had been with them for years, Curtis and Charlotte had decided they might as well inform her about Tabitha and his little girl.

"Yes, we welcome both of you," Curtis finally said when Lana continued holding the baby in one arm and placing her other around Tabitha.

After that, Curtis gave the shortest benediction imaginable and rushed out of the sanctuary. Normally, he hung around greeting members, but not today. Today, he ran to safety.

C harlotte stormed into Curtis's office and slammed the door behind her. Elder Jamison and Elder Dixon had gotten there ahead of her, and Curtis was glad they had. Although, from the way she was staring at him, he wasn't sure their being there was going to change anything she had to say.

"So do they know?" she asked, referring to the two elders.

"Yes, I told them before service."

"Did you know she was coming here?"

"No. I had no idea. I was just as shocked as you are."

"Well, this is it. I want you to call the police so we can get a restraining order in place."

"I don't think that's the right thing to do. Because if we push Tabitha too far, she really will tell everything she knows. And Elder Dixon and Elder Jamison have suggested I tell the board and congregation before they hear about this elsewhere."

"That's right," Elder Jamison said. "I know the road ahead is going to be tough for your entire family, but we have to handle this as soon as possible. What Pastor needs to do is speak to the board and then have his publicist prepare a press release for the national media. He's been out of the limelight for a little while, but he's still known everywhere throughout this country and we don't want him to lose his reading audience. We definitely don't want him to lose the support of all the churches that bring him in to speak for them."

Charlotte said nothing.

So Elder Dixon spoke instead. "Charlotte, I know you must be hurtin' but this really is the best way. We have to take care of this before it gets blown way out of proportion."

"I hate this," she said. "I always wondered why Tabitha was lying low and hadn't said a word to anybody, but now I know it was because she was always planning to do something like this. She walked in here like she owned the place, and, Curtis, you sat back like some scared little child and let her."

"Baby, I'm sorry. . . ."

"Don't. Please don't say that again. You've said that repeatedly, and I just don't want to hear any more of your apologies. I just can't take it."

"So, Pastor, what time do you want me to schedule the board meeting?"

"I think we should hold off on that and think this through. Because if Tabitha had truly wanted to reveal everything, she would have done it this afternoon."

"So what are you saying?" Charlotte wanted to know.

"That maybe I just need to talk to her. Maybe if we can work out something with the baby, she'll be satisfied and that will be the end of it."

"You mean like you agreeing to go see them?"

The elders looked at each other and then at Curtis, who remained silent.

"Is that what you're thinking? Because if you are, then you may as well forget it."

"What else can I do?"

"I've already made myself clear, and I'm not saying another word about it," Charlotte exclaimed and left the office.

"I'm telling you, Pastor," Elder Jamison said. "We need to call another emergency meeting so we can get this out in the open."

"Let's just wait to see what happens. I know it's a risk, but it's a risk I'm willing to take."

Elder Dixon disagreed. "It's a mistake, Pastor."

"I appreciate your concern but I have to tell you, I'm just not ready for the world to know I was sleeping around on my wife and then got some other woman pregnant. I know eventually I probably won't have a choice, but I need time to prepare for all the scrutiny and criticism you know I'll have to deal with."

"It's your call," Elder Jamison said. "And we'll be here when you need us."

"Call anytime," Elder Dixon told him. "Day or night."

"Thanks for everything. Thanks for standing by me."

The elders left and Curtis walked over to his window. People were still getting into their cars and leaving the parking lot. He watched for a few minutes and then he saw Tabitha walking toward her vehicle. He watched and then he saw her gaze up at him. She looked at him for only a split second and then sat the baby in the car. When she had her locked in, she walked around to the driver's side and glanced in his direction again. This time, though, she stared for almost an entire minute and then got inside and drove away.

Curtis stood watching until Tabitha and Curtina were no longer in sight.

Chapter 13

It was Thursday and Curtis and Charlotte were headed over to Matthew's school to see his last regular-season football game. Her parents were trailing behind, Tracy was following them, and they were only maybe ten minutes from their destination. Everyone was so proud of Matthew and no one was more proud than Charlotte, but this was one game she hadn't been looking forward to. The reason: David was going to be there front and center.

She'd been hoping and praying he wouldn't show up, that he'd call with some really great excuse, but to her dismay, he'd phoned them about two hours ago, saying that he was already in town and that he, Anise, and Aunt Emma would be driving to the school together. Charlotte had told him okay and had basically just hung up. She still wished he'd go away, and to add more misery, she was going to have to see Anise. Not to mention, Aunt Emma would be there and she wasn't feeling a lot of love toward her right now either.

So what a day this would be. One to remember. One for the history books. One she hoped would never happen again anytime soon.

"Did you set the alarm?" Charlotte asked Curtis.

"Yep."

"I told Mom and Dad that I wanted us to take Matthew to his favorite pizza place after the game, but I'm telling you now, David isn't invited."

Curtis turned and looked at her. "Do you really think that's right?"

"As a matter of fact, I do. This is something I want our family to share and as far as I'm concerned, David's not included."

"And how do you think that will make Matthew feel?"

Charlotte didn't say anything.

"Have you thought about that? Have you considered that he might want his father to come with us to dinner?"

"I don't wanna talk about it."

"Fine. And you're the one who brought it up anyway."

"So have you heard anything from Tabitha?"

"Where did that come from?"

"I'm just asking because if that heifer was crazy enough to show up at the church, she definitely wouldn't think twice about calling you."

"She hasn't called."

"Well, if she does, I want to know about it."

"Look, I thought we were gonna have a decent afternoon together. So if you don't mind, I'd rather not talk about Tabitha."

"Good. I don't wanna talk about that hooker anyway."

Charlotte switched the radio to a different channel and heard "Baby Hold on to Me" by Gerald and Eddie Levert. It was one of her favorite songs and while Curtis didn't listen to much R&B, him being a diehard gospel music fan and all, she knew he loved this one.

Which was the reason she switched the channel again. She saw the annoyed look on his face but didn't say anything. She knew her actions were childish but he deserved whatever she dished out. Sleeping with that tramp and then getting her pregnant. Humiliating her in front of Elder Jamison and Elder Dixon and then sitting back, doing nothing, when that hussy interrupted their morning service.

Although maybe now he'd finally realized what a lunatic Tabitha was and that he could never have a relationship with Curtina—that is, not unless he wanted to deal with her idiot mother. Maybe he'd finally come to his senses and realized that Tabitha's drama just wasn't worth it. At least, that's what Charlotte was counting on because she still hadn't changed her position on any of this. She still wanted him to have nothing to do with that baby and she was glad Curtis hadn't mentioned her or her mother ever since they'd left the church on Sunday.

When they drove into the parking lot, Curtis searched up and down the aisles until he settled on what seemed the farthest spot available. He was so touchy when it came to parking his vehicle next to others, thinking someone would open their door too forcefully, causing nicks and dents, but Charlotte didn't care about that. Especially since she had always parked wherever she wanted and she hadn't seen more than a small scratch on hers.

"It looks like we got here early enough to get decent seats," Charlotte said to her parents.

"It sure does," her mother said. "And the weather is holding up pretty well, too. It's definitely a lot warmer than it was this time last year."

"I just hope Matthew and them win," her father added.

"They've only lost one game all season," Curtis told him.

"I know. Matthew brags about it every time he calls me."

"Matthew brags about that team to everybody, even people he doesn't know," Tracy said.

They all laughed and strolled toward the football field. But when they arrived in front of the bleachers, Charlotte's blissful spirit diminished. David, Anise, and Aunt Emma were already sitting there, and Curtis was already taking a step up to where they were. Charlotte would have preferred to sit on the opposite end, as far away from them as possible, but it was too late. Curtis had already hugged Aunt Emma and Anise and was now shaking hands with David. Then, of all things, he took a seat next to him. Charlotte's mom and her aunt Emma made nice with each other the way they always did at family gatherings and Charlotte's mom and dad and Tracy sat just below the rest of them. Charlotte ended up sitting next to Curtis.

"Hi, Charlotte," Aunt Emma said.

"Hi."

Anise said nothing, and it was clear that Charlotte and Anise would never adopt their mothers' false admiration exchange. Anise didn't like her, and after begging for Anise's forgiveness and not getting it, Charlotte didn't care for Anise either.

Charlotte waved at Matthew when she saw him looking in their direction and everyone else yelled out to him. It was already evident that they were going to be a lively bunch but that was a good thing because Matthew would be proud.

"So, David, I hear you work for a pharmaceutical company," Curtis said.

"I do. I've been there for a while now."

"Matthew told us you were a big-time executive."

"I don't know about all that."

"He is," Anise said. "He's trying to be modest, but he makes a ton of money, and he's not ashamed of it. At least he wasn't when I was married to him."

Everyone laughed, all except Charlotte. She couldn't believe Curtis was sitting there laughing and talking with David like they were old friends. Didn't he know David was a threat to him? Didn't he know there might be a chance David was trying to maneuver his way into Matthew's life and was trying to take his place as Matthew's father?

"Well, I hear you had two very large congregations when you lived in Chicago, and that now you're a national bestselling author," David said. "I also heard you sold a million copies of your last book."

"Boy, Matthew's been talking a lot."

"He's very proud of you, man."

"He's proud of both of us."

Charlotte wondered how much longer it was going to be before kickoff because she was so tired of hearing all this small talk. Tired of Curtis and David going on and on about nothing.

"I'm really glad Matthew and David got to meet," Anise said to Curtis. "And it's so good to see you and David connecting the way you are, because it makes things so much easier for Matthew."

"Why don't you just mind your own business, Anise?" Charlotte spoke out loud before she knew it and even her parents turned to look at her.

No one commented but the atmosphere was beyond uncomfortable. But what did Charlotte care? She had a right to express her opinion any way she saw fit, and there wasn't a thing anyone could do about it.

Finally, after another twenty minutes or so, the game began and Matthew was already racking up yards. Then, as the competition continued, the best thing happened. Matthew ran across the fifty-yard line . . . then ran through the first defender . . . then he broke a second tackle and then. . .

"Touchdown!" Curtis and David yelled ecstatically and the entire family practically jumped off the bleachers. Matthew had made the first touchdown of the day and everyone screamed, applauded, and did whatever else they could think to do in order to cheer Matthew and his team on to victory. It was an exciting time and Charlotte was near tears, looking at her baby doing so well. She knew she'd let him down in the paternity department, but she was glad none of it had affected his playing ability. She was glad he was no longer pining around like he was depressed, and that he now seemed pleased with life again.

Eventually, the fans of Mitchell Prep Academy calmed themselves down and the game continued. But only seconds later, Charlotte was sure she'd heard Curtis's phone vibrate.

"Was that your cell?"

"What?"

"Was that your cell vibrating?"

"I don't know, but if it was, I'm watching the game."

"It could be an emergency."

"I doubt it."

Charlotte wanted to demand that he pull his phone from his jean jacket to see who was trying to contact him, but when she saw David looking her way, she changed her mind. Plus, she didn't want to make a scene. She would never purposely embarrass Matthew in front of his friends, teammates, or coaches. Not to mention some of his teachers who were in attendance or some of the parents she'd known for a number of years.

No, she would keep her mouth shut and deal with Curtis when they got home.

At the pizzeria, David reiterated to Matthew how great a player he was and told him for the third time how proud he was of him. Charlotte sat with her elbows on the table and her hands locked under her chin. She was livid. She'd thought she'd made it clear to Curtis that she hadn't wanted David tagging along with them, but lo and behold, Curtis had somehow, as he put it, "let it slip" when they'd been walking to the car. She'd wanted to tear into him about that and also for not checking to see who'd been trying to call him, but as it turned out, Matthew had ended up riding with them, and she hadn't wanted him to hear them arguing.

She couldn't wait until later, though.

"Matthew, you'll be way ready for high school football next year," his grandfather said.

"I hope so. I'm already counting down the months."

"You'll do fine," his grandmother said. "The newspaper will be writing about you every week."

"You'll be running touchdowns like they're nothing," Anise added.

"Isn't that the truth," Aunt Emma said.

"You'll be player of the week all the time," Tracy told him.

Curtis play-punched Matthew's shoulder. "I told him if he keeps this up, he'll definitely go in as a starter. No doubt about it."

"Aw, Dad."

"You really are an awesome player, sweetie," Charlotte finally said. Matthew was sitting between her and Curtis and it was all because she'd refused to have it any other way. She could tell when they'd walked in that David had been planning to take a seat next to Matthew, but she'd made sure it hadn't happened. And she would make sure he didn't get his way with any other plans he might be dreaming up, whatever those plans were.

"Curt, man," David said, "Matthew told me you wanted to get him into a camp next summer."

Curt? Where was that coming from? Charlotte just didn't get all this ho-hum camaraderie.

"I do," Curtis said.

"That's great. I'd be glad to help out with the cost."

"Thanks for the offer," Charlotte interrupted, "but Curtis and I have everything covered."

Everyone fell silent and Matthew turned toward his mother. She could tell he hadn't understood why she'd said what she'd said, and now she was sorry. She was allowing her disapproval of David to get the best of her, and she would do better at watching her conversation for the rest of the evening.

On the way outside, after paying the waitress, Curtis asked Charlotte if she minded riding with her parents.

"Why?"

"Because I received a call from Sister Nelson, asking if I could come to the hospital to pray for Brother Nelson. He's very ill, and since your mom left her sweater at our house and they were planning to stop by to get it before heading back home, I figured you could drive back with them."

Charlotte wanted to go off on Curtis right then and there. She was dying to ask him what hospital he was planning to go to when it was already shortly after 8:00 P.M. But since everyone was standing around listening, she never said another word to him. Instead, she got in her parents' car and once Matthew had said his good-byes to David, Anise, Aunt Emma, and Tracy, he slid in next to her.

Curtis drove away, and Charlotte couldn't help wondering where he was really going. Although maybe it was best she gave him the benefit of the doubt. Maybe he really was going to see Brother Nelson, because actually Charlotte had heard on Sunday that he truly was very sick.

As her father pulled out of the parking lot, Charlotte's cell phone rang.

"Hello?"

"I know you don't believe me, but I really am headed to the hospital. And if you want, I'll call you when I get there and you can speak to Sister Nelson. Actually, it would be good if you could offer her some words of encouragement."

Charlotte didn't let on, but she felt better already. She felt better because whenever Curtis offered to prove anything, he was definitely telling the truth.

"That's fine. Just call me when you get there."

Chapter 14

Curtina was just as beautiful as Alicia had been when she was born and Curtis could barely take his eyes off her. As a matter of fact, Curtina even favored Alicia. Her hair was coal black and she had a lot of it to only be six months old. She was as gorgeous as she could be and Curtis wished he never had to leave her. He wished he could spend as many hours with her as he wanted with no breaks in between, but he knew this wasn't possible. He knew Charlotte would never be okay with such an arrangement and she would die if she knew where he was at this very moment, sitting on the sofa in Tabitha's living room, holding his little girl.

He hadn't wanted to go behind her back but he hadn't seen where he had any other choice but to give in to Tabitha's demands. He knew the elders had pretty much insisted that he come clean to the board and the congregation, but no matter how he'd played the possible outcomes in his mind, he just couldn't see going public. He couldn't see where that would benefit him in the long run or how he would ever live it down. So, on Monday, one day after Tabitha had joined his church, he'd taken the plunge and gone over to her house to visit Curtina. And as of today, he'd seen Curtina four consecutive days this week, and he couldn't deny the fact that he was loving every second he spent with her. Yes, it was wrong to conceal his whereabouts when it came to his wife, but at least he hadn't lied to her, not even this evening when they'd left the restaurant. When he'd told her that Sister Nelson wanted him to come pray for her husband, he'd been telling the truth and he'd called Charlotte from the hospital the way he'd said he would. He'd even stayed there one full hour, but as soon as he'd left, he'd driven as fast as he could to see Curtina.

"Look how content she is sitting in your lap." Tabitha beamed as she sat down next to Curtis. "My mother used to say, blood knows blood, and you can tell she's already gotten attached to you. It's been only a few days, but she gets so excited when she sees you."

"I really feel bad about missing so many months of her life."

"I knew you would change your mind about not seeing her if only you could have a few hours with her. I knew you'd fall as much in love with her as I am. I knew you would love her, the same as you love your other children, if not more."

Curtis wasn't sure what the "if not more" comment meant, but he figured it was better to ignore it. He loved Curtina, but he could never love any of his children any more than the others.

"It's been really hard having to take care of her on my own. Trying to be both a mother and a father is very difficult. Not so much physically as it is emotionally."

"I'm sorry I haven't been there for her but from here on out, I will be. I'll do everything I can to help raise her."

"You don't know how long I've waited to hear you say that, and I apologize for all the threats I made and for confronting you at the church. I never should have gone that far, but I honestly didn't know what else to do. I guess desperate people do desperate things."

"Well, I'm sorry that the situation between us turned out the way it did, but let's just try to leave the past in the past and move on."

"I agree."

Curtina leaned her head forward and clapped her little hands when she saw some cartoon character singing on the TV screen. When the singing ended, she rested her head back against her father's chest all over again. Not since Alicia, Matthew, and Marissa were babies had Curtis felt so special and so needed. He hadn't really taken Tabitha's observation to heart, but now he had to agree with her. Curtina truly did seem comfortable when she was with him and he couldn't be happier.

Tabitha stood up. "Can I get you something to eat or drink?"

"I'll take some bottled water if you have it."

"I'll be right back."

Curtis surveyed Tabitha's home and couldn't help remembering all the days he'd spent there with her. He hadn't spent the night on more than just a few occasions, but he'd come over for general visits on a regular basis. That is, when they weren't traveling together.

He glanced above the fireplace and saw the Lashun Beal painting he'd purchased for Tabitha a couple of years ago for her thirty-eighth birthday. It was the one Lashun had named *Divine* and it was one of Tabitha's favorites. At first, Curtis had figured he'd ask his assistant to purchase a print version and have it set in an elegant frame but as it had turned out, she'd contacted a gallery that had an original for sale. Then, in the corner, there was the light wood and glass étagère she'd wanted from Plunkett, a top furniture store in Hoffman Estates.

As Curtis scanned the entire family room, he realized that most everything he saw was something he'd purchased with money he and Charlotte had been blessed with. Because whether he'd wanted to admit it back then or not, everything he earned was as much his wife's as it was his. They were two separate individuals but in God's eyes, when they'd gotten married, they'd become one and Curtis had violated the precious vows he'd taken with her. Charlotte had done the same, but finally, after all these years, Curtis knew the tit-for-tat mentality wasn't the right way to be thinking. Once upon a time, he'd believed one bad turn deserved another. He'd wholeheartedly believed he had the right to pay Charlotte back for every terrible thing she'd done to him.

But that was then and this was now, because today he knew better. And when one knew better, he or she had an obligation to act accordingly. It was the reason he was no longer the man Tabitha had come to know six years before. It was the reason Charlotte had not a thing to worry about if she was worried about him sleeping with his ex-mistress. It was true that Tabitha was still as beautiful as ever but he had prayed to get over her and had succeeded. He did care about her but only in a way any man would care about the mother of his child.

"You sure I can't get you anything else," she said, sitting back down.

"No. This is good."

"She looks like she's dropping off to sleep. Do you want me to take her?"

"She's fine."

"Can I ask you something?"

"Go ahead."

"Did you ever really love me?"

"Actually, Tabitha, I don't think we need to discuss that. There was a time when you and I were together, but that part of our relationship is over."

"I realize that, but I just wanna know. I wanna know if everything I thought you felt for me was a lie."

Curtis wasn't sure why she was bringing up this particular subject. He knew she'd been hurt when he'd ended their affair but it was time she moved on. Time she accepted the fact that they could never be together again and time she found someone else she could have a relationship with.

"There was always a part of me that did love you but at the same time, I never stopped being in love with my wife. There were moments when I thought maybe I didn't love her anymore and that maybe I even hated her, but eventually I realized it was only because of the way she'd hurt me."

"But there's no way she could possibly love you. Not after the way she slept with your best friend behind your back."

"She was wrong and yes, her affair with Aaron is what drew me to you, but still, Charlotte and I do love each other."

"Baby, I'm really shocked that you're being so naive."

"You know, I think it's time for me to go."

"No. I'm sorry. I didn't mean to upset you. And all I'm trying to say is that no matter what happened between you and me, I still love you and I always will. I've never loved any man the way I love you and nothing will ever change that."

Curtis hadn't wanted to believe what Charlotte was saying but she'd been right all along. Tabitha was thinking there was a chance for them to be together.

"Do you want me to lay Curtina down or do you want to do it?" he asked.

"Can't you stay a little while longer?"

"No, I really have to go."

Tabitha reached for their daughter and Curtis eased his hand from beneath her head.

Then Tabitha followed him to the entryway. "Baby, I meant what I said. I love you, and I can make you so much happier than your wife ever has. She doesn't love you. I know you think she does, but she's only pretending to care about you."

Curtis opened the front door and turned to look at Tabitha. "I know this is hard for you, but I love my wife. I love her, and I'm committed to her. I'm committed to our marriage and somehow you're going to have to accept that."

"But how committed is she to you? And what do you think is going to happen once she finds out you've been spending so much time with Curtina?"

"I'll find a way to tell her the truth, and we'll work through it."

"If you believe that, then I feel sorry for you because your wife will never understand. And she'll do everything she can to stop you from seeing your daughter."

Curtis looked toward his jacket when he felt his phone vibrating but tried to ignore it.

"I'll bet that's her calling now."

"Look. I'll stop by to see Curtina tomorrow, okay?"

"Fine."

"You take care."

Curtis turned the key inside the door leading into the kitchen, walked in, and typed in the four-digit code, turning off the security system. Then he turned it back on. Without even realizing it, he'd spent nearly two hours at Tabitha's and now his watch read midnight. He'd left the hospital at nine thirty and since Tabitha lived only fifteen minutes away, he'd arrived at her house around nine forty-five. It hadn't been until eleven thirty before he'd finally left. Which wasn't good because he was going to have a hard time convincing Charlotte that he'd been with Sister and Brother Nelson for three hours. Plus, he didn't want to lie to her, but there was no way he was telling her where'd he'd just come from.

After removing his shoes, he headed upstairs and, no surprise, Charlotte was sitting in bed with her light on. Her arms were folded and he knew she'd probably spent the last hour practicing exactly what she was going to say, word for word.

"So where were you?"

"I went to the hospital, remember?"

"Uh-huh. And you were there all this time, I guess?"

"Baby, not tonight. Matthew had a great day today, so please let's not ruin that for him."

"Don't even try it. Matthew has been asleep for the longest, and it's not like his room is right next door to ours anyway."

"I told you where I was and if you don't believe it, there's nothing I can do about it."

Curtis hated having to do this. Hated deceiving her the way he was, but he didn't see any other way out. At least not one that would allow him to tell Charlotte the truth and at the same time allow him to still see his child in peace.

"I hope you weren't with that tramp."

"What tramp?"

"Please. You know exactly who I'm talking about. Tabitha."

"How many times do I have to tell you I don't want her?"

"So what you're saying is that you haven't seen Tabitha at all today?"

Curtis paused and then realized that since it was after 12:00 A.M., he actually hadn't seen her "today."

"No. I haven't. I really haven't."

"So you say."

Curtis knew his before midnight/after midnight theory was nothing more than a cop-out, but what else could he do? Certainly not tell her he'd been with his daughter every single day this week and that her mother was now confessing her undying love for him. There was no way.

He would tell her, though, eventually. He wasn't sure when, but he knew there was no way around it.

Chapter 15

Charlotte slipped on her black spandex workout pants and fitted sports tank and sat on the side of the bed so she could put on her socks and gym shoes. Since Matthew would be spending this afternoon and evening with David, Curtis had taken Matthew out to breakfast. And actually, Charlotte was sort of happy they were gone. Relieved was more like it, because she needed some time to cool down. Of course, Curtis had denied seeing Tabitha on Thursday night, but Charlotte wasn't sure what to think, especially since he had such a long history of lying. Which was why she wondered if maybe she should hire Mr. Perry, the private investigator who had gotten her all the information on Tabitha before she'd even known Tabitha existed. But in all honesty, hiring him again really wasn't necessary because all she actually had to do was park near Tabitha's house herself and then wait to see if Curtis showed up.

When she'd tied her Nikes, she went down to the main floor, pulled a bottle of water from the refrigerator, and continued down to the lower level and into the workout room. She set her water inside one of the open slots on the side of the treadmill, straddled the belt, and pressed manual. Sometimes she chose specific programs, but today she wanted to control her activity on her own. She attached the magnetic key, pressed three and a half miles per hour, and took the incline up 3 percent.

After about two minutes, she flipped on the television, searched for CNN, and turned down the volume. She liked watching various programs, but more than anything, she loved listening to her iPod. She could still remember how excited Matthew had been when he'd gotten his and for the longest time, she'd figured it was basically just a gadget for children. But then one day, she'd borrowed his and realized it kept her walking with great rhythm and her time passed very quickly. She hadn't loved some of Matthew's music selections, though, and had even made him delete a couple once she'd heard them. But still, she'd been impressed enough to purchase an iPod for herself.

So now she had everything on it from Luther Vandross to Trinitee 5:7 to Howard Hewitt to Mary J. Blige to Yolanda Adams to Beyoncé, and the list went on and on. She was only thirty-one, but she loved music by both young artists and some who were older. She loved gospel and R&B.

Charlotte listened to one song after another and as soon as twenty minutes flashed on the screen, she elevated the incline to 6 percent. She normally stayed on for only thirty to forty minutes total, but she liked doing at least ten minutes of a more uphill climb. So far, in all her years, she hadn't had any weight issues, but still, once she'd begun doing higher inclines, she'd noticed how much more toned her legs and butt were. Her stomach had always been flat but even that seemed more muscular as well.

As she entered the cool down phase of her walking routine, she heard Mary J. Blige singing "Your Child," which had been out for a few years now, but still sounded as good as anything current. Charlotte sang along but then suddenly snatched out both earpieces. She must have heard this song more times than she could count, but for some reason it bothered her more today than ever before. Especially when she heard Mary singing about a man denying his own flesh and blood and how he needed to face reality.

She knew the lyrics were on key, but no matter what Mary, or anyone else for that matter, said, she just couldn't accept another woman's baby. She knew, just as Aunt Emma had told her, that Curtina was completely innocent, but Charlotte couldn't help the way she felt. She couldn't help the anger and resentment she was feeling and all she wanted was for Tabitha and her baby to vanish. She'd even considered offering her a hundred thousand dollars, anything to get her away from Mitchell. Although she knew Tabitha would never agree to it.

When Charlotte stepped onto the carpet, she unclipped her iPod from her waist, sat it on the window ledge, picked up a couple of five-pound free weights, and toned her biceps, triceps, and shoulders. After that, she did fifty crunches and a couple of other abdomen and leg floor exercises.

When she went back up to the second floor, she debated whether she should jump right into the shower or go online to check her e-mail, something she hadn't done in a couple of days. Matthew and Curtis wouldn't be home for a while so maybe she would spend some time on the computer.

In her office, she pushed the space bar on her desktop keyboard and waited for the system to boot up from hibernation and when it did, she signed onto AOL. She saw that she had thirty messages but she knew most of it was probably junk. Still, she clicked on the mailbox icon in the upper left-hand corner of the window and scrolled down the list. She stopped when she saw a message with a subject line that said "Re: Your Husband" and actually, if she hadn't seen those particular words, she would have probably decided it was spam and just deleted it, because she didn't recognize the address it was being sent from.

But when she clicked the mouse and opened it, she felt her nerves racing.

Charlotte,

I thought long and hard about whether I should tell you this
or not, but I really feel you have every right to know . . . your
husband has been with his other woman and his baby five days
in a row. He's seen them every day this week, and if for some
reason you don't believe me, just ask him where he went on
Monday after he left the Christian bookstore, on Tuesday, after
he left the church, on Wednesday, before both of you went to
Bible study, on Thursday after he left the hospital to pray for
one of your members, and then yesterday evening between
five and seven. He'll probably deny everything I've told you, but
I guarantee that every bit of what I'm saying is one hundred
percent true.

 I'm only telling you this because I think it's a terrible shame
for him to go behind your back the way he is, and if it were me,
I wouldn't let him get away with it. I wish I was contacting you
with better news, but the reality is that your husband is the
same lying, cheating minister he's always been.

Sincerely,

A Friend

Charlotte was fuming and had no doubt this message was from
Tabitha. What a nightmare this woman had turned out to be, and
Charlotte couldn't wait until Curtis brought Matthew home and
for David to pick him up. All morning, she'd been dreading the
idea of David taking Matthew on another outing, but right now
she welcomed it because Matthew's absence would give her and
Curtis just the kind of privacy they needed. The kind where she
could say whatever she felt like with no restraints.

atthew had left with David about ten minutes ago, and
Charlotte was curled up on a chaise in their bedroom sit-

ting area, reading a novel. Her initial plan had been to confront
Curtis as soon as Matthew had left the house but she'd decided
that maybe it was better to wait. Wait and see if he would come
up with some lame reason why he needed to leave the house.
Right now, he was walking toward the armoire but Charlotte
kept reading or at least that's what she wanted him to think.

"I know you're not happy about David, baby, but it's really
amazing how well he and Matthew are getting along."

Charlotte never looked up.

"So I guess you still don't have anything to say."

Again, Charlotte refused to look at him. Never even moved a
finger.

"Hey, I forgot some of my notes at the church, so I need to run
by there to get them."

Now she lowered her book onto her lap. "Oh, okay, then why
don't I get my shoes so I can ride over there with you, and after
that, we can get something to eat."

She was suddenly and purposely more cheerful toward him
than she'd been in weeks but Curtis stood there with what
appeared to be a shocked look on his face, obviously not expecting that she would want to go with him.

"What's the matter?"

"Nothing. It's just that I was planning to work on the rest of
my sermon while I was there so that I won't have to worry about
doing it when I get back home. I was even thinking I could go
pick up something for us right now from Big Italy's, so we can eat
dinner before I go."

"You know, actually, that sounds good because that way I can
keep reading, and I won't have to go out."

"Are you sure?"

"Positive."

Curtis went into the bathroom and then came back out. "Do
you mind calling it in?"

"That's fine. Do you know what you want?"

"What are you having?"

"Lasagna."

"Then I'll have the same."

"Is that it?"

"I think so."

When Curtis left, Charlotte called the restaurant and placed their order, and they told her everything would be ready in about twenty minutes.

Now she was back on the chaise again, reading. And she kept reading until she heard Curtis coming in with the food and then went down to the kitchen. All twenty-five copies of the infamous e-mail she'd received were either spread out on each counter, taped to the refrigerator, or positioned all across the island and now Curtis was reading one of the copies he'd just picked up. The look on his face was worth a million bucks, and it was the reason Charlotte hadn't argued about him going to the restaurant to pick up carryout. She'd wanted time to print the copies and then display them in a way that would catch Curtis off guard. She hadn't even thought of doing it until he'd made that dense and deceitful claim about needing to run by the church, but now she was glad she had. It was petty, she knew, but petty was exactly what her lying, scheming husband deserved. That and then some.

Curtis turned to look at her. "Baby, I am so sorry. I wanted to tell you but I knew you wouldn't understand."

Charlotte looked at Curtis as if everything were great and wonderful in their lives, went over to the glass and wooden cabinet, pulled a silver-rimmed plate from their stack of casual china, took a knife and fork from the drawer below, and came back over and sat down.

Curtis gestured with the e-mail toward her. "Who sent you this?"

Charlotte took the lasagna out of the bag but didn't say a word.

"Baby, I'm telling you right now. Tabitha means nothing to

me, and I've already made that clear to her. I told her face-to-face that I love only you, and that I'm committed to you."

Charlotte opened the container, cut a square of lasagna, and placed it on her dish.

"I know I messed up but as God is my witness, baby, I haven't touched Tabitha in any way. Whenever I go over there, I spend the entire time with Curtina."

Charlotte lifted the selector, turned on the wall-mounted flat-screen TV, and cracked up when she saw JJ making some crazy face at Thelma. She loved every rerun of *Good Times* she'd ever seen.

Curtis sat down next to her. "Baby, talk to me."

Charlotte took a bite of her food and laughed at JJ again.

"Baby, please." Curtis's tone was loud.

"Please what?"

"Please let's work this out."

"You know, I practically begged you not to go around Tabitha, but you did it anyway. So, as far as I'm concerned, we have nothing else to say."

"I don't believe you. I just don't believe you're taking such a cruel stance on this when you've done the same thing to me. And twice for that matter."

"You're right. But this is different. In your situation, you were able to be a father to Marissa without ever having to deal with Aaron. But with Curtina, I'll have to deal with Tabitha all the time and I'm not doing it."

"Well, what about David? I'm dealing with him, and I'm fine with it."

"Yeah, but it's only because you know David and I didn't sleep together while I was married to you, not to mention that was years ago."

"But you and I were still seeing each other, and then you led me to believe Matthew was my son when you knew full well he might not be."

"Nonetheless, I'm through arguing with you about this."

"So you're still saying I can't see my daughter?"

"No. Not anymore. I told you over and over how I felt, but as of this moment, you're free to see her whenever you want to. You do whatever it is you feel you have to do."

"But where will that leave us? Are you saying you want a divorce?"

"I'm not saying anything of the sort."

"I hate this."

"Why?"

"Because somewhere in your heart you had to know it wasn't right for me to disown Curtina. I mean, baby, what if she was your child and I wasn't having anything to do with her?"

"But that's just it." Charlotte spoke coldly. "She's not mine, and frankly I couldn't care less about her. You hear me. That's *your* baby. And I'm telling you right now, I'd better never once catch you bringing her around Matthew. As a matter of fact, I don't even want you telling him about her and if you do, I'll take you for everything you have. I'll make you wish you never laid eyes on me, let alone married me. Now get out of my face."

Curtis went outside, got into his SUV, and Charlotte resumed eating her dinner.

She ate one bite after another but couldn't help wondering if Curtis really thought she was going to allow these visits with Tabitha to continue—allow him, Tabitha, and Curtina to pretend as though they were this happy-go-lucky family, living happily ever after. She wondered if he was naive enough to believe she would ever accept any of what was happening when her own little girl had died so tragically less than two years ago.

If he did, he was dead wrong.

And in for a rude awakening.

Chapter 16

It had been three days since Charlotte had plastered copies of that e-mail all over the kitchen, but Curtis still couldn't stop thinking about it. He'd known it was probably only a matter of time before she found out where he'd been going, but what he'd wanted was to tell her himself. He'd wanted to tell her from the very beginning, but his hesitation in doing so had stemmed from his assumption that she would never understand. He'd worried that her reaction would be way over the top, and he hadn't wanted to deal with yet another confrontation between them.

Now, though, he wished he'd handled this head on because there was no telling what Charlotte was planning to do to get back at him. Especially since she was the type of woman who felt a strong need to hurt those who'd hurt her and who felt a strong obligation to protect what was rightfully hers. Sadly, he knew he was at the center of every ounce of revenge she was probably considering. He knew this because she still wasn't speaking to him, and just this morning she'd looked at him in a way that screamed pain and hatred. He'd wanted to say something to her, anything, but he hadn't found the right words and had ultimately left the house as soon as he could.

"Yes," Curtis said to Lana when she called into his office.

"Pastor, Elder Jamison is on the line for you."

"Thanks. Put him through."

"So I know you're calling with good news," Curtis said to him.

"I wish I was. But unfortunately, Reverend Tolson finally called and said he's not signing any agreement and he's not accepting two years of pay. He wants four years or else."

"I'm sorry to hear that."

"I just don't get why he's doing this."

"I do. Tolson is consumed with greed and all he's trying to do is manipulate us."

"Well, if that's the case, he should be ashamed of himself."

"He should be but I doubt that he is."

"So what do you want to do now?"

"At this point, I think we should let him know that if he doesn't take the deal, we'll be rescinding our offer and that he can forget about any future job recommendations."

"Sounds good to me and maybe once he realizes we're finished with this, he'll come to his senses."

"We can only hope."

"On a different note, have you heard anything else from that Tabitha woman?"

"I won't go into details, but let's just say, I think I have everything under control."

"Look, Pastor, I know I'm one of the elders of this church but I'm also your friend. And as your friend, I have to say I still think you should tell the board and the congregation. I know it may seem like you have everything under control, but you and I both know that secrets always have a way of getting out. No matter how well we try to hide them."

"I hear you, and to be honest, I know you're right. But the thing is, I'm just not ready to face everyone yet. I'll do it soon, but I need time to prepare myself first."

"That's all well and good, but I just hope you don't take too long."

"I won't. And I want you to know I appreciate your friendship. It means a lot, man."

"Same here."

Curtis heard his cell phone ringing and saw that the call was restricted.

"Hey, I need to take this, but let me know if you hear from Tolson again."

"I'll be in touch."

Curtis hung up his office phone and picked up his cell.

"Hello?"

"Hey," Tabitha said. "I was just checking to make sure you were still coming."

"You don't have to be at the salon until two, right?"

"Yes, but it'll take me about thirty minutes to get there."

"Then I'll be at your place around one fifteen."

"That'll be fine. And thanks so much for watching Curtina. Her babysitter is out of town this week, and you know my two best friends work until five."

"It's no problem."

"Okay, then I'll see you in about an hour."

Curtis was truly looking forward to spending time alone with his daughter but the idea that he was going to be babysitting for Tabitha while she got her hair done made him feel guilty. Visiting Curtina was one thing, but if Charlotte ever found out he was helping Tabitha out personally, he couldn't imagine what might happen. Of course, he didn't see anything wrong with watching his own child while her mother did something she needed to do, but given the circumstances, he knew Charlotte would never see it that way. She would jump to conclusions and decide hands down that he was doing favors for his ex-mistress and that this also meant he was now sleeping with her again. Something that couldn't be farther from the truth.

Curtis finished working on a few more items and left his office.

"Lana, I'm leaving for the day but if you need to reach me, just call my cell."

"That's fine, Pastor. We'll see you in the morning."

Curtis said good-bye to Lana's two assistants and headed out to the parking lot. He grunted when he saw Leroy standing near his vehicle.

"Hey, Pastor, gotta few dollars you can spare?"

"It depends on what you need it for."

"Food. What else?"

"I don't know. You tell me. Because the last time I gave you money, one of my members told me they saw you going into that liquor store down the street."

Leroy smiled, gritty teeth and all, and said, "You talkin' about your member that drives that black Lexus? Howard?"

"I'd rather not say who."

"Hmmph. I know it was him. And while he all up in my business, did he tell you he was in there, too? Shoot, that fool bought enough liquor to make every drunk in town jealous."

Curtis wanted to laugh out loud but he didn't.

"That's beside the point, Leroy, because what I want you to do is clean yourself up and get off the bottle. And it would be nice if you started coming to service on Sundays."

"Aw, Pastor, you know I'm here every week."

"Yeah, out here harassing my female members."

Leroy chuckled. "Okay, you got me there. But I don't come in because I don't have anything to wear."

"Really? Well, what happened to all those clothes we gave you not too long ago?"

"I got 'em."

Curtis shook his head and pulled out his wallet. "I pray for you, Leroy."

"I pray for you, too, Pastor. All the time. Every single day."

Curtis couldn't help smiling and then passed Leroy ten dollars.

"God bless you, Pastor. This'll get a nice bottle of . . . I mean a nice dinner at that restaurant a few blocks down the way."

"Bye, Leroy."

"See you tomorrow, Pastor."

Curtis sat in his vehicle and wondered why Leroy didn't see a reason to change. Because it wasn't like he couldn't do better. He was able-bodied and he'd told Curtis about a year ago that he'd graduated from high school and had one semester of college. Not to mention, the church had tried to help him get on his feet more than once. All Curtis could hope was that one day Leroy would listen to his advice and would realize how much better his life could actually be if he made more of an effort.

Curtis snapped his seat belt and turned on the ignition, but he rolled the window down when Leroy approached him again.

"Don't tell me that ten isn't enough."

"No, Pastor, it's fine. But since you've always been so generous with me, I figure the least I could do is tell you something you might need to know."

"What's that?"

"You know that preacher who takes your place when you're gone sometimes?"

"Reverend Tolson?"

"Yeah, that's him. And his first name is John, right?"

Curtis nodded yes.

"Well, a buddy of mine told me that the reverend sleeps with prostitutes just like they're going out of style."

Curtis raised his eyebrows. "Leroy, you should be ashamed of yourself."

"No foolin', Pastor. I wouldn't lie to you. And I also hear he sleeps with hookers so much that they've had to give him a nickname."

Curtis pursed his lips.

"I'm serious. They call him Johnny the John."

"That's too bad."

"I think it is, too. Sad. A man of God out here sleeping with women, left and right. Just pitiful if you ask me."

"Pitiful it is, Leroy. And thanks for the information."

"No problem. Glad I could be of service."

When Curtis pulled into Tabitha's driveway he got out and walked up the sidewalk. He still couldn't believe what Leroy had told him, but he knew it was definitely possible. When Curtis had first hired Tolson, he never would have believed Leroy or anyone else who might've had something negative to say about Tolson, but with the way Tolson was acting now, totally indignant, Curtis knew he was probably capable of anything.

Curtis rang the bell and Tabitha opened the door within a couple of seconds.

"Hey," she said.

Tabitha was wearing an expensive, pure white silk robe but Curtis ignored it. "How's it going?"

"Good."

"Where's the little one?"

"Asleep. Just dropped off about twenty minutes ago."

"Oh. Well, then, I guess I'll just watch some television."

Curtis wasn't sure why Tabitha was just standing there, staring at him, so he started toward the family room.

But Tabitha grabbed his arm. "Baby, I know this is a touchy subject, but the truth is, I want you so badly I don't know what to do."

"What?"

"I can't stop thinking about you and no matter how hard I try not to, I can't help myself."

"Tabitha, please. We've already discussed this. What you and I had is no more and the only connection we have is Curtina."

"I know you keep saying that, but if you would just let me show you how much I still love you, I know we can make things right again. Baby, please," she said, untying her robe and slipping it away from her shoulders.

Curtis watched it drop to the floor and couldn't resist staring at Tabitha's body a second longer than he should have. She didn't have a stitch of clothing on and though she'd recently had a baby, her body was practically rock-solid again.

But then he came to his senses.

"Tabitha, please put your robe back on. And if you think I came over here to have sex with you, you're sadly mistaken."

"I'm sorry."

"You should be. And you know what, I shouldn't even be here."

"No, please don't leave," she said, grabbing him when he turned toward the door, but Curtis snatched away from her.

"I'm out of here."

"Baby, please. I'm sorry. I was wrong for doing this, and I promise it won't happen again."

Curtis opened the door. "You're right. It won't ever happen again."

Tabitha begged and pleaded until Curtis was in his car and could no longer hear her, and he could kick himself for being so thick-headed about all of this and for trying to make himself believe Tabitha truly only wanted him there to see Curtina. He hadn't wanted to admit it, but now he knew Charlotte had been right about Tabitha all along and that he never should have gone behind her back to see Curtina. And while Tabitha had totally denied it on Saturday evening when he'd asked her about it, he couldn't help but believe she was in fact the person who'd sent that convicting e-mail message. He wasn't sure how she would have gotten Charlotte's address, but after today, her motives were crystal clear.

Actually, they'd been clear since day one, but he'd been so caught up with Curtina that he'd chosen to overlook the excitement that seemed to overcome Tabitha every time he came for a visit. She'd never given up on having a relationship with him again and Charlotte had a right not to want him around her. The only thing was, he didn't know how to not be around Tabitha and yet still be able to see Curtina. She was only six months old and it wasn't like Charlotte would ever allow him to bring her to their home.

So, bottom line, he was at a crossroads and didn't know which direction to proceed in.

He drove away from Tabitha's subdivision and called home.

"Hey, Tracy. Is Charlotte around?"

"No, Mr. Curtis. She has her weekly hair appointment and some other errands she needed to run."

"Okay, then I'll try to catch her on her cell."

"Bye-bye."

"See you, Tracy."

Curtis dialed Charlotte's number but it rang four times and went to voice mail. He debated whether he should leave a message and then decided he would.

He decided any apology, recorded or otherwise, was the very least he could offer her.

The very least he could do after witnessing the crazy stunt Tabitha had just tried pulling.

Chapter 17

For the life of her, Charlotte couldn't understand why every well-to-do, black-owned salon in town always had women stacked on top of each other. Not in the literal sense but it was just that every time she came to Robin's Hair Creations there was a minimum of two clients waiting for each of the four stylists to finish up with another client that individual was already working on. She didn't understand this because it just wasn't logical for any stylist to assume he or she could service more than one person at a time. It was also the reason she paid Robin whatever she needed to in order to have her undivided attention. She paid her almost double her normal prices, so that Robin could do her hair nonstop with no one-hour delays in between steps. It was true that some customers had basically resorted to using salon time as their magazine- or novel-reading time and didn't mind playing musical chairs with each other, but Charlotte refused to do anything there that she could easily do in the comfort of her own home.

"Hey," Robin said, smiling. "I'm all ready for you."

"So how's it going?" Charlotte said, sitting in the chair.

"Everything's good. How about you?"

"Fine. I think it's time for a touch-up, though."

Robin picked up Charlotte's client information card. "It looks like I just gave you one five weeks ago."

"I know, but feel my roots and you'll see what I mean."

Robin pulled the plastic cape in front of Charlotte and tied it behind her neck. Then she took a comb and parted her hair down the middle.

"Yeah, I guess you're right. You've got quite a bit of new growth. It grew out fast this time."

"I know."

Robin pulled out a large jar of relaxer and set it on her station's counter. It wasn't one of the most widely used relaxer systems or one of the most expensive, but it was mild and still strong enough to straighten Charlotte's hair the way she liked it. Robin always said she loved it because it wasn't harsh and because it helped keep Charlotte's hair extra healthy.

Next, Robin parted her hair from side to side so that it was now divided into four sections. Then she slipped on her gloves and applied the first portion of chemicals.

"So how's Pastor Black?"

"He's doing well."

"Did you tell him what I said?"

"About not writing fast enough?"

"Yep."

"I told him. And he said to tell you he's getting ready to start another one."

"Good. You know I love his work. Helped me tremendously when I was seeing that jerk, Roscoe."

"I remember you saying that, and I'm just glad you finally left him alone. You deserved so much better than that."

"I realize that now but back then I just couldn't see it. I really thought I was in love with him."

"It happens to the best of us. We've all been in that situation at one time or another."

"And how's Mr. Matthew?"

"He's wonderful. His football championship is this Thursday, so of course he's excited about that."

"You're so blessed to have such an amazing young man. And he's a gorgeous little thing, too. Looks just like his daddy."

Charlotte heard this all the time, which was why she'd been so sure Matthew was Curtis's son. She knew she'd slept with David around the time Matthew had been conceived, but Matthew looked nothing like him. David was fair, the same as his Caucasian and Native American mother, and Matthew was medium brown. They had no resemblance whatsoever, but that just went to show that not every child was the spitting image of his parents.

Charlotte crossed her legs. "You still planning to take one of those extension courses you were talking about?"

"I think so. I've been researching a few of them, but what I like about two of the methods is that they can bond other brands of hair if I needed them to."

"Why wouldn't you want to use the hair they manufacture?"

"Because most of the samples I've seen look way too silky to match most black hair. Our hair is so much coarser than most anyone else's, and you would have to use a ceramic flat iron on it all the time in order to make sure it blended properly."

"So can they do it?"

"Yes. There's an extra charge, but I think it's worth it. All I'd have to do is order the hair I need, send it to them, and then they would cut it from the weft and bond individual strands together."

"Sounds neat. Maybe I'll have to get me some extensions once you start doing them."

"Yeah, right."

"I'm serious. You know I don't care for sewn-in or glued-in weaves, but I saw the strand-by-strand process being done on *Today*, and I really liked it."

"Well, it's not like you really need it. Your hair will grow past your shoulders on its own anytime you want it to."

"Still, it would be nice to have a lot more volume every now and then."

"That's true. Well, we'll see what you think once I start doing it."

When Robin finished working in the relaxer, she and Charlotte walked over to the shampoo bowl so she could rinse it out. Next she added a special conditioner that would bring the pH back to normal and then she rinsed that out as well and saturated Charlotte's hair with a neutralizing shampoo. She washed her hair a second and third time and then squeezed all the water out. When Charlotte sat up, Robin massaged a liberal amount of deep conditioner so that it covered every strand and then placed a plastic cap on her head. Afterward, Charlotte followed her over to the dryer area and sat in a chair between two other women. Robin set the dryer for twenty minutes and then lowered it.

Then she brought Charlotte the latest issue of *Upscale,* which was fine because she did think dryer time was the one time it was okay to read something at the salon.

When her twenty minutes were up, Robin took her back to the shampoo bowl and Charlotte almost laughed when she saw the two women she'd been sitting between still sitting under their respective dryers. Their stylists must have set their timers for forty-five minutes, and Charlotte knew it was all because they were trying to buy themselves more time with the other clients they were working on. Clients they were trying to maneuver and were doing so unsuccessfully.

"Do you want it wrapped today or just blow-dried?"

"Blow-drying is fine. Especially since you have that new ionic blow-dryer."

"I love it, too. Doesn't dry the hair out the way regular ones do."

They walked back over to Robin's station and Charlotte sat down again. "Did you know that most of the black salons here in Mitchell are still using marcel equipment to flatten and curl hair?"

"That's what I keep hearing, and I think a lot of it has to

do with the fact that so many stylists in this area don't attend regional or national hair shows on a regular basis. Which means they're not always aware of new trends. Plus, switching over to new trends usually means you'll have to make a certain investment and in all truth, the really decent ceramic flat irons do cost a pretty penny. But to me, they're so worth it because they're so much better for our hair. They get the hair silky straight, and they don't overheat or damage it the way the marcel curling irons can. That is, if you use the expensive ones. And they can curl the hair the same as a curling iron."

Robin pulled out a large round brush and turned on the blow-dryer. Charlotte looked around the shop and then up at the television at Dr. Phil.

But she thought she would pass out when she heard the front door of the salon opening and saw that witch, Tabitha, walking in. Charlotte locked eyes with her and she took a seat.

"You must be Tabitha?" Melanie, one of the stylists, said.

"Yes."

"Welcome. I'll be with you in just a few minutes."

If only everyone in there knew what Charlotte was thinking. If they did, they would run for cover and would probably lose all levels of respect for her. She knew her thoughts were heartless, but she just couldn't stand Tabitha. She couldn't stand her, and the mere sight of this woman made Charlotte sick. Made her want to jump up and rush over and knock Tabitha out of the chair she was sitting in. Better, she wished she could drag that heifer outside to the middle of the street and leave her there.

Charlotte tried to focus on Dr. Phil and the two guests he was conversing with, but every now and then she couldn't help glancing in Tabitha's direction. She did this for about fifteen minutes until finally Melanie called Tabitha over, which was worse because Melanie's station was directly next to Robin's.

"So how are you today?" Melanie asked, shaking Tabitha's hand.

"I'm well. And you?"

"I'm good. Please have a seat," she said, and Tabitha sat down. "On the phone you mentioned that you wanted to get a hot oil treatment and then a roller set, correct?"

"Yes."

"You have really nice hair. It's very nice and thick."

"Thank you."

Charlotte cringed and took a deep breath. Robin was now curling her hair, and Charlotte was glad no one in the place knew who Tabitha was or what her connection was to Curtis.

Melanie asked Tabitha a few questions and jotted down some information on a card. "Are you on any medications?"

"No. I take a multivitamin every day but that's pretty much it."

"Do you color your hair?"

"Not really. I've gotten a few highlights here and there but not on a regular basis and not in a long time."

Melanie jotted down more information and then pulled a cape from the hook on the side of her station. "So are you from Mitchell?"

"No, but I've been here for a while. My husband's job transferred him here but even after we were divorced, I decided to stay."

Yeah, and why don't you tell her the reason? Why don't you tell her it's because you're a lousy tramp, you started sleeping with my husband, and then you got knocked up by him?

"So do you like it here?"

"It's okay. I just had a little girl six months ago, and I definitely think it's the right place to raise her. Plus, her father lives here, and he comes to visit her every day. Actually, he's the one who offered to come by and watch her so I could have some me time to come and get my hair done."

Charlotte wanted to scream a thousand words, none of which God would be happy about, and it was all she could do to keep still. It was all she could do not to grab Tabitha and yank her across the room. On the other hand, she wanted to cry her eyes out because the whole idea that Curtis, at this very moment, was sitting at his woman's house, looking after their child, was enough to tear her heart out.

Melanie and Tabitha went over to the shampoo bowl and Robin said, "She seems nice, doesn't she?"

"Actually, I wasn't paying all that much attention," Charlotte lied.

"She's beautiful and she dresses with a lot of class. The more I think about it, she reminds me of you."

Charlotte felt like she was suffocating. Like she was dying a slow death and if she didn't get out of there soon, she wasn't sure she'd be able to hold her tongue.

But thankfully, Robin finished her hair before Tabitha returned to Melanie's chair.

Charlotte and Robin walked to the front of the salon; Charlotte paid her and then left as quickly as she could.

She dialed Curtis's number before she even made it to her car.

But he didn't answer.

So she groaned and threw her phone inside her purse and drove away from the hair salon. She was steaming and the more she replayed everything that Tabitha had just told Melanie, the more she realized there was no way she could allow Tabitha to get away with all her boasting.

Which is why she drove down to Subway to get a quick bite to eat and then returned to the parking lot and waited. It was now after five and with it being so close to November, it was already dark outside, which was good because she didn't want to be noticed. The temperature was actually starting to cool down, so she kept the car running and turned on the heat.

Then she waited some more. She waited until she saw Tabitha practically sashaying out to the parking lot and over to her vehicle.

Charlotte got out of hers and headed toward her.

"Of all the salons in town, I guess you decided my salon was the best one for you to go to, hunh?"

"Charlotte, leave me alone."

"No, you leave me alone. I don't know how you found out where I get my hair done or how you knew I was getting it done today, but I'll tell you this. I'd better never see you here again."

"Ha! And you think that's going to stop me? Sweetheart, please," Tabitha said and opened her door.

But Charlotte slammed it back shut.

"You may have slept with my husband and then had a baby by him, but you'll never have him as your husband."

Tabitha opened her door again. "We'll see about that."

Charlotte slammed it shut a second time and shoved Tabitha against the vehicle. "If you think I'm playing with you, just keep messing with me."

Charlotte looked around to see if anyone had witnessed their little altercation and then went back to her car. Tabitha yelled out a bunch of threats but Charlotte left her standing there. She drove away and tried to calm herself down. She was so upset and even embarrassed about the way she'd put her hands on Tabitha. But then again, Tabitha deserved that and so much more. She knew Curtis was at fault, but now she had a feeling this lunatic was stalking her and she hoped this wasn't going to become a habit.

She pulled out her phone and saw that she had two messages. The first was from Curtis, saying he was sorry about everything and to please call him back. The second was from Matthew, saying he'd gotten an A on his math test, that he would call her later from Jonathan's, and that he loved her. Charlotte hadn't remembered him saying he was going over there after practice, but Jonathan and Elijah had been his best friends since elementary school and she was sure Elijah was probably over there as well and they were happy to be doing whatever thirteen-year-old boys do when they get together.

The third and final message was another message from Curtis.

"Baby, it's me again. Where are you? Tracy told me you had some errands and that you had to get your hair done, but I was thinking you'd be home by now. Anyway, Tabitha crossed the line today and, baby, I can't tell you enough how sorry I am that I didn't listen to you. You were right all along about her intentions, and I never should have made the decision to start going over there. I was wrong, and I'm through doing that. I know none of this changes the fact that I have a child with her or the fact that I love Curtina, but I will never, not under any circumstances, allow any woman to come between you and me ever again. So please when you get this message call me. I told Matthew he could spend the night at Jonathan's because I really wanted you and I to have some time alone. But, most important, baby, I love you. I love only you and that should mean everything. Don't you think? Anyway, I'll see you soon."

Charlotte saved his message and wasn't sure what to think. She was so confused. Only a short while ago, she'd just learned from Tabitha that Curtis was at her house babysitting and now Curtis was saying he was never going over there again.

She dropped her phone onto the seat and drove toward the side of town they lived on. She drove and for the first time in a while, she prayed.

She prayed that Curtis really was finished with this Tabitha and Curtina business for good.

Chapter 18

H ey, baby," Curtis said when Charlotte walked into the kitchen. He was pulling a bottle of sparkling white grape juice from the refrigerator, but then he set it down on the counter. She could smell salmon and possibly spinach and she knew Tracy must have put dinner on before leaving.

Charlotte set her tote on one of the chairs and started out of the room.

"Baby, wait."

She stopped abruptly and turned toward him. "Curtis, don't you dare baby me."

"Look, I really, really need to talk to you."

"Is that right?"

"Yes."

"Oh, so what you're saying is that you spent pretty much the entire day at Tabitha's and now you finally have time for me."

"I what?"

"Curtis, don't even try to deny it."

"Deny what? I did go over to Tabitha's, but I was only there for maybe five minutes, and that's what I need to talk to you about."

"You are such a liar, because I just saw Tabitha at the hair salon and she was going on and on to her stylist about how her baby's father offered to watch her baby while she came to get her hair done."

"You saw her at Robin's?"

"As if you didn't know."

"I didn't. And I didn't stay with Curtina. I mean, I admit I was planning to, but then Tabitha sort of tripped out when I got there."

"Why would she say you were there if you weren't?"

"I don't know. I've been here for the past few hours, and if you don't believe me, you can call Tracy. She just left maybe an hour ago."

Actually, Charlotte had wondered how he'd gotten home so quickly because she'd left the salon before Tabitha and there really hadn't been enough time for Tabitha to drive to her house and also for Curtis to drive to their home after that.

"I'm telling you, baby, whatever she said, she was only saying it to upset you, and she must have asked someone else to watch Curtina."

Charlotte didn't respond.

"Look, just have a seat so I can talk to you."

At first she hesitated, but then she did what he asked.

"First of all, I want you to hear me loudly and clearly. I wasn't at Tabitha's all afternoon. I went over there because she said she needed someone to watch Curtina but when I got there, she said Curtina was asleep. So I told her I was going to go watch television but before I left the entryway, she opened her robe and let it slide to the floor. And while I know you won't want to hear this, I'm going to tell you because I want you to know the whole truth. She dropped her robe and she didn't have anything on."

A lump settled in Charlotte's throat and her heart ached terribly. "And then what, Curtis?"

"I told her to put it back on and that I was leaving. She tried to stop me, but I left anyway. And that was it. That's all that happened, and I meant everything I said to you in my voice mail. I shouldn't have handled this situation the way I did, and I'm sorry. I'm sorry. I'm sorry. I'm sorry."

Curtis reached across the island and grabbed Charlotte's hand. "Baby, do you hear me? I'm sorry, and if I have to spend the rest of my life making this whole thing up to you, I will. You and I have hurt each other so much over these last six years, but I'm through causing you pain, and it's my goal to never hurt you like this ever again."

Charlotte wanted desperately to lash out at him. She wanted to hurt him in a way like she never had before. But she couldn't. She couldn't because no matter how hard core she'd been trying to be and no matter what Curtis had done, she still loved her husband. She loved him and for some reason, right now, she believed what he was saying. She wasn't sure why, but his words seemed more than sincere.

Then, with no way to control them, tears rolled down her face and Curtis stood and went around to where she was sitting. He pulled her up and they held each other in a tight embrace. They held each other and Charlotte felt more and more at ease. She was relieved to know that Curtis finally understood what she'd been trying to tell him all along.

Curtis leaned away from Charlotte and lifted her chin. "You still love me?"

"I never stopped. Not once."

"Because I definitely love you. It's the one thing you'll never have to question."

"This has all taken a huge toll on me, and I'm just glad you saw what Tabitha was trying to do before it was too late."

"I guess I saw what I wanted to see, but it was only because I knew I wasn't ever planning to be with her again."

"Well, you know this isn't the last we'll hear from her."

"Maybe not. But at least now, you know where I stand and that I won't be doing anything to jeopardize our marriage."

"But what about Curtina?"

"I won't lie to you. I do love her, and there's nothing I can do to change that."

Charlotte gazed into his eyes and while she didn't know where this feeling of sympathy was coming from, she sort of felt sorry for him. Maybe because she couldn't imagine ever being separated from Matthew. Not to mention, she still longed to see Marissa, even though she'd been gone a year and a half now.

Curtis kissed her on the lips. "So are you hungry?"

"A little, but I was thinking maybe we could turn the oven off and head upstairs for a while."

Curtis smiled. "Really? Now?"

"Yep."

"Then let's go."

You just don't know how much I've missed you," Curtis said, turning on his side and facing Charlotte. He was happier than he'd been in a long time and glad he and Charlotte were no longer at odds with each other.

She snuggled closer to him. "I've missed you, too. More than you could possibly ever know."

"And I've missed this."

"So have I."

"There were days when I didn't know which way to turn, but the good news is that I didn't turn to another woman. Something I wouldn't have thought twice about doing in the past."

"You are a changed man. It's one thing for people to say they've changed, but your actions have been proving it for a while now, and I love you for that."

"Oh, and hey, before I forget. Did Matthew call you about his math test?"

"Yeah, he left me a message, and he said he would call me back."

"He was so proud of his grade."

"He's always done so well in school, and I really think he'll do great things one day."

"No doubt about it," Curtis said, and his stomach rumbled.

"Have you eaten anything at all today?"

"No. What about you?"

"I had a sandwich right after I left the salon, but to be honest, I'm actually starting to feel hungry again."

"Then let's go eat." Curtis kissed her on the forehead and then they both got up and took a shower.

Charlotte set two place settings in the dining room and Curtis lit two candles and set them on the table. When they'd fixed their plates, they sat down and ate and laughed like two teenagers who'd just fallen in love. They were having the best time and as Curtis sat there admiring how beautiful his wife was, he couldn't help thinking back to the day they'd gotten married. Everything had been perfect and Matthew had been ecstatic. He'd been thrilled to know that his parents were going to be together forever, and Curtis was planning to make sure nothing ever changed that.

Charlotte took another bite of her salmon and then a forkful of sautéed spinach. "Tracy is such a great cook. Even when her food has to be warmed up, it tastes like it's just been prepared."

"I know. And I'm not sure what we'd do if we didn't have her."

"Neither do I, because you know I'm not the one when it comes to cooking anything."

"That's for sure," he teased her.

"Shut up, Curtis."

They laughed and then Curtis said, "Hey, but on a more serious note, guess what Leroy told me today?"

"Leroy who?"

"You know. Homeless Leroy. From the church parking lot."

"Oh. What did he tell you?"

"That Tolson solicits prostitutes."

"Yeah, right."

"I know it sounds way out there, but Leroy does seem to know a lot about other people's business."

"But Reverend Tolson? Buying sex from sleazy women?"

"That's what he said."

Charlotte and Curtis finished eating, but when Charlotte began gathering their plates from the table the phone rang.

"If it's not Matthew, I'm not answering it," she said, and went into the kitchen.

But it was him, so she picked it up.

Charlotte and Curtis felt full and relaxed and now they were resting in the center of their bed, watching *Sophie and the Moonhanger* on Lifetime. Curtis was beginning to doze off, but Charlotte was enjoying every minute of it. She'd seen it one time before but to her it was just as good as when she'd watched it the first time.

When a makeup commercial came on, the phone rang again and Charlotte sighed.

"I'm asleep," Curtis told her.

But when she looked at the screen, she saw David's phone number. She debated answering it but figured it might be best to hear whatever it was he had to say so she could get back to her movie.

"Hello?"

"Charlotte. Hi. Do you have a few minutes?"

She paused the DVR. "Yeah, what is it?"

"I need to talk to you about Matthew."

"Okay. And?"

"I've been thinking long and hard about this and because I've already missed so much of Matthew's life, I really want to spend more time with him."

"You've seen him two weeks in a row, so how much more time are you talking about?"

"Every weekend, every holiday, and every summer."

"David, you must be kidding."

"Wait. Just hear me out. What I was thinking was that I could have a car service pick him up after school on Fridays and then I would bring him back on Sunday afternoons."

"And what weekends do you expect us to have with him?"

Now Curtis was wide awake.

"This wouldn't be forever, but at least for the next couple of years or so. Just until we have a chance to really bond and get to know each other the way a father and son ought to. The way we should have bonded way before now."

"No."

"Charlotte, I'm asking you nicely so please don't turn this into something ugly."

"Excuse me?"

"All I'm saying is that if you're willing to cooperate, we can work this out with no problems."

"I'm Matthew's mother, David, and I don't have to work out anything with you."

"You know, maybe this is a little overwhelming for you and you just need a little time to get used to the idea."

"No, I'm telling you right now. Matthew won't be spending any weekends in Chicago. You can continue to come here maybe a couple of Saturdays a month, but that's where it ends."

"I'm sorry you feel that way because if you don't agree to what I'm asking, then you'll be hearing from my attorney. And I should also add that if you force me to hire an attorney, I'll be filing for full custody. I'd already decided I was going to file for joint custody anyway, but now full custody makes a lot more sense. Meaning, I'll either have him every weekend, holiday, and summer until he graduates from high school, or I'll have him year-round and you'll have him every now and then. So if I were you, I would think long and hard about all of this because once any judge learns that you kept Matthew a secret from me for thirteen years and then tried to pass both him and a second child of yours off on Curtis, I'm pretty much guaranteed to win."

Tears welled up in Charlotte's eyes when she realized Anise must have told him everything. "David, why are you doing this?"

"Because he's my son, and I want to be with him."

Charlotte held the phone in silence.

"So you think about everything I've said, and I'll check back with you in a couple of days. Good-bye, Charlotte."

She slowly hung up the phone and then looked at Curtis.

"Baby, what's wrong?"

"If we don't allow Matthew to spend every weekend, every holiday, and every summer in Chicago, David is threatening to file for full custody of him. Can you believe that?"

"Where did all this come from?"

"I don't know. But we can't let him do this, Curtis, because the next thing you know, we won't get to see our son at all."

"See, I had no problem with him getting to know Matthew or with them spending time together, but filing papers in court is something totally different."

"We have to fight him until the end."

"We'll try to work this out with David, but if he refuses to cooperate, we'll contact our attorney as well. We'll do whatever is necessary to protect Matthew. No matter what it takes."

Charlotte sat down on the side of the bed and began praying. She prayed because when she'd prayed earlier about Curtis and that whole Tabitha and Curtina situation, God seemed to already have begun answering her request.

So just maybe He would fix this problem with David, too.

Maybe He would fix things so that David never bothered them again.

Chapter 19

Charlotte signed onto her e-mail account to check her messages and saw that she had a new one waiting for her. It was from the same bogus address the other message had come from, informing her about Curtis and his visits to Tabitha. To be honest, Charlotte hated having to open it because the last thing she needed was more bad news. Last night, she and Curtis had enjoyed their evening together, and she was now feeling good about the way he'd come clean with everything. But now there was no telling what this latest note might actually reveal. She had a mind to just delete it but the problem was, her curiosity was already getting the best of her.

So she clicked the mouse and opened it.

Charlotte,
I can't believe that after finding out where your husband has been spending all his time—with the mother of his child—that you're still hanging in there. And then to think how yesterday, you stooped low enough to physically attack his other woman at the salon, just because you can't stop him from being with her. I mean, does the money and all the status really mean that much to you? Is it really that important for you to live a certain

lifestyle even though you and your husband are so ridiculously miserable with each other?

If so, then I feel very sorry for you and all I can say is that whether you realize it or not, you would be so much better off without him.

My advice: Let him go. And move on with your life.
Sincerely,
A Friend

Why was this woman harassing her this way? Why couldn't she just take her child and leave the country without ever looking back? Why in the world did Curtis ever have to sleep with her in the first place?

But Charlotte knew her questions and cries for understanding didn't mean much of anything because the truth was, Curtis had slept with Tabitha, and from the looks of it, she had no plans of leaving Mitchell, Illinois, let alone the entire United States. Charlotte knew there was no sense agonizing about it and that the only way to end this nightmare was to take action.

When she signed off, she went into her bedroom and closed the door behind her. She had a few calls to make and didn't want Tracy to hear what she was saying. Although, interestingly enough, the phone rang before she could pick it up.

"Hello?"

"I don't care how long it takes me, but just know that I will make you pay for what you did to me yesterday," Tabitha said.

"And what? I'm supposed to be terrified or something?"

"If you know what's good for you."

"No, if you know what's good for you, you'll make this your last time calling here and you'll never contact Curtis or me ever again. I've warned you over and over but, Tabitha, this is it. You hear me? This is where it ends."

Tabitha laughed. "You're pathetic. You know that? Absolutely pathetic and you'll be even more pathetic when Curtis leaves you."

"Look, you can fantasize all you want to, but the bottom line is this. Curtis doesn't want you, and I think he proved it yesterday when he walked out on you, butt naked and all. Am I right?"

Charlotte waited for some long-drawn-out response.

But the next thing she knew, Tabitha hung up—hard.

Charlotte wasn't at all happy about the call she'd just gotten, but what she was happy about was the fact that Curtis really had told her the truth. He really had walked out on Tabitha the way he'd claimed, and she was glad she'd told Tabitha what she knew.

Still, it was time Charlotte made the phone call she'd been getting ready to make earlier, the one to her cousin.

"Who dis?" he answered.

"Who dis?" Charlotte repeated, laughing.

"Yeah, who dis?" he said again.

"Boy, I can't believe you're answering your mom's phone like that."

"Charlotte?"

"Yeah, Dooney, it's me. So how are you?"

"Shoot, caught a forgery charge a few months back, but other than that, I'm straight. So what's goin' on with you?"

"Don't even get me started."

"That bad, hunh?"

"It is, and I really need to talk to you about it."

"Well, hey, let me call you back in a few because I was just about to make a run. You know, so I can take care of a lil business. Plus, Moms wants me to pick up a couple of things for her from the store."

"How is Maydora?"

"She's good, but working way too hard, the same as always."

Maydora was Charlotte's mother's first cousin, whom her mother had grown up with when they were children. As a matter of fact, Charlotte's mother was closer to Maydora than she was to her own sister, Emma.

"Well, I won't hold you, but when you call me back, call me on my cell," Charlotte said, and told him the number.

Dooney hung up and Charlotte wondered if she was making the right decision contacting her cousin, the one who'd been in and out of juvenile delinquent facilities and prison since he was twelve. He was now twenty-eight, but from the sound of things, he was still getting into trouble and, as he put it, still "catching" charges. But at this point, she really didn't see where she had any other choice. Curtis would die if he knew she'd hooked up with the likes of Dooney and she didn't even want to think about how her parents would feel about it, but Dooney was the type of person who could help make Charlotte's problem go away. He was caring enough when it came to his own family but he had absolutely no sympathy for anyone who violated him or his loved ones. He'd proven it time and time again and dealing with him was just a chance she was going to have to take.

Next Charlotte called her mother to tell her about David and the threats he'd made about Matthew. Now she was talking to Janine, who was taking a break between classes.

"I can't believe he's making such serious demands so quickly," Janine said. "Especially since he's known Matthew for only a couple of weeks now."

"I know. I don't get it either, but for whatever reason, he wants Matthew with him."

"What is Curtis saying about all of this?"

"He's not happy about it either, and he says we'll do whatever we have to in order to stop David. I mean, this is just insane. Because how can any man decide he wants to take a child away from the only parents he's ever been with and think it's okay?"

"Have you guys discussed this with Matthew?"

"No, and apparently David hasn't either because Matthew hasn't said anything. But if he does, we'll explain to him exactly the way we feel."

"Have you spoken to your cousin Anise or your aunt? Because maybe they can talk to him for you."

"No. I haven't spoken to my aunt since the football game and, of course, you know my relationship with Anise is horrible. She would never help me even if she could."

"Yeah, but even Anise would probably want what's best for Matthew."

"Maybe, but she seems thrilled about David and Matthew finally having a chance to be together. Plus, I didn't tell you this, but David knows about Marissa and how she wasn't Curtis's daughter either, and I know Anise had to tell him that."

"You think?"

"I know she did because where else would he get that from?"

"I hate that you and she are so at odds with each other."

"I hate it, too, but at the same time, there's nothing I can do about it."

"Girl, what you're going to have to do is stay prayerful."

"I am and I'm ashamed to say that I hadn't done much praying in a long time, but this week, I've prayed like never before."

"I think we all get lax from time to time when things are sort of going our way but when they go bad, we tend to lean on God just a little more than usual."

"It's true, J. It really is."

Charlotte felt her cell vibrating and saw a Chicago area code.

"J, I have a call coming in on my other phone, but thanks for listening, okay?"

"Of course, and call me this evening when you get a chance."

"I will. Love you."

"Love you, too."

Charlotte pressed the end button and picked up her Treo.

"Hello?"

"Yeah, Cuz," Dooney said. "It's me."

"Thanks for calling back."

"So what's up? Whatchu need?"

"I have a situation, and if you take care of it, I'll make it worth your while."

"Whoa. Sounds serious."

"It is. And long story short, Curtis had an affair with a woman who won't leave us alone. She's calling and showing up places she shouldn't, and I'm sick of it."

"Wow, Cuz. I'm sorry to hear that."

"Not as sorry as I am."

"Well, is it over?"

"What?"

"Curtis's affair with her. Is he finished with the chick?"

"Yes, and he has been for a long while."

"Has he tried to talk to her?"

"More than once, but she's not hearing it."

"That's too bad. Well, how do you want me to go at her? I mean, do you want her out of the picture completely . . . like you never wanna see her again? What exactly?"

See, it was this sort of thinking that made Charlotte nervous. It was true that she really did want Tabitha completely out of the picture but now that Dooney was making the possibility more of a reality, she was having second thoughts. For months she'd been counting the number of ways she could rid herself of Tabitha, violently and otherwise, but now, after speaking with her criminal cousin, she wasn't so sure this was the answer. She wasn't sure because, deep down, killing someone wasn't something she could do.

"I don't want you to hurt anybody. I just want you to mess with her and make her think she's in danger."

"Make her *think* she's in danger?" Dooney roared with laughter. "You want me to come all the way to Mitchell, ninety miles to be exact, just to play a few kiddie games?"

"This isn't funny, Dooney. I'm serious."

"Okay, okay. So how much we talkin'? You know, for making someone *think* they're in danger," Dooney said, and cracked up again.

Charlotte couldn't help chuckling herself. "I don't believe you."

"I'm sorry. I thought you really had this big job waiting for me."

"I do."

"Then how much?"

"How much do you require?"

"It depends on how long I'll have to be over there because if I have to leave my real business for a few days, I've gotta make up for that. I've gotta pay my boys to handle things while I'm gone."

Charlotte wanted to ask him what his real business was but decided it was better if she didn't know. She could just about imagine anyway.

"Name your price."

"You think I'll be there longer than a week?"

"No. I doubt it, but if you are, I'm prepared to compensate you."

"Will I be staying with you?"

Charlotte didn't know what to say and she hoped he wasn't serious.

"Relax, Cuz. I'm only kidding because you and I both know Curtis would never stand for that."

Charlotte was relieved. "I'll just put you up in a hotel."

"That'll work. And I'm thinking I'll need at least three thousand for the week and the same thing if I have to stay longer."

"Done."

"Dang. If I'd known you were going to be that easy, I'd've asked for twice that amount."

"I'm sure you would have."

"So when do you want me to get started?"

"In a couple of days, but if you can, I want you to come over here tomorrow, so you can get settled into your room and so I can show you where she lives."

"Bet. I'll try to be there late morning or early afternoon."

"Sounds good. And Dooney?"

"Yeah?"

"This is just between you and me. I'm trusting you not to tell a soul. Not one person."

"Definitely. This is you and me, Cuz. Period."

"See you tomorrow."

"Peace."

C urtis drove out of the church parking lot and turned on his radio. Normally, on Wednesday evenings, he taught Bible study, but this morning he and Charlotte had decided that tonight they should have dinner together with Matthew and then spend some quality time at home. Which was fine, except right now he was beyond frustrated. Tabitha had called his cell phone no less than five times in the last two hours and now she was calling again, at this very moment. He didn't answer, the same as he hadn't with any of the others, but she was starting to get on his nerves. She just wouldn't stop and the second time she'd called she'd left a message, practically begging his forgiveness. She'd apologized for her actions and then promised it would never happen again. She'd gone on and on about how wrong she'd been and how she didn't want her mistake to come between him and Curtina.

But Curtis still hadn't called her back. He hadn't called because the more he thought about the way Tabitha had tried to come on to him, well, he didn't want anything to do with her. He'd tried to make things work for the sake of seeing his daughter, but Tabitha had gone too far.

Curtis heard his phone ringing again and sighed loudly. But when he looked at the screen, he saw that it was Alicia.

"Hey, baby girl."

"Hi, Daddy. How are you?"

"I'm okay. And you?"

"I'm fine, and I'm coming home this weekend."

"Glad to hear it. I can't wait to see you."

"I'm calling because I wondered if I can see the baby?"

"Actually, that might not be possible because Tabitha did something I'm not happy with and for right now, I think it's best for me to keep my distance."

"What happened?"

"I don't want to go into it, but maybe you'll get to see her another time."

"Oh. That's fine. But I definitely want to spend Saturday with Matthew."

"You know he'll be excited."

"I'm thinking I'll take him to the movies and then to the arcade."

"Sounds good to me."

"Well, I won't keep you, Daddy. Plus, I need to call and check on Mom."

"Is she okay?"

"She has the flu. She was doing a lot better when I called her earlier, but I still want to talk to her again before the night is over."

"Tell her I hope she feels better."

"I will."

"Take care, baby girl, and I'll see you this weekend."

"See you, Daddy. I love you."

"I love you, too."

Curtis ended the call and drove another ten miles or so in deep thought. He couldn't remember when he'd had so many problems all going on at the same time, and it was tiring. First, they'd been dealing with the Tabitha situation, then Tolson had become an unexpected problem, and now David suddenly wanted to take Matthew from them. Right now, he was claiming all he wanted was more visitation time, but just the fact that he'd thrown out the words *full custody* was enough to make Curtis stand up and take notice. It was enough for him to realize they couldn't ignore David's demands.

When Curtis looked at the fuel indicator on the instrument panel, he noticed his gas tank was nearing half full. He never liked it to move any lower than that, so he pulled into the gas station, parked in front of a dispenser, and turned off the ignition.

Then he stepped out onto the pavement and waved his Mobil Speed Pass across the activation sensor. But as soon as he lifted the hose and prepared to position the nozzle inside his vehicle's fuel entry, Tabitha pulled up on the other side. Curtis turned away and once he saw that the gas was pumping, he sat back down inside the SUV.

But that didn't matter to Tabitha, because she got out of her car and walked over to him.

"Curtis, please roll down the window," she said.

He ignored her. Or at least tried to.

"Curtis? I really need to talk to you."

She was now speaking loudly and Curtis realized it might be better to hear her out and then be on his way. So he cracked the window.

"Tabitha, what do you want? And what are you doing here?"

"I called you several times, but you didn't call me back."

"That's because there's nothing for us to say."

"I'm so sorry. I never should have approached you the way I did, and I apologize."

"Fine," he said, hoping it would get her to leave.

"Please don't stop seeing Curtina. She loves you and she needs you, so please don't do this to her."

"You ruined my visits with her. And then you disrespected my wife yesterday."

"What? How? I went to get my hair done the same as anyone else and she's the one who waited for me to come out and then forced me against my car."

Curtis wasn't sure if her claim was true or not, but regardless, it still didn't change his position.

"Look, I have to go," he said when he heard the nozzle click.

"Curtis, please. I was wrong, but you have to understand how tough this is for me."

"No, what you have to understand is that I have a wife and that I won't allow you to cause problems for her. Not anymore."

Curtis pushed open his door and Tabitha stepped away, watching him as he placed the nozzle back onto the dispenser, pressed a button, waited a few seconds, and took his receipt.

"Do you want to see her? She's in the car. She's asleep, but the least you can do is look in on her."

"No. I have to get going."

"I can't believe you're doing this."

"Good-bye, Tabitha."

"No, this is far from being good-bye," she said, walking back to her car. "Trust me."

Curtis watched her drive away and then he left as well.

He tried to figure what Tabitha was planning to do next.

There was just no telling.

Chapter 20

Charlotte spooned out a helping of cheddar cheese potatoes and set it on his plate. "So how was school today, Matthew?"

"Fine. Tomorrow is the deadline for this month's newspaper, so we had a lot of work to do. That's why I had to stay so late after my last class."

Curtis cut into his slice of prime rib. "Did you hear anything from your coach about the camps?"

"No, but David said he'll find a good one near him, so I thought we could just wait for that."

Charlotte and Curtis looked at each other.

"When did he tell you that?" Curtis asked.

"When he called me this afternoon. He called me on my cell to see if I wanted to spend the weekend with him at his house."

"And what did you tell him?" Charlotte said.

"That I had to ask you and Dad. So can I?"

"Actually, Matthew, Alicia called me this afternoon to say she's coming home this weekend and that she's going to spend all day Saturday with just you."

Matthew looked disappointed, and this bothered Charlotte because for as long as she could remember, he'd never thought anything was more important than being with his big sister.

"David can see you next weekend," she said. "And anyway, your dad and I want to spend some time with you, too."

"But you and Dad see me every day."

"Yeah, but we still want to do things with you on days when you're not in school."

Matthew drank some of his lemonade but didn't look at either of his parents.

Charlotte glanced over at Curtis and she could tell he was at a loss for words.

Then Matthew looked up. "So can I?"

"Don't you even care that Alicia is coming here to see you?"

"She's coming to see you and Dad, too, and I can see her next time."

"She's really going to be disappointed if you're not here," Curtis tried to explain.

"I think you can stay home this weekend and you can see David on the next one."

"Can I be excused?" he asked.

"Why?" Curtis said.

"I'm not hungry anymore."

Charlotte set her fork down. "Sweetie, I know you don't understand, but sharing you with someone else hasn't been all that easy."

"Yeah, but David says we've lost so much time that we have to work hard to make up for it. He says he wants me to visit him every single weekend, and that's what I want, too."

Charlotte could kill David for saying these things to Matthew without their consent. It was one thing for him to contact her about it last night, but he had no right discussing anything so crucial with Matthew.

"We think it's a good thing for you and David to spend time together," Curtis said. "But not every single weekend."

"But why? He's my father."

Charlotte watched Curtis lean back in his chair and she could tell his feelings were hurt. She could also tell that Matthew regretted his last comment.

"I didn't mean anything by that, Dad, because you're my dad, too. But I think it's unfair for you and mom to say I can't be with David. He doesn't want to take me away. He just wants us to spend weekends together."

Charlotte wanted so badly to tell him that David was in fact threatening to take him away. She wanted to explain to Matthew what full custody actually meant and how his father was threatening to file for it. But she didn't.

"Mom, Dad, please. Can I go stay with him until Sunday?"

"No," Charlotte said matter-of-factly. "You heard your dad say that Alicia is coming here, mainly to see you, and that's that."

Matthew frowned. "I wanna go to my room."

"Then go," Charlotte told him.

Matthew left the table in a hurry and never said another word to either of them.

"Curtis, what are we going to do?"

"Baby, I don't know. Things are worse than I thought, because I had no idea David was already talking to him about this frequent visit thing."

"He really has a lot of nerve. And I don't care if he is his biological father, as far as I'm concerned, he has no rights. None."

"I know you feel that way, but by law he does. And that's what worries me."

"This is just crazy."

"Well, if you think that's crazy wait until I tell you what happened tonight."

"What?"

"I stopped at the Mobil on Aventura, and guess who pulled up next to me?"

"Not Tabitha?"

"Yeah."

"What did she want?"

"To apologize and to ask me why I won't return her calls. She called multiple times today, and then left a message."

"She's never going to give this up."

"It seems not."

"I think it's time we called the police, because the next thing you know, she'll be showing up here."

"I hate having to get them involved, but I do agree that this is starting to spin too far out of control. I never expected her to start following me, but if she knew I was at the gas station, she had to be."

"No, what she's doing is stalking us. She showed up at my salon yesterday, and then I didn't tell you that she called here this morning."

"Saying what?"

"Everything. And she definitely believes you're going to leave me for her."

"But you know that's not true, right?"

"All I can do is hope."

"No, you don't have to hope anything. I know I messed up in the past, but the only way you and I won't be together is if you make that decision. But it won't be my choice."

"I'm glad to hear you say that, and I need you to keep saying it."

"I told you, I'll do whatever you need me to do to reassure you."

Charlotte and Curtis finished their meals and then she removed everything from the table, including Matthew's plate, which was still half full.

But then, without warning, they heard a window shattering and then a loud thud against the floor.

Curtis rushed into the living room area and Charlotte hurried behind him. Then they dashed over to the door and Curtis opened it. A car screeched away and while it appeared to be some sort of dark-colored, compact car, they couldn't make it out exactly. Curtis shut the door, turned on the light, and Charlotte saw a palm-size rock lying on the carpet.

"Baby, look," she said.

Curtis grabbed her into his arms and now Matthew ran into the room.

"Mom? Dad? What was that?"

Charlotte reached out to him and her son hugged her. "We don't know. It looks like someone threw a rock through one of the front windows."

Curtis started out of the room. "I'm calling the police."

"Mom, who would do something like this?"

"I don't know," she said, but her intuition told her that Tabitha's name was written all over this.

Curtis hung up with 911 and within minutes, the doorbell rang.

"Thank you for coming, Officers," Curtis greeted them. "Please come in."

Both men in blue did a quick investigation and then took a seat in the kitchen. Curtis, Charlotte, and Matthew did the same.

"Do you have any idea who might've done this?" the muscular officer asked.

"No," Curtis said. "We don't."

Charlotte gazed at Curtis and wished she could tell them exactly who she thought it was. She wanted to tell them how Tabitha had been harassing them and how she was the only person they were having problems with. That she was the only person angry enough to vandalize their property. But she didn't. Instead, she kept her mouth shut and found peace in knowing that Dooney would be in town in less than twenty-four hours. She was happy to know Tabitha was finally going to get what was coming to her.

When the officers finished the report, they examined the window and the rock again, and then took a look outside.

"I don't think you can get this fixed tonight but if you call any of the top glass companies in town, they'll at least send someone out to cover it for you," the second officer suggested. "That way, you won't have so much cold air blowing into your home."

"Thank you. We'll call right now."

"The report will be available downtown in a couple of days but please call us if you have any more trouble."

"We will."

"Also, we'll check with your neighbors to see if by chance anyone saw who did this, because with your house sitting quite a few feet away from the street, there's no doubt the perpetrator would have had to step outside of their vehicle in order to throw something through your window. It looks like there are only four or five other houses in your subdivision, but maybe someone saw the car leaving and can give a better description of it."

"Maybe."

"We'll let you know."

"We appreciate whatever you can do."

"You folks have a good evening."

"You, too," Curtis and Charlotte said.

"Man, just wait until Jonathan and Elijah hear about the police being here. They'll love it," Matthew said, heading toward the stairway.

"Honey." Charlotte stopped him. "Let's just keep this to ourselves for right now, okay?"

"Why?"

Curtis locked the door. "Your mother is right. Let's not talk about this to everyone. Maybe family and close friends, but that's it."

"But Jonathan and Elijah are my close friends. They're my best friends."

"I know," Charlotte said. "But—"

"It's fine, Matthew," Curtis interrupted. "Go ahead."

"Thanks, Dad. And Mom, are you okay? You look upset."

"I'm fine, honey. You just go ahead and call your friends to tell them about your big crime story."

"I will. I'm telling you, they'll love this."

Matthew skipped stairs on his way up and Charlotte looked at the glass on the carpet. "What made you change your mind about him telling his friends?"

"Because that's what any other child would do if a rock was thrown through their window, and the only reason you and I didn't want him to say anything is that we're always worried that something is going to get out to the public and then get twisted around."

"Exactly."

"But it's probably going to make the news anyway, just because of what I do for a living. You can bet someone will be calling here before the night is out."

Curtis called the glass company and just as the officer had mentioned, they couldn't fix it until tomorrow, but someone did come out to cover the window with very sturdy plastic and secured it with thick tape.

"You know Tabitha had something to do with this," Charlotte declared after she and Curtis had gone up to their bedroom.

"I don't know. I'm not defending her, but any woman who would be out this late with a baby and tossing rocks through windows is a bit insane."

"I'm not saying she physically did it, but I'll bet she had someone do it for her."

"This is ridiculous."

"I'm telling you, baby, if Tabitha keeps calling here or calling your cell or if any other strange incident takes place, we have to report her. I know you don't want your affair with her to go public, but after tonight, my concern is for our safety. Either one of us could have been near that window and could have gotten hurt. And I don't even want to think about anything happening to Matthew."

"You're right," he said, pulling her into his arms. "Baby, I'm really sorry about this."

"What happened, happened, but now we have to stick together."

"That we do."

"And hey, did Elder Jamison or the attorney hear anything from Reverend Tolson?"

"I forgot to tell you, but he turned down the two years of pay and we haven't heard anything from him since."

"Really? Do you want me to talk to Vivian? She's such a nice woman. She's seems a bit timid, but still, she's his wife and maybe she knows why Reverend Tolson is acting this way."

"Maybe if we don't hear anything in a couple of weeks or so, but for now, let's just wait to see if he changes his mind."

"Gosh, it's so strange. Although, the more I think about it, Reverend Tolson did seem real comfortable running things when you were on the road. Sometimes he seemed drunk with power, but he was always nice to everyone. The whole congregation liked him and so did I."

"I liked him a lot too, that's why I chose him to fill in for me. But maybe it's the loss of power that has made him so angry. Once upon a time, your own husband used to be drunk with power, too. Remember?"

"How could I forget? That's why I was so drawn to you when I was only seventeen."

"Don't remind me."

"You know it's true. I would have done anything to be with you and I did."

"Maybe, but as much as I hate to admit it, I'm not proud of that."

"Of what? Robbing the cradle?" she teased.

"Yeah. Although now that you're thirty-one and practically over the hill, it really doesn't matter anymore, does it?"

"Okay, that's enough of that."

"That's what I thought. But you know I'm just kidding, right? Because even at thirty-one, you're still just as young and vibrant as ever. You're a beautiful woman, and I'm glad you're my wife."

"I love you, too," she said, and Curtis kissed her.

They held each other closely and Charlotte felt safe.

Safe and content.

At least for now.

Chapter 21

Curtis unfolded his arms and leaned forward when Elder Jamison and Elder Dixon walked into his office. Curtis had called both of them this morning and asked them to come in to meet with him. He wasn't looking forward to telling them about the incident last night because he knew they would suspect that Tabitha was behind it and they'd want him to move forward with disclosing everything publicly.

"Thank you both for coming on such short notice. Especially you, Elder Jamison, because I know you have a business to run."

"No problem at all. It's a lot easier to get away when you're self-employed. Plus, it just so happens that I don't have any clients to meet with today or tomorrow."

About three years ago, Elder Jamison had left corporate America to start his own consulting company and he loved the fact that he had so much more flexibility in his schedule.

"Well, the reason I called you here is because, last night, we had a bit of a situation at our home. Someone threw a fairly large rock through one of our front windows and glass shattered everywhere."

Elder Dixon was shocked. "Was anyone hurt?"

"No."

"And who would do somethin' like that?"

"We don't know."

"Do you think that Tabitha woman had something to do with it?" Elder Jamison asked.

"It's hard to say. Because by the time I opened the door and looked out, we saw a car flying out of the subdivision, but we didn't see the driver."

Elder Dixon shook his head. "My Lord."

"I just spoke to Charlotte maybe a half hour ago and the glass company was there measuring the window, and, thankfully, they should have the new one installed late this afternoon."

"Well, that's good, because the last thing you need is to have your home unsecured," Elder Jamison said.

"Well, Pastor," Elder Dixon began. "I know you still won't want to hear this, but I really think it's time you go to the board and the congregation about everything."

"I agree," Elder Jamison added. "Because if this Tabitha woman is responsible for this, you need to tell the truth before she does something worse."

Elder Dixon said, "Have you heard from her again?"

"Actually, I have and I hadn't told either of you this. But right after she joined church a couple of Sundays ago, I called her up and started going to see my daughter. I figured that would fix everything and then I wouldn't have to tell anyone anything. But then on Tuesday, I went over there and, well, let's just say, she came on to me in the wrong way and I left. Then, she came to Charlotte's hair salon while Charlotte was there, and then last night, she showed up while I was at the gas station."

Elder Dixon sat up straight in his chair. "Boy, you gotta do somethin' about this now. 'Cause you got a real live fatal attraction on your hands. You hear me. A real, real live one."

"Pastor, Elder Dixon is right. This woman is a problem. I knew she was a piece of work that first day she showed up here before service and I brought her up to your office. And she's not crazy.

She seemed as sane as sane can be, but she wants what she wants and she's obviously willing to do whatever she has to in order to get it."

"Pastor," Elder Dixon pleaded. "We're beggin' you. Tell the board and the congregation as soon as possible."

"You have to," Elder Jamison said. "Because if you don't, I'm afraid a lot of the members won't be very forgiving once they find out the woman who joined church was actually talking about you when she said a married man got her pregnant and then dumped her before she had his baby.

"And they'll feel even more betrayed because you stood there and never acknowledged her accusations," Elder Dixon explained. "They'll feel like you deceived them right to their faces and then just simply went on about your business."

Curtis didn't want to face the board, his congregation, and definitely not the entire country, but he knew the elders were right. He knew he no longer had a choice and that it was time—finally time—to come clean about his five-year affair and the child that had resulted from it.

"Let's do it," Curtis said. "Set up the meeting with the board, and we'll go from there."

"I'll schedule a mandatory meeting for Saturday around noon, and then you can tell the congregation during Sunday morning service, first thing."

"You really are doin' the right thing," Elder Dixon assured him. "It may not feel like it right now and I'm not sayin' it'll be easy on you and your family, but the sooner you do this the better off you'll be."

"I think so, but as you said, it won't be easy. Not for anyone involved and especially not for my children."

Elder Dixon stood up. "You just hang on in there."

"That's right," Elder Jamison added. "Because we support you and stand by you one hundred percent."

"That means everything."

After a few more parting words, the elders left the church. Curtis called Charlotte.

"Baby, I just met with Elder Jamison and Elder Dixon and I've made a decision. I probably should have discussed it with you first, but there really is no other way. I have to go to the board and then to the congregation this Sunday to tell them everything."

"Are you sure?"

"I'm positive. I'm not looking forward to it, but no matter how I try to figure this, it's the only way."

"This is bad, Curtis. I mean, can you imagine how much embarrassment we're in for? And the worst thing of all is the fact that Matthew will have to face his schoolmates, his teachers, and everyone else. He'll be so humiliated once everyone learns that his father has a baby with another woman. It'll be horrible for him."

"I know. I've already thought about that and that's my biggest regret. Alicia will be just as affected, and all I can say is that I'm sorry and that if I could erase all of this I would. But unfortunately, I can't and now I'm going to have to deal with it. We're all going to have to pay for my mistake."

"So what's the overall plan?"

"I have to tell the truth. And when I hang up with you, I'm going to call Lisa so we can start preparing a statement for the media. I'll see what she says, but I was thinking she could release it on Sunday evening, so that it airs on radio and TV Monday morning."

"Is there anything I need to say or do?"

"I'll ask her and if there is, I'll have her talk to you."

"I just wish we didn't have to do this."

"I wish we didn't either but look what happened at my other two churches in Chicago. Someone told everything, and I ended up being ousted from both of them."

"But we founded Deliverance Outreach, so there's no chance of that happening this time."

"No, but people can leave, and what good is a church if you have no congregation? So it's really important for me to be honest with them before someone else discloses everything. They need to know that I came forward on my own and that they heard every detail from me first."

"If it's okay with you, I'm going to call Mom. I just need to talk to her about this."

"I understand, but with the exception of her and your father and Janine, we need to keep this to ourselves until Sunday."

"I guess the upside to this is that we'll no longer have to worry about what Tabitha is going to say and who she's going to say it to."

"True. And actually, that'll be a relief. There's nothing worse than lying and hiding secrets, and I certainly won't miss doing that. I've done it for too many years as it is."

"I guess. Well, hey, I'll let you call Lisa, and just call me when you get a chance. I have some errands to run this afternoon but that's about it."

"I will. And, baby, thanks for trying so hard to understand."

"I told you we have to stick together. It's the only way we're going to survive this."

"I love you. And I'll talk to you later."

Curtis pressed the flash button, but instead of calling his publicist, he called his assistant first.

"Lana, do you have a few minutes?"

"Of course, Pastor. I'll be right in."

Curtis stood up, slipped his hands into his pockets, and gazed out the window. He smiled when he saw one of the church maintenance guys passing Leroy some money. He couldn't make out whether it was a one, five, ten, or twenty, but it was money just the same and now Leroy was patting the man on the back, thanking him. Curtis watched Leroy leave the parking lot with not a major care in the world and it dawned on him that, at this moment, Leroy was probably happier than he was and wasn't worried about a single thing—except how much liquor he'd be able to purchase with the handout he'd just been given.

Lana walked in and shut the door and Curtis turned toward her.

"This will be the most difficult thing I've had to tell you, but I just feel it's time."

Lana already looked concerned. "Should I sit down?"

"Yes. We both need to sit down for this one."

Curtis began with no hesitation and told her everything. That he'd made the decision to see this woman the very night Aaron set Curtis and Charlotte's house on fire, that he'd started seeing her before Marissa had been born, that the woman had pretty much traveled with him on the road full-time, that he'd paid all of her bills for her, that for five years, he'd slept with her far more times than he had with his wife, that a baby was born six months ago, that they'd paid the woman to keep quiet, and that now she was becoming a major problem.

Then, lastly, he told her who the woman was.

"Her name is Tabitha and she's the new member who joined our church two Sundays ago. And the baby you held is my daughter."

"My, my, my."

"I'm sorry. I'm sorry I led you and everyone else to think I didn't even know who she was, when all the time, I knew she was talking about me."

"Pastor, I guess I'm at a loss for words. I'm just so shocked to hear you say all of this."

"I know. It's a lot, and I just hope you can forgive me."

"Of course I forgive you. I'm disappointed. Very disappointed, but that doesn't change the way I feel about you as my pastor. I still love you and as long as you don't plan on ever doing anything like this again, I'll even try to forget it."

"Lana, thank you. That really helps me more than you know."

"Mm, mm, mm. Poor Charlotte. I can't even imagine how she must be feeling."

"It's been very hard for her. Especially, now, with Tabitha calling and harassing her the way she has been."

"I guess so."

"Then the thing I'm worried about is whether I'll ever live this down because so many thousands and thousands of people have looked up to me and supported what I do as a minister, speaker, and author. I know they'll be just as disappointed as you are and that's what hurts the most."

"They may be, but, Pastor, you just keep your head up. I know things don't look so bright at the moment, but as time goes on, things will get better. And don't think you're the only one to ever go through something like this. President Clinton and the Reverend Jesse Jackson made some mistakes with women, too, but most people still love and respect them just the same, including me. And so do most of my close friends." Lana smiled and then continued.

"No one is perfect, but what will make all of this okay is what I said to you earlier. You can't do anything like this ever again. You have to repent before God and accept responsibility when it comes to everyone else. I'm not saying the road won't be rocky, because it will be, but what I am saying is that everything will work out the way it's supposed to in the long run. It'll work out and what you and Charlotte have to do is stand together on this, at all times, and you have to pray together. You have to surrender completely to God and before you know it, life will be good for you again."

"Thank you, Lana. Thank you for your kind words and for being such a wonderful Christian woman. A lot of people are going to judge me for this but deep down, I always knew you wouldn't."

"Judging you or anyone else is not my job, and I've always tried to stay away from that. Always. My job is to love people in spite of themselves and if everyone adopted that philosophy, the world would be a much better place to live in."

"Now I wish I'd come to you before today."

"Well, just know that from now on, you can come to me about anything."

"I will. And we'll have to talk about this a lot over the next few days because by Monday, the phones will be ringing off the hook."

Lana got to her feet. "Just tell me what you need and it's done."

"Thanks again."

Lana left, and oddly enough, Curtis felt a lot better. Nothing had changed in terms of what he had to do, but it was good knowing that Charlotte, Lana, Elder Jamison, and Elder Dixon were all in his corner.

Good to know he wouldn't have to stand alone this weekend.

Chapter 22

Charlotte pulled into the parking lot of the roach motel where Dooney had told her to meet him and waited. She wasn't sure if he was planning to stay here or not, but she didn't like what she saw. People who looked like prostitutes and drug addicts. Actually, since he lived in Chicago, she wasn't sure how Dooney even knew about this place, which was about twenty miles east of Mitchell, but there was no telling with him. No telling at all and she would be glad when their business with each other had come to a close.

Charlotte made sure her doors were locked and turned the radio to 106.3. *The Michael Baisden Show* was on and based on what the current caller was saying, she knew the topic must have been Pimps in the Pulpit, a topic Michael had spotlighted on a few occasions over the last year. She listened and couldn't help thinking about Curtis and how it was only going to be a matter of days before listeners everywhere would be calling their local radio talk shows, discussing Curtis, Tabitha, and their baby. Everyone was going to have an opinion and Charlotte cringed at the thought of it all.

She listened for a few minutes and while she loved Michael's show, she switched the channel to an XM music station and gazed through her rearview mirror. "How disgusting," she said out loud when she saw some trashy-looking woman and man standing in front of a room with their hands all over each other. Both of them looked as though they hadn't showered in weeks, and Charlotte wished Dooney would hurry up.

Thankfully, her phone rang and it was him.

"Where are you?" she asked.

"About fifteen minutes away. I'm runnin' a little late."

"That's fine, but I hope this isn't where you're planning to stay because this place is horrible."

"Of course not. But I figured no one you know would be out there, and that's why I chose it as a place to meet."

"That's probably true, but how did you even know it existed?"

"I've done a little business in the past with some associates in Mitchell, and that's where we made our transactions."

"Whatever."

"I'll see you in a few."

Not ever in Charlotte's wildest imagination would she have thought she'd be teaming up with Dooney for anything. They were as different as Las Vegas and Peoria, Illinois, and they had been since childhood. They had nothing in common but right now, she needed his thuggish mentality—she needed his help with Tabitha, and there was no one else she could turn to. Of course, Charlotte did worry that if something happened to Tabitha, she and Curtis might end up suspects, especially now that Curtis was going public about the affair, but she had to admit it was a chance she was willing to take.

Finally, when Dooney pulled up, Charlotte left her vehicle and got into his tinted-window Escalade, which was just as new as Curtis's.

"It's about time."

"Traffic was a trip. There musta been some sort of accident or somethin'."

Charlotte pointed her finger. "Go right and then left at the light."

"Cool."

"I really appreciate you doing this."

"That's what family is for."

"I know, but this is serious, and I hate involving you. Maybe you could find someone else to do this for us."

"For what?"

"Because I don't want you to get into trouble. I don't want to be the reason you go back to prison."

"Look, Cuz, I appreciate you carin' about that and all, but I got this. Everything is straight. Plus, I'm not tryin' to go back to the pen. Lockdown is nothin' but a bunch of madness, so I'm definitely not plannin' on gettin' caught."

"Does anybody plan on getting caught when they commit a crime?"

"Oh, I see. You got jokes, hunh?"

They both laughed. "All I'm saying is that I don't want you to get arrested on my account."

"And I won't. Like I said, I got this."

"Fine. Whatever you say."

"But . . . just in case somethin' does go wrong, you have nothin' to worry about. The one thing I'm not is a snitch and to prove it, I turned down a DA twice when he tried to make a deal with me. He wanted me to give up one of my boys but there was no way I was doin' that. Did eighteen months for somethin' I didn't even do, but that's the way that sh . . . I mean that's the way that is. Sorry. I forgot you're a preacher's wife," he teased. "Can't just be usin' my usual words around you, now can I?"

"Shut up, Dooney, and just drive."

Charlotte smiled to herself and couldn't deny that Dooney made her laugh and she felt comfortable around him. He'd always been a fun person and even after his convictions and prison stints, his personality hadn't changed.

"Turn here," she said.

"So, Curtis really got himself caught up in some serious junk this time, hunh?"

"Yeah. He did. It's bad and it's only a matter of time before it all comes out."

"Well, at least if we can put some fear in this trick's heart, that'll help tone her down."

"That's what I'm hoping. And thank you again for coming to help me."

"Please. To be honest, I would have done it for free because I would never let some tramp mess up the good thing you got goin' with Curtis. You got the most dollars in the family and the most bling, too, and we gotta protect that. I'm proud of you, Cuz."

"That's nice of you to say."

They drove a few more miles and Charlotte told Dooney about the way Tabitha was stalking them and how she'd shown up during church service. Then Charlotte directed her cousin into Tabitha's subdivision.

"That's it," she said. "The tan-colored brick ranch."

"Cool."

"Now, just so we're on the same page, I better say this again. I don't want her hurt. I just want you to scare her. I want you to let her know if she doesn't leave town, something bad is going to happen to her."

"Okay, but what if that doesn't work? Then what?"

"Let's just hope it does."

"Yeah, but what if it doesn't?"

"We'll worry about that only if it becomes necessary."

"Well, if this trick is as bold as you've been telling me, I might not have a choice. This might have to get physical. I'm not talking about ending her life or even sending her to the hospital, but a few bruises might be in order."

"We'll see. But what are you planning to do first?"

"Haven't decided for sure, but she'll get my message loud and clear."

"Maybe you should run it by me beforehand."

"Cuz, I'm tellin' you, I got this. Don't worry. I'm givin' you a money-back guarantee."

"Fine. Let's go."

Dooney drove out to the main street and headed back toward the motel. "So how's Anise and Aunt Emma?"

"They're good. I don't really talk to Anise that much anymore, but I do visit Aunt Emma."

"What happened to you and Anise?"

"It's a long story."

"What you mean is that it's none of my business."

"I didn't say that."

"You didn't have to."

"I just don't want to talk about it."

"She was older than you, but you guys used to be as thick as thieves."

"I know."

"Actually, we all used to have the best time. Our family was close."

"We really were. And it's too bad that we're all spread out in different areas and we don't get to see each other that often."

"At family reunions, but that's about it."

"Or funerals."

"Yep. Or when husbands cheat on their wives."

"I don't believe you."

"Well, if Curtis hadn't cheated, would you have called me?"

"Probably not."

"See."

Charlotte chuckled and so did Dooney.

"So which hotel are you planning to check into?"

"Haven't really decided. But I think I'll just find one in Elgin or Dundee."

"That's thirty to forty minutes away."

"Yeah, but the farther away the better, because I don't wanna run up on anyone in Mitchell. Can't take the chance of somebody tryin' to ID me. That's also why I asked you to drive outside of the city limits today. It's also the reason I'm usin' this cell phone

I got here. It's not registered in anyone's name. It's totally rigged, but you shouldn't call me that often because you don't want the number showin' up in your records way too many times."

"That makes me feel a little more at ease."

"I keep tellin' you, I got this."

Charlotte pulled an envelope from her handbag and passed it to him.

"What's this, a down payment?"

"No, it's the whole 3K."

"Thanks."

"And you be careful."

"No doubt."

Charlotte heard what he was saying, but she still worried about the outcome. She worried that Dooney might get caught or worse, the police could easily connect him and her as relatives. She did believe him when he said he'd never implicate her but even still, she knew that might not mean a thing if the police did their research.

She worried, but on the other hand, Tabitha had to be dealt with. And this was the only way.

D ad, why can't I go stay at David's this weekend?"
Matthew and Curtis were sitting in the family room, watching *SportsCenter* on ESPN and waiting for Charlotte to get home so they could have dinner.

"Because you spent the last two Saturdays with him and we want you home with us this weekend. Plus, don't you want to see Alicia?"

"Yes, but I could spend the morning with her and then I could go with David in the afternoon and stay until Sunday night."

"But Alicia hasn't been here to stay an entire weekend with us in over a month."

"But, Dad, she'll understand that I have something else to do this time."

Curtis wasn't sure how to respond. He was trying to see Matthew's point of view, but he couldn't forget David's threat of full custody. He didn't want to keep Matthew away from his father, but there was a part of him that now felt the same as Charlotte. He was hesitant and didn't know if it was a good idea for Matthew to spend so much time with David. Not to mention, he really wanted Matthew home this weekend because of everything that was about to happen, specifically the confession he would be offering to the church and public.

"We'll talk about this when your mom gets here."

"But you already know what she's going to say. She doesn't want me seeing David at all."

"That's not completely true."

"Yes, it is, Dad. You know it. And I don't understand why."

"This isn't an easy situation, son, but we'll work it out."

"Well, it's not my fault that she slept with David behind Cousin Anise's back."

"Matthew! You watch your mouth."

"Sorry."

"Look. You listen to me. Don't you ever talk like that about your mother. Do I make myself clear?"

"Yes, sir."

Curtis left the family room and went into the kitchen. Not once could he remember Matthew speaking so negatively toward anyone and certainly not toward his mother and this bothered Curtis. Matthew had always been a good kid and this change in attitude was so unlike him. It was almost as if his being with David was the most exciting thing in his life. He was acting as if nothing else was important.

When Charlotte walked inside the house, she pecked Curtis on the lips and slipped off her leather jacket.

"So how'd it go with Lisa? Did you figure out what you need to say?"

"Pretty much. She's drafting my statement and she said she'll get it to me in the morning so I can look it over. Then, if I don't have any changes or additions, which I'm sure I will, we'll be ready."

"Is the board meeting set?"

"Yeah. Elder Jamison called me about an hour ago, saying that everyone has been notified."

"Did he tell them why?"

"No. He just told them that it was imperative that they be there and that was it."

"Then I guess there's no turning back now."

"No, I guess not."

"Where's Matthew?"

"He's in there. All upset about this weekend."

"But I already told him he's staying home."

"I know, but he doesn't understand why."

"Well, he's not going and David's not coming here either."

"I think we need to go talk to him right now, so we don't have to discuss this again."

They walked into the family room and Matthew looked at both of them.

"Matthew, your dad told me that you're still upset about having to stay home this weekend."

"Mom, I just want to go see where he lives. That's all."

"But you know Alicia is coming and you can go to David's the next weekend."

"I don't wanna go next weekend, I want to go this one."

"Okay, that's it, Matthew. I'm not arguing with you about this. You're not going and that's final."

"But, Mom—"

"I said, *that's* final."

Matthew rolled his eyes at her and turned back toward the television.

"Go get washed up for dinner."

"I'm not hungry."

"Then go to your room. And stay there until I tell you to come out."

Matthew tossed the TV selector onto the sofa and left.

"Baby, what are we going to do?" she asked Curtis.

"I don't know. But as much as I hate to say it, we can't keep him from David. David has rights, and he's already made it clear that he's prepared to fight for them."

"Maybe if I talk to him again, we can try to come to some sort of agreement."

"I think you should. He said he wants to see him every weekend, but maybe you can get him to compromise. Maybe Matthew can stay at his house every other weekend instead of all of them."

"We'll see. I'll call him in the morning."

"Actually, you should try him tonight."

"You're right. I'll call him after we eat."

"David, this is Charlotte."

"How are you?"

"I'm good, and if you have some time, I'd like to talk to you about Matthew."

"Okay."

She looked at Curtis, who was sitting over on the chaise, and then said, "I've been thinking about our last conversation, and I was wondering if you would consider alternating weekends with us."

"Meaning?"

"Matthew could come stay with you every other weekend, and he could be here with us on the opposite ones."

"But that would mean I'd only have barely four days a month with him."

"I know, but, David, you have to understand that we want some weekend family time with Matthew as well."

"Which is what you've had for thirteen years."

Charlotte could already tell that this wasn't going to turn out as well as she'd hoped, so she decided to offer something she really didn't want to.

"But every other weekend wouldn't be all. You could also have him with you every other holiday and every other summer."

"Unfortunately, that's not acceptable to me."

"Why?"

"Because it's like I told you before, I've already lost so much time and I want Matthew and me to make up for it."

"But do you think it's right to take him out of his environment so frequently so soon after just meeting him?"

"Yes, because Matthew wants this, too."

"Did he say that?" Charlotte knew Matthew did want this, but she was curious to see what he'd discussed with David.

"He did. As a matter of fact, he called me on my cell phone a little while ago, saying that you told him he couldn't come here on Saturday."

"But only because his sister is going to be here."

"I don't see where that has anything to do with my visitation time."

"It doesn't, but Alicia doesn't come home all that often."

"He can see her next time."

"Yes, but that won't be anytime soon because the next time she spends a weekend away from campus, she'll probably spend it in the Chicago area with her mom and stepfather."

"I understand that, but the bottom line is that I want to see Matthew on a regular basis."

"Okay, fine. But, David, can you just please let us have this weekend with him? I can't go into details, but we really need to have our family together."

"I don't know about that."

"Please. I'm begging you. Just let us get through the next few days and then you and I can talk about this again. Please."

Charlotte hated groveling to him this way, especially about her own son, but she could tell this might be her only solution.

"Fine. But if I don't hear from you by Monday, I'm moving forward with my attorney."

"I'll call you then. And thanks for agreeing to this."

"Good-bye."

Charlotte returned the phone to its base.

"So what did he say?" Curtis asked.

"He's fine with this weekend, but he wants me to call him by Monday."

"Is he still talking legal action?"

"Yes."

"Then that means we need to find representation."

"I agree, but at least now we have a few days to do it."

"Yeah, but trust me, Monday will be here before we know it, and then we'll be dealing with David and the backlash from my announcement all at once. So the timing couldn't be worse."

"I was thinking the same thing. How our lives are basically going to be unbearable."

Chapter 23

Curtis repositioned his headset and slightly turned up the volume. He was pacing back and forth inside his home office, speaking with his publicist, Lisa, on the phone and Charlotte was sitting behind his desk reading what Lisa had faxed over to them.

"The statement looks fine, and so does the press release."

"I think it says everything we need it to say, but in a very remorseful and humble manner."

"I agree."

"But what we have to discuss now is how you should handle interviews. Both local and national. For television, radio, and print. Because the requests are going to be rolling in immediately."

"Just tell me what I need to do."

"Well, most important, I want you to be as open and as forthcoming with information as you can because what we want is for the public to truly see how genuine your confession and apology are. We want the public to sympathize with you and your entire family."

"That won't be hard to convey because I truly am sorry for what I've done."

"I know you are, and, Pastor, while I haven't said this yet,

I'm glad you're doing this. I'm glad you ended your affair with Tabitha because even though you never told me, I knew she was always around you way too much for something not to be going on. And I have to tell you, even the thought of it was sometimes very difficult for me because I didn't want to lose respect for you. So, for the most part, I pushed the whole idea of it from my mind and just did my job. I told myself it wasn't any of my business and that what I needed to focus on was getting you publicity."

"I'm sorry I put you in such an awkward position, but I'm glad you hung in there. You're the best, and I definitely need you in my corner. Now more than ever before."

"Not to worry. I'm going to do everything I possibly can to get you through this."

"So what's next?"

"Your family. It will be crucial that you stress your newfound commitment and faithfulness to Charlotte. You need to make sure you mention the fact that you're the one who ended the affair with your mistress and that you've been faithful to Charlotte ever since."

"Should we say when I ended it, so people will know it's been well over a year?"

"I was considering that, but then I decided you shouldn't because we don't want to encourage conversation that will force you to admit you ended it when you found out Tabitha was pregnant. It won't look good because people will say that's the only reason you stopped seeing her. They'll say you dumped a woman who was carrying your child."

"You're right."

"Then as far as Charlotte's part in these interviews, it will be important for her to do them with you, side by side. Proving that she has forgiven you and that the love between both of you is stronger than ever. But I'll prep her later today or tomorrow."

"Sounds good."

"The other thing is that I don't want you saying Tabitha's

name. There will come a time when you won't be able to avoid it, like when the media eventually finds out who she is, but until then, just refer to her as "a woman" or "the woman" the way I have it written in your statement. Then, once the media knows who she is and you run into situations where you can't avoid saying her name, I want you to refer to her as Ms. Charles. But never call her by her first name."

"Is there a reason?"

"Because we don't want it to sound like your relationship is still very personal. We want you to speak about her in a very respectful way, but that's as far as you need to go with it."

"That works for me."

"Also, I know you were saying we should submit the press release over the wire late Sunday evening, but the more I think about it, I think we should release it as soon as you've told your congregation. And the reason I say this is because we don't want anyone from the church leaking information to the press. We want your side of this to get out well before people start twisting and adding their own opinions to your statement, because as soon as that happens all sorts of rumors will be flying. Rumors are going to be running rampant anyway, but still, it will be better if we get a head start on them."

"I'm willing to do whatever you suggest, and I'll have Elder Jamison call you on his cell as soon as I begin telling the congregation."

"That's perfect. I think that's it for now, but I'll be in touch again later. Also, don't forget to let Charlotte know that I'll need to talk to her."

"I will. And, Lisa, thanks again for everything."

"You're quite welcome, Pastor. We're in for a fight, but I think you'll be fine when this is over. Especially since you decided to come forward on your own before anyone found out about it."

"I hope you're right."

"I'll speak to you later."

"Take care."

Curtis removed his headset and laid it on his desk.

"So is there anything I need to do?"

"Lisa said she'll call you later to fill you in. She wants you to be with me during all the interviews."

"That's fine. Whatever it takes."

Curtis sat on the edge of his desk where Charlotte was sitting and smoothed his hand down the side of her face. "Thank you."

"For what?"

"Everything."

"I'm standing behind you because I love you and because I don't want to see our marriage ruined, but I need you to know that my feelings haven't changed when it comes to Tabitha. From this day forward, I don't want you communicating with her. Not about anything. I know you love your daughter, but I can't deal with her mother. I won't allow Tabitha to continue stealing my joy the way she has been."

"I hear what you're saying, and I'll respect your wishes."

"Good. That's all I want."

Charlotte stood and Curtis hugged her.

He hugged her tightly, and he also thought about Curtina.

He pictured her sweet little face and prayed that one day God would make it possible for him to be a father to her.

He hoped that one day Charlotte's heart would soften and make her okay with it.

It had been a long while, at least two weeks, since Charlotte had gone to Mitchell's most popular mall, and she was looking forward to checking out what Macy's had in their misses department. Normally she drove to Schaumburg to Woodfield Mall so she could shop at Nordstrom's or their Macy's or over to Oakbrook Mall so she could shop at Nordstrom's or Neiman's, but now that

Federated had acquired Marshall Field's and renamed it Macy's, the local clothing selection was a bit more upscale than it used to be, and now she could at least find a variety of dressy casual garmênts, which she loved. She also wanted to see what they had in the baby department because she was dying to get something for Janine's baby. Of course, the new bundle wouldn't be here for a while and in only a few months, Charlotte would be throwing the absolute best shower for her, but she still wanted to pick up a few items right now.

When Charlotte entered the store, she went directly into the shoe department. She browsed from one table to the next and then spotted a beautiful, three-and-a-half-inch basic pump. She had a ton of black shoes, actually a ton of shoes period, but these particular ones screamed pure class and she had to have them.

"Hi. Do you have these in a size eight?" she asked the salt-and-pepper-haired woman heading her way.

"Good choice. We've been selling a lot of these, but let me check."

"Thank you."

Charlotte browsed the athletic table and thought about trying on a couple of pairs of those, but decided not to since she had just about every color imaginable. She had gym shoes to match each of her fitness outfits, and she also had shoes that she didn't even have outfits for and had never worn.

"I'm so sorry," the saleslady said. "The closest thing we have is a seven, but I could check the system for you to see if any of the other locations have them in stock."

"I have some more shopping to do, so maybe I'll stop back by here on my way out."

"That'll be fine."

After passing through fine jewelry, and then passing by the Lancôme and MAC counters, she took the escalator up to the second floor and turned right. Just as she'd hoped, they had a lot of new pieces, so she headed over toward a stack of folded sweaters. Cashmere was her absolute favorite, and they had every color from black to red to royal blue to hot pink to orange. She already had two in black and also one in red, so she picked up the blue and pink and laid them over her arm. They were on sale for $69.99, which was a great sale given the original price was thirty dollars more.

Next, she walked into the Ralph Lauren section and pulled a navy blue wool blazer with beautiful gold-toned buttons from the rack it was hanging on and glanced up at the woman on the other side of it. To Charlotte's surprise, it was Reverend Tolson's wife.

"Vivian?"

"Oh, hi, Charlotte, how are you?"

"I'm well. And you?"

"Good."

Charlotte knew Curtis had told her not to say anything yet, but she at least had to find out what their plans were now that Reverend Tolson was no longer interim pastor.

"I'm really sorry that I didn't get to say a proper good-bye before you and Reverend Tolson left the church."

"I know. It happened pretty quickly, so I really didn't get to talk to anyone at all."

"So are the two of you planning to stay on here in Mitchell?"

"We haven't decided yet, but I'm hoping we go back to Dallas."

"That's where you lived before coming here, right?"

"Yes, we were both born and raised there, so that's really where home is for me."

"I can imagine."

"So how's Mr. Matthew?"

"He's fine."

"And Pastor?"

"He's fine as well."

"Please give them my best."

"Of course."

"Vivian, let's go!" Reverend Tolson said, appearing out of nowhere.

"I'm so, so sorry for everything," she whispered and hurried toward her husband, who clearly wasn't happy to see her talking with Charlotte. As a matter of fact, he seemed just a little too angry and almost like some lowlife abuser—either verbal or physical, or both.

Charlotte watched Vivian step onto the escalator behind her husband and wondered what he was going to say to her once they were out of the store and in their vehicle. She wondered what terrible thing he might do to her, and she couldn't wait to tell Curtis what she'd witnessed. Then, the more she thought about it, she wondered what Vivian had been apologizing for. It was true that her husband wasn't being cooperative with the board's decision, but Vivian had stressed how sorry she was in an almost passionate way—too passionate to merely be referring to Reverend Tolson's rejection of his termination offer.

After paying for the sweaters and blazer, Charlotte went down to the main floor and then to the lower level. She thought about stopping to look at sheets, but continued into the children's department. Once there, she immediately picked up two of the cutest onesies she'd seen in years. They were even cuter than the ones she remembered receiving as gifts when Marissa had been born, so she had to buy them. Then, over to the left, she saw the most beautiful, white satin christening dresses and suits and she would gladly have purchased one of those, too, except she didn't know if Janine and Carl were having a boy or girl. Nonetheless, she was so proud and happy she and Curtis were going to be the godparents.

Charlotte browsed through the rest of the section, but was saddened when she picked up a little pink sweater and matching hat that was almost identical to a set she'd purchased for Marissa. Charlotte still missed her terribly, and she longed for the day when the loss of her child would be easier to live with.

"Well, well, well," the voice said, and Charlotte looked in the woman's direction. "It seems you and I simply just can't stop running in to each other."

She didn't want to believe she was staring Tabitha straight in her face.

"Why are you following me?"

"Please. You give yourself way too much credit because I would never even waste my time."

"First it was the salon, then you confronted Curtis at the gas station, and now this."

"And?"

"You're stalking us like some madwoman."

Tabitha snickered. "Do you actually think you're worth all that? Because if you do, I have big news for you . . . you're not."

Charlotte looked down at Curtina, who was sitting in her stroller, smiling. She was so innocent and thankfully much too young to know what was going on.

"You're sick. Very sick, because no woman in her right mind would chase behind a man and his wife and bring her baby along for the ride," Charlotte said.

"You're just jealous. Of me and my daughter."

Charlotte dropped the onsies and the blankets onto a table where they didn't belong and moved closer to her adversary. "Don't ever say I didn't warn you, Tabitha."

"Whatever."

Charlotte brushed by her and left the area.

But as soon as she stepped outside the mall, she called Dooney.

She didn't even bother with saying hello to him. "I know we agreed that you would start tomorrow, but if you're ready, I need you to pay that tramp a visit tonight."

"Done."

Chapter 24

It was Friday evening and, as usual, Pelley's Seafood was jam-packed. Charlotte, Curtis, Matthew, and Alicia had been waiting for more than forty-five minutes, but the hostess had just informed Curtis they were next on the list. This was by far one of their favorite restaurants, but Charlotte wasn't sure if the long wait was worth it. Of course, Matthew and Alicia definitely thought otherwise and would have waited any amount of time they had to. At least four seats on a padded bench had become available and they were now sitting down.

"So, Matt, how long are you going to keep doing all that pouting, like some tiny little baby?" Alicia said, elbowing him.

"Quit it, girl." He was trying not to smile but Charlotte could tell it wasn't going to be long before he did.

"Maybe you're just not that happy to see me. With that big head of yours." She nudged him again.

And he was now slightly grinning. "I told you to quit that. And anyway, you're the one with the big old water head."

He and Alicia both cracked up, and then she wrapped her arm around his neck and pulled him closer to her. "I knew you couldn't stay mad for long. You never can."

Charlotte felt relieved and she could tell Curtis did as well, because ever since she'd told Matthew he couldn't spend the weekend with David, he'd been walking around the house sulking and not saying a word to anybody. Not even to Tracy, which was totally unusual. He'd been acting as if he'd never been more miserable, and Charlotte had hoped Alicia's presence would make a difference and it had.

"Black," the hostess said, and they all stood and walked toward her. "This way, please."

They followed behind her and waved at a couple of their church members as they were passing. Then, right after, they spotted another couple who'd just joined the congregation maybe three months ago.

"We'll have to go speak to them once we place our order," Curtis said.

"Definitely."

When they arrived at a full-length booth, large enough to seat three people on each side, they slid down into it. Curtis next to Charlotte and Matthew next to Alicia.

The hostess opened the menus as she passed one to each of them. "Your server will be with you shortly."

"Thank you," Curtis said.

Then he scanned the menu and closed it. "I think I'll have my usual. Lobster and shrimp."

"Me, too, Dad," Alicia added.

Matthew set his menu on the table. "And me three."

Charlotte kept perusing the various food items. "I think I'll wait to see what the specials are for tonight."

"I'm really glad you came home this weekend, baby girl," Curtis said.

"So am I. So I can harass my bonehead *little* brother."

"Girl, who are you calling little? I'm thirteen."

"Like I said, my *little* brother."

"Whatever, Alicia."

When the waitress returned to the table, she took their orders and Charlotte ended up choosing a combination of shrimp scampi and seafood pasta. Then Curtis and Charlotte went over to greet the two couples they'd seen on the way in.

They stopped at the new couple's table first. "Brother and Sister Carter," Curtis said, shaking both their hands. "It's good to see you."

Charlotte smiled. "Yes, it is," she said and the four of them chatted for a few minutes.

Next they headed over to the Allens, who'd been members of Deliverance Outreach since the first year it was founded, and spoke to them.

As they headed toward Alicia and Matthew, Charlotte thought about Brother Allen and how, for as long as they'd known him, he'd always had the same beautiful smile. He was one of the most genuinely friendly people she'd ever met and so was Sister Allen. Which is why she wasn't looking forward to having to face them on Sunday. She dreaded having to face the Allens, the Carters, or any other members of the church but there was no sense dwelling on the inevitable. No sense pondering and stressing over something that had to happen.

Back at their table, Matthew and Alicia were already eating their salads and rolls, and they were talking nonstop.

"Wow, son, it's great to see you in such a good mood," Curtis observed.

"I'm fine, Dad. I just wanted to go visit David. That's all."

Charlotte placed her hand over Matthew's. "And you will get to visit him. Next weekend. Okay?"

"And I get to stay at his house?"

Charlotte paused and then said, "Yes. You can stay until Sunday afternoon."

"Thanks, Mom."

"You're welcome."

Alicia drank some of her strawberry lemonade. "Matthew was telling me that his dad works at a pharmaceutical company."

"Yeah, he does," Curtis confirmed.

"There were recruiters from some of the top pharmaceutical companies at the job fair we had on campus a couple of weeks ago. They were looking for people to join their sales team."

"You're not thinking about that, are you?"

"No, but Sonya is," she said, referring to her roommate. "Her major is marketing and her minor is in sales, so she's gotten interest from a bunch of different companies."

"That's wonderful," Charlotte said.

"Well, I'm hoping you stick to law and writing," Curtis told her.

Alicia playfully rolled her eyes toward the ceiling. "We know, Dad."

"I'm serious. I keep telling you, you'll be great at both."

"I do love writing, and I also love the law, so I'll decide by the end of this semester whether I'm going to law school or not."

Curtis opened his mouth to say something else, but stopped abruptly . . . when Tabitha walked up, holding Curtina.

"Well, hello, Reverend and Mrs. Black. Remember me? I recently joined your congregation."

Charlotte was stunned. And thought maybe she was dreaming, because there was just no way this woman was standing at their table, speaking to them like they were lifelong friends. She couldn't be. Not in a million years.

But she was.

"How are you?" Curtis said, obviously trying to ignore the tension and trying to keep their communication cordial.

"I'm well. And so is my little one here," she said, looking at her daughter and then at Alicia and Matthew.

"Good," he said. "Glad to hear it."

"Well, I'd better get back to my table. My girlfriend is over there waiting, but there was no way I could miss speaking to all of you. Have a good evening."

Curtis and Charlotte looked at each other.

"Dad, who was that?" Matthew wanted to know.

"She joined our church, but there's something else I need to tell you about her when we get home."

"Is she sick?"

"No. But we'll discuss everything later."

Matthew glanced over at his sister and then shrugged his shoulders. Charlotte could tell he didn't see what the big deal was.

Alicia looked at her father but quickly averted her eyes, and Charlotte realized Alicia knew exactly who Tabitha was.

It was true that Tabitha had gone back to her table as planned, but Charlotte was still taken aback. Tabitha always seemed to know where she and Curtis were. The woman was showing up everywhere they went, and Charlotte was glad that after Sunday, they'd finally be able to report her to the authorities. The entire ordeal would be out in the open, and they'd be free to file for a restraining order.

When they'd finished their meals, they left the restaurant and went to a movie. Matthew had been dying to see the latest PG-13 comedy and actually, they all enjoyed it. Of course, Charlotte knew she would have enjoyed it even more had she not been thinking about Tabitha and the way she'd showed up at the restaurant this evening. The whole idea of it was so ridiculous.

When they got home, Curtis called Alicia and Matthew into his and Charlotte's bedroom.

"What is it, Dad?"

"I've already told Alicia, but now I need to tell you."

"About what?"

"The lady at the restaurant who was carrying the baby."

"Who is she?"

"She's the mother of your little sister."

"How?"

Charlotte saw the look of horror on Matthew's face and wanted to die. First, she'd disappointed him with her affair with David, and today Curtis was giving him more news he clearly didn't want to hear.

"I made a terrible, terrible mistake, son."

"So you have a baby with another woman?"

"Yes."

Tears filled Matthew's eyes. "Why do you and Mom keep doing stuff like this? Why can't you just love each other?"

Charlotte moved toward him. "Honey, we do. Your dad and I have had a lot of problems over the last few years but we finally have things right."

"But that's what you said after Aaron tried to burn down our house. And then you said that again when Marissa died."

"I know, sweetie, but this time, we really mean it."

"That's right, Matthew," Curtis agreed. "Nothing like this will ever happen again."

Matthew turned toward his sister. "Alicia, do you believe them?"

Charlotte could tell she'd been caught off guard and wasn't sure what to say exactly. But she did the best she could.

"Matt, sometimes life can be real hard, especially when you become an adult, but yes, if Daddy and Charlotte say this won't happen again, I have to believe them."

"So is this new baby and her mother going to be coming over here to visit?"

"No," Curtis said. "They won't be."

"Why? Because you're going to go over to their house instead?"

"No."

"Then I don't understand."

Curtis sighed. "Son, it's all very complicated. And there's more that we have to tell you. And you, too, Alicia."

"What?" she asked.

"We've decided to talk about it to the board and the congregation, and we're also releasing a press release to the public."

Alicia seemed confused. "Why would you do that?"

"Because we can't go on trying to cover this up and because it's only a matter of time before people start finding out on their own."

"Nooo," Matthew protested. "I don't want all my friends to know about this."

"I'm sorry," Curtis apologized. "I'm sorry, but unfortunately, it has to be done. We've thought about this long and hard and there's just no other way."

The tears Matthew had been trying to hold back finally fell.

Alicia hugged him and told him everything was going to be all right.

Charlotte tried consoling him as well. "It'll be tough for a while, but in the end, we'll be fine."

Matthew loosened his embrace with his sister and left the room.

"I'll go talk to him," Alicia said.

Charlotte hugged her. "Thanks, sweetie."

"No matter what, Daddy, I'll always love you."

Curtis kissed her on the forehead. "And I'll always love you."

Charlotte watched her leave and felt helpless.

Curtis and Charlotte were both just about to climb into bed when Curtis's cell phone rang.

He frowned when he saw the phone number.

"Who's that?"

"Tabitha."

"Answer it."

"For what?"

"Because now I want as many calls to come through from her as possible, so we can show the police all of our phone records."

The last thing Curtis wanted to do was talk to this woman, but he knew if he didn't pick it up, Charlotte would think he was hiding something.

"Hello?" he said.

"Oh my God, Curtis, you have to come over here quick."

"Why?"

"Someone slit all four of my tires. They did it while Curtina and I were inside my girlfriend's house, and I had to have my car towed. Then, when we got home, I noticed that someone had broken the glass on my front door and they'd forced a note through it. And I know that witch you're married to had something to do with this, because the note said if I didn't want to get hurt, I would leave town by the end of next month."

"Tabitha, why are you doing this? Why are you resorting to all these lies just so you can get me over there?"

"But I'm not lying. I'm telling you the honest truth, and I'm so afraid for Curtina and me to stay here tonight all by ourselves."

"Just stop it. And after tonight, don't you ever call my number again," Curtis yelled and dropped the phone on his nightstand.

"What did she want?" Charlotte asked.

"She claims her tires were cut and that someone broke her door window and left some sort of note. Oh, and she thinks you're the person behind it."

Charlotte snuggled into her pillow. "I told you something's wrong with Tabitha. The woman is crazy."

Curtis tried once again to get comfortable in bed, but then his cell rang again. This time it was Reverend Tolson. He didn't want to speak with him either, but he answered it just in case Tolson was finally ready to agree to their terms.

"Hello?"

"I just thought I would give you one last chance to pay me what I asked for. Or even better, I'd be more than willing to come back as interim pastor, as long as you're prepared to step aside until my contract is up."

"Man, we've already told you what we were willing to pay you, and if that's not good enough then so be it."

"Then I guess your decision is final?"

"Didn't you just hear me?"

"I heard you, but I think you should know that I've known about that illegitimate baby of yours for quite some time."

Curtis ended the call and dropped the phone on his nightstand even harder than he had when he'd hung up with Tabitha, and he hoped he hadn't damaged it. Tolson had gotten on his last nerve, calling him this late at night and then threatening him. A couple of weeks ago, he'd sort of been worried about what Tolson might know, but now that Curtis was going to reveal everything to everyone, he couldn't have cared less about any of Tolson's blackmail attempts.

"What did he want?"

"Money, of course, and he definitely knows about Tabitha and Curtina."

"But how?"

"I don't know, but he does."

"Well, it's not like any of what he says will matter to anyone after this weekend, but I still wonder what Vivian meant when she told me how sorry she was."

Charlotte had told Curtis how she'd seen the Tolsons out at the mall and how rude Tolson had been when he'd summoned his wife away from her.

"Maybe she just meant she was sorry for the way Tolson is trying to swindle money from the church," Curtis suggested.

"I guess."

"I'm sure that's what it was."

"Yeah, you're probably right. It was probably nothing at all."

Chapter 25

There was a frantic knock at the bedroom door and Curtis sat up. "Come in."

"Dad, Charlotte, you have to turn on the television!" Alicia exclaimed.

"You have to turn it on now," Matthew added.

"Why?" Curtis asked. "What's on?"

Charlotte picked up the selector and pushed the power button.

Alicia dropped down on the foot of the bed. "BBN just ran a clip, and we saw Reverend Tolson. We heard him saying something about how the nationally known Reverend Curtis Black is not the upstanding Christian people think he is."

Curtis's heart sank and he could already see the look of astonishment on Charlotte's face. Would Tolson actually go this far? Would he actually go on national television, trying to pay Curtis back?

As they sat waiting for the commercials to end, Lisa called Curtis's cell.

"Pastor, are you watching?"

"Yes. My children just came in and said they saw Tolson, so I'll call you back as soon as the interview is over."

"Okay," she said, and they hung up.

Charlotte raised the volume of the television and now the home phone was ringing.

"It's Janine," she said, and picked it up.

Curtis could tell Janine was also calling to inform them about the news broadcast, but he heard Charlotte tell her she'd get back with her. Then, finally, the anchors, a man and a woman, appeared on-screen again, and the male newscaster began speaking.

"We now take you by satellite to Chicago to talk with Reverend John Tolson. Good morning, Reverend."

"Good morning, and thank you for having me."

"Well, why don't we start with the reason you wanted to come on with us. Because it's my understanding that you have some very surprising information to share with everyone."

Reverend Tolson laughed. "The question is, where do I begin? There's so much to cover, but I think what most people will be shocked to learn is that Pastor Curtis Black has a six-month-old baby, and it's not with his wife."

"Hmmm. Well, if it's not with his wife, then who's the mother?"

"For right now, I'd rather not say, but what I will say is that the entire time I was serving at his church as interim pastor, he was out on the road with his mistress, living the good life. They traveled together, slept in the same hotels, and now they have a baby."

"And just so we can clarify this for our viewing audience, you're talking about *the* Reverend Curtis Black, the *New York Times* bestselling author and national faith-based speaker, correct?"

"Yes. That's exactly who I'm talking about."

"Well, you do know that these are some very strong allegations you're making."

"Of course. And that's why I would never make them unless I was telling the absolute truth. Pastor Black has been keeping secrets for years, and I finally decided that the public has a right to know what he's really about. Especially when millions of people have such high regard for this man. There are millions who see Pastor Black as one of the nation's top spiritual leaders, and I felt it was time for the chickens to come home to roost. It's time for Pastor Black to take responsibility for his actions."

"Do you think Reverend Black and the mother of his child will now come forward?"

"I have no idea, but if I were him, I'd do the right thing. And that would be to come clean."

"Reverend, we're almost out of time, but just quickly, if you don't mind us asking. Are you still serving as interim pastor at Reverend Black's church?"

Tolson smiled wide into the camera. "Not after today, I'm not."

"Well, thank you again for coming on."

"No. Thank you. I appreciate the opportunity."

When the screen focused back on just the anchors, the female shook her head. "Amazing. Just recently, we heard about Pastor Haggard, head of the largest Evangelical organization, and how he'd been keeping secrets and now Reverend Black."

"It's pretty interesting news."

"It is, but I do have to say that my heart goes out to both families involved, Reverend Black's and the alleged mother of the child, because something like this is never easy to deal with."

"I couldn't have said it better," the male anchor agreed and turned his attention back to the camera. "I'm sure we'll have more coverage on this story as the day continues, so please stay tuned for further developments."

Charlotte frowned. "Why did he try to make it seem like he was still serving as interim pastor?"

"He was just trying to make himself look good."

"But he's been out for over two weeks or so."

"Yeah, but they don't know that, and to be honest, I'm surprised they didn't try to contact us first before just letting him go on live the way they did."

"So now what, Dad?" Alicia asked.

"I'm going to call Lisa back right now to see what she suggests."

"This is bad," Matthew said and stood up. "This is so embarrassing and after this, I'll be the biggest joke at school. No one will ever stop talking about it, and I wanna transfer somewhere else."

"Honey, I understand how you feel," Charlotte told him. "But once the media gets wind of this, people will find out at the other schools, too, so I think it would be best if you just stayed where you are."

"I don't mean another school around here. I want to transfer to a school in Chicago."

"But the news is going to be out over there as well."

"I still want to leave here, and maybe David will let me come live with him."

"Matthew, you don't mean that."

"I do, Mom," he said, and walked out of the room.

Curtis wanted to run after him, but he simply didn't have the energy. He wanted to beg Matthew to forgive him, but he knew Matthew wasn't in a forgiving mood. His son was angry and disappointed at both him and Charlotte and it wasn't like anyone could blame him. Curtis and Charlotte had failed him as parents, and now Matthew had actually told his mother that he no longer wanted to live with them. Curtis had known the news about Tabitha and Curtina would be devastating, but what Curtis hadn't counted on was David's being in the picture when this all came to light. He hadn't counted on David's wanting to have a regular relationship with Matthew, one that involved frequent visitation.

"Dad, is there anything I can do?" Alicia asked.

"No, baby girl. Just being here is help enough."

"Well, I'm going to go get in the shower, and I'll also try to talk to Matthew."

Charlotte headed toward the doorway. "That'll be good, and while you're getting ready, I'll go talk to him now."

When Charlotte and Alicia left, Curtis dialed Lisa back.

"So are you just as shocked as I am?" he said.

"Probably even more so."

"And this is all because we wouldn't agree to pay him double what we owed him."

"But that's what doesn't make sense to me. I mean, who would go on national television, trying to defame someone, just because they didn't get a few thousand dollars?"

"Apparently, the money was worth more to him than we realized."

"Or maybe it was never about the money at all, and he has some other motive."

"Well, if he does, I don't know what it is."

"This is not good. And what we have to do now is issue a statement to the media right away because it's only going to be a matter of minutes before the calls begin coming in. They'll be calling me as your representative and if they can get access to your number, they'll be calling you as well. The other thing we have to do is decide which national news channel or talk show we should get you and Charlotte an interview with. We should do something on Monday, and the more I'm sitting here thinking about it, I think the best platform might be *Live with Michael Price*. Michael is watched and respected by millions of viewers every weeknight and he's extremely fair. He asks very good questions, but he never takes sides."

"When are you thinking we should do this?"

"Monday evening. You should still go speak to your congregation tomorrow but if I can get you on, we'll need to fly to New York first thing Monday morning."

"Just let us know."

"I will, and for now if you get any calls, please check the caller ID and only answer calls you recognize from family and friends. Don't answer anything from the media or any numbers showing as private, restricted, or unavailable."

"Fine, and I'll let Charlotte and the children know, too."

"Anyway, let me get this statement out over the wire and call up the producer for Michael Price's show, and I'll get back to you as soon as I can."

"Thanks, Lisa. And what I'm going to do now is call my agent at home, so I can discuss with her the letter of apology I want to send to everyone at my publishing house."

"That's a great idea. And if you can speak directly to your editor and your publisher that would be good as well."

Curtis started into the bathroom but stopped when he heard the home phone ringing to check the display. It was the local NBC affiliate. Then the ABC affiliate. Then the CBS affiliate, and the top local FM radio station.

But Curtis did as Lisa had told him and ignored every one of them. He ignored them and then he went to tell the rest of his family how they were to do the same thing.

How they were to dodge the media at all costs because of him.

Within a few hours, Charlotte and Curtis were dressed and still waiting to hear back from Lisa about their possible trip to the East Coast two days from now. In the meantime, however, they'd called their friends and family members. Charlotte called her parents, Janine, Tracy, and even her aunt Emma, and Curtis called Lana, Elder Jamison, and Elder Dixon. He'd even called his sister, but as usual, they hadn't gotten an answer and Charlotte felt sorry for him. She could tell just how badly Curtis was hurting and still not being able to make things right with his sister wasn't making him feel better.

Then there was Matthew, who seemed a lot more cooled down now that Charlotte and Curtis had sat and talked with him, but Charlotte still worried that he was serious about going to live with David. Something she would never be able to stand.

Charlotte poured diet ginger ale into a glass filled with ice and did the same with a bottle of spring water for Curtis. Matthew and Alicia were upstairs in his game room, but she and Curtis were sitting in the kitchen. They sat talking about what had happened earlier with Reverend Tolson's interview and all that they would probably have to endure in the days ahead. Charlotte tried to see the bright side of things, but no matter how hard she searched, she couldn't find one positive element when it came to their predicament. Curtis kept saying that the good thing about all of this was that they no longer had to hide any secrets, but she didn't see it that way. What Charlotte saw was a ton of slander and humiliation they'd have to deal with for months and years to come.

When the phone rang for the umpteenth time, Charlotte closed her eyes and refused to go see who was calling. So Curtis left his seat to check instead.

"It's David."

"Let it ring."

"I think you should talk to him. Because I'm betting he's heard the news by now."

Charlotte hesitated and by the time she took the receiver, the ringing stopped. But at Curtis's urging, she called him back.

"David?"

"Hi."

"I'm sorry I didn't answer in time."

"I wanted to talk to you about that BBN broadcast this morning. I didn't get to see it live, but I've seen a ton of replays, and I have to tell you, Charlotte, I'm not happy about any of it. I'm not happy about the type of environment Matthew is living in."

"I know this looks bad, but Matthew is fine."

"That's not what it sounded like when I spoke to him earlier."

Charlotte had had no idea a conversation had taken place between David and her son.

"What did he tell you?"

"That he wants me to come pick him up for the rest of the weekend."

"This isn't a good time. Not with everything going on. Plus, you agreed to pass on seeing him this weekend, as long as I called you in a few days."

"That was then. But now things have changed."

"I understand how you feel. And I appreciate you caring about Matthew's well-being, but we need him here with us. We need our family here together until we can try to get past this."

"So the answer is no?"

"I'm sorry."

"Not as sorry as I am because now you're leaving me no choice."

"David, if you could just try to understand. If you could just give us a week or maybe even until after Thanksgiving, which is only a couple of weeks away."

"I've waited long enough. Thirteen years, remember? So I'm through talking about this."

"David, please."

"I'll see you in court."

"But . . ." Charlotte tried to reason with him again, but he hung up. Curtis clasped his hands together and rested them atop the island. "Well, I guess that didn't go over too well."

"Not at all, and we have to hire an attorney first thing on Monday."

"What did he say?"

"That he'll see me in court."

"Why is he pushing so hard about this?"

"I don't know," she said, lowering her voice and looking behind her to make sure Matthew was nowhere in sight. "But I wish Matthew had never asked to see him because David has been nothing but trouble ever since then."

"What we have to do is get the best custody attorney we can find, either here or from the Chicago area."

"I hope that'll be enough, because just like you were saying before, David is his biological father and he has rights. Not to mention, he's made that very clear to me more than once himself."

"What I'm hoping is that the court will think twice about removing a child from a home he's been in for so many years and giving him to a father who has a very demanding job and who can't be home every day right when Matthew gets out of school."

"Baby, I'm scared."

"I know you are, but we have to face this."

"Well, just so you know. I'll die if Matthew is taken away from us."

"That's not going to happen."

"But what if it does?"

"We have to believe it won't. We have to pray for all of this to work out in our favor."

"I have been praying. Every single day about every single thing. But it just seems to me that no matter how hard I pray, things only tend to get worse. I'm so frustrated, and I'm to the point where I feel like I was better off when I wasn't praying at all."

"You can't be serious."

"I am."

"And you've heard me preach on the power of prayer how many times?"

"Still."

"I know we've been through a lot, but the worst thing you can do right now is lose faith. The worse thing you can do is stop praying."

Charlotte heard him and while she would try to do what he was telling her, she couldn't promise anything. It was the reason she changed the subject.

"So was Lisa leaving right after you spoke to her?"

"She had a couple of calls to make, and then she said she'd be on her way. She should be here in a couple of hours."

"I'm glad she decided to be here for tomorrow's service."

"So am I."

"Did she hear anything about *Live with Michael Price*?"

"She doesn't have final confirmation, but they're definitely interested."

"Of course they are. I was sure of that just based on all the people who've called here today. They're still calling, and I wonder how they got our phone number."

"For all we know, Tolson could have given it to them."

"I wouldn't doubt it, and to be honest, I'm surprised we haven't heard from Tabitha yet."

"Maybe we won't," Curtis said. But he spoke too soon because now the phone was ringing and it was in fact Tabitha.

Charlotte answered it on the first ring.

"Hello?"

"Well, well, if it isn't Miss Thing, the schizo who had my tires slashed."

Charlotte wanted terribly to tell Tabitha how right she was and how more than that was going to happen if she didn't leave them alone. She wished she could tell her how she'd smiled herself off to sleep right after Tabitha had called Curtis crying on the phone. She'd wanted to laugh because Curtis hadn't believed one word of what Tabitha had told him.

"Think whatever you want to," Charlotte finally said.

"I don't have to think. I know you did this. And that's why you and Curtis are getting everything you deserve. Yeah, that's right, I saw the broadcast and the media has already begun calling me. And as soon as I meet with my attorney, I'm planning to tell them everything they want to know."

"Do whatever you want, Tabitha, because we no longer have a single thing to hide."

"We'll see. Because at the least, I'm sure the public will be

more than interested in hearing the details of my affair with
Curtis and how you were basically sitting home alone for five
years. And I also wonder what people will think when they hear
about all the other schemes you've concocted."

"Good-bye, Tabitha."

Charlotte put the phone down. Curtis was breathing heavier
than normal. "I don't know why you insist on talking to her."

Charlotte wasn't sure why she kept talking to Tabitha either
but what she did know was that she couldn't wait to speak to
Dooney again. She'd spoken to him earlier and thanked him
for the way he'd carried out phase one, but now it was time for
phase two. Now it was time he showed Tabitha just how serious
this was.

Chapter 26

Charlotte and Curtis were in the limo, on their way to O'Hare, Alicia had driven back to school yesterday evening, and Charlotte's parents had driven over to pick up Matthew, so he could stay with them while Charlotte and Curtis were in New York. He'd mentioned that he wanted to stay with David instead but Curtis had somehow miraculously been able to talk him out of it. They still hadn't told him about the custody battle they were going to be in for, and all they could hope was that David wouldn't say anything to him either. So far he hadn't, and Charlotte could only assume that the reason David was keeping quiet was that he wasn't sure how Matthew might feel about him taking his parents to court.

"I'm glad one of Attorney Hallstrom's partners has so much experience with custody cases," Curtis said. "Because now we don't have to look for anyone."

"And it was nice of him to talk to us last night, especially with it being a Sunday."

"Attorney Hallstrom said Attorney Vellman was very good, that he rarely lost any cases, and that he was an expert when it came to making the other party look bad. He said that if David has any skeletons whatsoever, it'll all be brought out in court."

"Let's just hope David even has something to hide because

what I remember is that he was always so self-righteous. And
the more I think about it, Anise used to talk about that all the
time, and still I remember how terrible he used to make her
feel because she was dark-skinned. She used to tell me how he
thought he was better than other black people simply because
his skin was lighter and that because his father was dark he was
ashamed to be seen with him."

"Are you serious?"

"Yes. Which is why I'm shocked to see Anise getting along
with him so well."

"Maybe they get along fine now that they're not married."

"I guess. And maybe David doesn't feel that way anymore
because Matthew is definitely on the darker side, yet David is
acting as if it doesn't matter to him in the least."

The shiny black stretch limo moved into the far right lane of
I-90, curved around the O'Hare exit, and went through the toll-
way. They'd arrived in record time, and Charlotte was glad traffic
wasn't heavy at 4:30 A.M.

The limo continued toward terminal one and parked in front
of one of United's entryways. Curtis and Charlotte gathered
together briefcases and carry-on pieces, and Curtis opened the
right door. When they stepped out, Orson, one of their usual
drivers, removed their rolling garment bags from the trunk and
Curtis passed him forty dollars.

"The gratuity was already included when you made your res-
ervation by credit card."

"I know," Curtis said. "But you know I always give you a little
more than I give the others. You always take such good care of us."

Orson smiled. "Thank you so much, Pastor."

"Anytime."

"And, Pastor, I hope you don't let all that junk I saw on television this weekend discourage you any."

"I won't."

"You and Ms. Charlotte will be just fine."

Charlotte hugged him. "Thanks, Orson. Thanks for everything."

"Your support means a lot," Curtis added.

"You all have a safe trip, now."

Inside the airport, they immediately spotted Lisa standing near first-class check-in.

"How are you?" she said, hugging Charlotte and then Curtis.

"We're hanging in there," Charlotte told her.

"Good," she said and they entered the pathway leading up to the counter. No one was in line, so they were able to check their luggage and get their boarding passes pretty quickly.

Next they walked over to the line reserved for first-class security and showed their passes and IDs to the young female agent on duty. Charlotte saw the funny look on the agent's face, right after she checked Curtis's photo, and Charlotte wanted to tell her to mind her own business and to just do her job. But she knew the woman couldn't help taking a second look, not with Curtis being so well known and now having been attacked on BBN. And she wasn't the only curious one anyway because at this very moment, there were at least a dozen pairs of eyes from the general security line, staring in their direction. Which is why Charlotte was glad Lisa had suggested they take a 6 A.M. flight, because she couldn't even imagine how bad the gawking would have been had they flown out later in the day.

"I know it's difficult," Lisa said. "But just try to ignore them."

Charlotte set her carry-on luggage and tote onto the moving belt and took off her coat and shoes. "If it's this bad this early in the morning, I hate to even think what it'll be like by the time we get to New York."

Curtis laid his briefcase on next and then pulled out his notebook computer so it could roll through separately. "So do I."

Lisa removed her blazer. "Unfortunately, this is the way it's going to be for a while, but I promise, it will get better. It always does. Because, believe me, I've heard and seen a lot worse situations than yours, and today you never hear anything about them."

At the gate, Curtis and Charlotte sat down but Lisa walked a few feet away, making one phone call after another.

"I still can't believe how understanding everyone was at church yesterday," Charlotte said. "There was barely a dry eye in the room when you finished speaking."

"It was definitely a blessing but my only worry is that at least twenty-five percent of the church was empty when normally just about every seat is taken."

"Well, we knew there was a chance we might lose a few people, but even the entire board offered you their love and support. They made it very clear that they were behind you all the way."

"It just goes to show that what most people really want is the truth, and I'm just sorry that I didn't come forward when Elder Jamison and Elder Dixon told me I should. If only I had listened to them, Tolson never would have been able to do what he did. He wouldn't have had anything to tell that I hadn't already told."

"Well, what's done is done and now we're going to have our time tonight to give our side of the story. You'll have an opportunity to apologize and to explain things in our own words."

Curtis smiled at Charlotte.

"What?"

"You're doing so well with this. Better than I ever would have expected."

Charlotte smiled back at him and opened the magazine she'd purchased on their way from security. She smiled because regardless of what they were going through, they were happy with each other. And to her, that meant everything.

One of the producers attached a tiny speaker to Curtis's lapel and then did the same with the turtleneck of Charlotte's wool dress. They were only minutes away from the interview with Michael Price, and Charlotte was suddenly starting to feel nervous. She wasn't sure why, but maybe because all the bright lights were beaming down on them and because there were so many people rushing around, trying to get everything ready.

Producers, assistant producers, camera people, teleprompter coordinators, they were all there, and it was the first time Charlotte had paid attention to just how much work went toward shooting a talk show. She'd done a number of interviews with Curtis in the past, both local and national, both taped and live, but she'd never sat in on anything of this magnitude. Curtis, of course, had been on everything from *Oprah* to the *Today Show*, to *Fox & Friends*, and that was pretty obvious because even though he was fully aware of the reason he was there, he was still noticeably calm.

"Are you okay?" he asked.

"Actually, I'm a little nervous."

"You'll be fine once we get started. You'll feel more and more comfortable as the interview progresses."

Charlotte looked over at Lisa and saw her point both her thumbs up and Charlotte nodded.

"Reverend Black, can you say your name and a few other words for our mike check, please?" a very handsome, late-twenties producer asked.

"Sure. Reverend Curtis Black. Testing, one, two, three. Testing, one, two, three."

"Now, Mrs. Black, if you could do the same."

"Charlotte Black. Testing, one, two, three. Charlotte, testing, one, two, three."

"Perfect."

Next Michael Price walked onto the set, looking as distinguished as always.

"Reverend and Mrs. Black," he said, smiling, taking a seat and shaking both their hands. "It's so good seeing you again, Reverend. Thank you so much for being here and for giving us your first interview on this particular subject."

"We appreciate you having us," Curtis said.

"I'm sure my producers have explained the format and told you approximately how often we'll have to break for commercials, but for the most part, I just want you to relax and answer questions the same as you would if we were having a personal conversation. And, of course, please feel free to let me know during the breaks if you want to cover something specific."

"No problem," Curtis said.

Michael adjusted his microphone. "So, did you have a good flight in?"

"Yes, it was fine."

"No delays at all," Charlotte added.

Michael laughed. "Now, that's always a plus. A major one."

They chatted for a few more minutes and then the lead producer did the final countdown. It was now showtime.

"Good evening, and welcome to *Live with Michael Price*. I'm Michael Price, and tonight we have on with us world-renowned pastor, bestselling author, and speaker Reverend Curtis Black. And sitting beside him is his lovely wife, Charlotte. Welcome to both of you."

"Thank you," they said in unison.

"So let me just begin by saying that it is always an honor to have you on the show, Reverend. I think the last time you were here, you were promoting your latest book, *How to Love Everyone, Even Your Enemies*, which topped all the national bestseller lists the first week of publication."

"Yes."

"Are you working on anything right now?"

"Sort of. But my plan is to get something finished by the middle of next year."

"Of course, we'll certainly be looking for it. But the reason you're here tonight is because of an interview that was done with a man by the name of Reverend John Tolson, which aired on BBN two days ago. So why don't you start by telling us your connection to him."

"Well, Michael, Reverend Tolson was the interim pastor I hired for my church when I first began traveling on the road, promoting my books and doing speaking engagements. As a matter of fact, he served as interim pastor for about five years, but I've been back in the pulpit on a regular basis for the last twelve months or so."

"I see. So is there a reason why he went forward with making public allegations against you?"

"As far as I'm concerned, he had no reason at all, but I will say that he was pretty unhappy about my being back. He came to me about three weeks ago and said that he hadn't signed up to be a lowly assistant and that this was what he was starting to feel like. So, I told him he could leave if he chose to and that we would pay him the remaining two years of his contract. But unfortunately, he didn't think that was fair and said he wanted four years. My board and I refused his request and he began making threats."

"Such as?"

"He talked about having ammunition and how he would use it if he had to. And, of course, now we know what he was talking about."

"You mean the woman and baby he referred to over the weekend?"

"Yes."

"Well, you know I have to ask this, but was he telling the truth? Was there an affair with Ms. Tabitha Charles and is there a baby?"

Charlotte should have known they'd have her name by now and she wondered if Tabitha had already spoken with some of Michael's staff members.

"Yes. I'm sad to say that I did have an affair with Ms. Charles, that it lasted almost the entire time I was on the road, and I now have a six-month-old daughter with her."

"Have the two of you spoken recently?"

"Yes. We've spoken on several occasions and until a week ago, I was actually visiting my daughter."

"Is there some reason you stopped?"

"I won't go into details, but what I will say is that I have no interest in being unfaithful to my wife. I hurt her in the worst way, and I can never put her through anything like this again. I do love my daughter, and I want to see her, but not if the arrangement means being unfaithful to my wife."

"So are you saying that Ms. Charles still wants a relationship with you?"

"As I said, I don't want to go into details, but the important thing is that I'm committed to my wife."

"And Mrs. Black," Michael said. "Have you seen your husband's daughter?"

"Yes. Maybe three or four times."

"At your home?"

"No. In public places."

"This must be very difficult for you."

"It has been. I will say that it's better now, but the whole ordeal really caused a heavy strain on our marriage. It's really been tough, trying to work through this. But we have. Curtis has proven to me that he only wants me, and I have forgiven him. It took me a while, but I was finally able to do it, and life is so much better for us. To be honest, we're closer and more at peace with each other now than we were before all this happened. Somehow this disaster made us and our marriage stronger."

"That's amazing. I've had on a number of marital counselors in the past, and I've heard a few of them say exactly what you just stated. That many times, an affair makes the marriage better. That it was the best thing that could have happened to certain couples."

"It's strange, and it's not something I would have expected, but it's true. It's almost as if Curtis and I really know how to appreciate each other now, and we've both come to realize that we could never truly be happy with anyone else."

"Exactly," Curtis agreed. "My eyes are so open, and I'm more in love with Charlotte now than I was when we first got married. Which is a very blessed change of pace for me because there was a time when I just couldn't imagine being with just one woman, and I hurt two wonderful women in the process. I was married twice before, and I pretty much did whatever I wanted when I wanted. I lost two churches, and even that didn't stop me. And that's why I'm sitting on your show tonight, trying to make amends for the terrible choices I've made. Choices I take full responsibility for."

"When we come back," Michael said, "we'll talk more with Reverend and Mrs. Black, and we'll take calls from our viewers."

Charlotte breathed deeply and relaxed her body. Michael asked if she and Curtis needed anything, but mostly they sat quietly until they were on air again.

"Welcome back. For those of you just tuning in, we're talking with *New York Times* bestselling author and faith-based speaker Reverend Curtis Black and his wife, Charlotte."

"Is there anything, Reverend, that you'd like to say to your readers or the thousands and thousands of people who have enjoyed hearing you speak?"

"Yes. That I'm sorry. I'm sorry for the awful sins I committed, and I pray that everyone can forgive me. There's no excuse for the pain I've caused for so many people, but I have changed. I'm a new man with a new dedication to God, and I feel good about the road I'm now traveling on. It feels good to have everything out in the open. It feels good to be honest. It's good not to have to sneak around doing something I have no business doing and then putting every ounce of energy I have into hiding it. From my wife, from my children, and from all of you. Words will never be able to express how ashamed I am for letting so many of you down, but as time goes on, I hope you'll see the change in me through my actions."

"And Mrs. Black. Is there anything you'd like to share?"

"Just that I believe in my husband, and I love him with all my heart. I also want to add that we love our children, and that they are our priority. They've been very hurt by all that has happened, and we plan to do everything we can to protect them."

"Meredith from Birmingham, you have a question for Reverend Black?"

"Good evening, Michael. And good evening to you, Reverend and Mrs. Black."

They all greeted the first caller.

"Actually, I have more of a comment than I do a question. First, I want to say that I was very disappointed in you once I learned about you having an affair on your wife and especially about you having a baby. But I prayed about it and realized it wasn't my place to judge you or anyone else. And then I thought about how much all of your books have helped me. They've changed my life and the lives of my children, and I'll forever be indebted to you for that. So I just wanted to say that here in Alabama, we still love you."

"Thank you so much," Curtis responded. "Your words are very kind."

"Next, we have Jasper from Los Angeles."

"Hello, Michael."

"Hello."

"I just wanna tell Mrs. Black that I'm very happy to see her standing by her husband the way she's doing. A couple of years ago, I made some mistakes in my marriage and my wife walked out and took everything with her. And it wasn't even an affair. She left because I had a major gambling problem, and I lost most of my retirement savings. And please know that I'm not saying I wasn't wrong, because I was. But if only she could have loved me enough to stick by me, maybe I could have gotten help and we would have been okay."

"I'm sorry to hear that you're no longer together," Charlotte said. "Do you have children?"

"Yes, we have two teenage boys, and now that I've stopped gambling, I see them all the time. But my wife still barely speaks to me."

"You're still married?" Curtis asked.

"Yes, Pastor, I am."

"Then maybe there's still a chance. I don't know your whole situation, but I'd like to talk to you privately if you're okay with that."

"Jasper, if you'll stay on the line and give your contact information to one of our producers, we'll see that Reverend Black gets it," Michael assured him.

"I will, and thank you so much, Reverend. And God bless you."

"God bless you."

"Does he do this all the time, Mrs. Black?"

"You mean counsel people?"

"Yes."

"He does. And as you can see, he doesn't even have to know them," she said, and they laughed.

"Our next caller is Sharon from Boston."

"Good evening, Michael."

"Good evening."

"I debated whether I was going to call in or not, but as I continued watching, I just couldn't sit here, not saying anything. Pastor Black, I have to say I'm completely appalled at the way you're sitting on *Live with Michael Price*, trying to make all of us believe that you've changed. You're a total hypocrite, and, Mrs. Black, you should be even more ashamed than he is, because you're pretty much sitting there telling every woman in this country that it's okay for a man to cheat on his wife, so long as he apologizes for it."

"I'm sorry you feel that way," Curtis said.

"No, you're the sorry one. You're just as sorry as my ex-husband because he was just like you. He went out and got himself a baby, too. Had it by some wild piece of trash but I'm not like your little wifey. I dropped him like he never existed."

Charlotte felt her nerves racing, and she hoped there weren't going to be many more calls like this one. Thankfully, Michael moved on to the next caller and never even acknowledged Ms. Boston, Massachusetts.

"Theresa from Chicago, go ahead with your question or comment."

"Actually, my name is Tabitha, and I'm the woman the three of you have been discussing."

Michael looked at Curtis and Charlotte, and Charlotte could tell he was waiting to see whether they were okay with Tabitha being on the line or not. So Curtis looked over at Lisa and she gave him the go-ahead. She'd already warned them that something like this might happen, and she'd prepped them well enough to handle it.

"Okay, Tabitha, you're welcome to stay on," Michael told her. "But if at any time this turns into something I'm not comfortable with, we'll have to end our dialogue with you."

"Not a problem. Because what I mainly want to say is that I'm not proud of the affair I had with Curtis, especially since he's a married man, and I do regret it. However, I still think it's wrong for Curtis to neglect my daughter when she had no say in being born. Curtis and I were both two consenting adults when we conceived her, and he owes her everything. She deserves to be given the same love he's giving his other two children. Not to mention, if Charlotte really loves Curtis the way she's been claiming on your show tonight, then she should have no issues with accepting her stepdaughter. She needs to accept her, the same as Curtis accepted her two children that weren't his, her thirteen-year-old son and her daughter who passed away, the one she had by some mental case."

Charlotte wanted to crawl under the desk they were sitting at, and she wished Michael would signal his producers to drop Tabitha from the broadcast. It was one thing for her to talk about Curtis and Curtina, but it was something far different now that she was bringing up Matthew and Marissa. She had no right, and it was all Charlotte could do to try to stay calm and in control of her emotions.

"Would you like to respond, Reverend Black?"

"First of all, I don't think it's even slightly appropriate for us to talk about our children this way on national television, and I won't be a part of that."

Charlotte nodded in agreement. "Neither will I. I'd just mentioned earlier how we're working very hard to protect our children, and I would hope that every adult in the viewing audience would respect that, regardless of who that viewer is."

"Why should I respect your children when you're not respecting my daughter?"

Michael interrupted. "We'll be right back, so please stay with us." Then, when the producer cued him to relax, he said, "I'm sorry about that. I was hoping she would keep her comments on the cordial side, but no such luck, I guess."

"She's a real piece of work," Charlotte said. "More than anyone will ever know."

When the break ended, they discussed Curtis's plans for the future and took more calls from viewers, which interestingly enough were very positive. There had been a couple of other calls like the one from Boston, but the majority of callers had wished them well and had told Curtis to please keep doing what he was doing.

When the interview was over, Michael thanked them again for coming on the show, and Charlotte, Curtis, and Lisa headed out to the car.

Charlotte felt relieved. Relieved that they'd made it through the interview and that it was now over.

And happy to know Dooney would be taking care of business in only a matter of hours. He'd take care of things just as soon as all the lights were out in Tabitha's subdivision.

Chapter 27

Charlotte and Curtis had just walked inside their front entrance, and Charlotte couldn't have been happier. They'd extended their stay and had been in New York for two full days instead of one, thanks to the other television and radio interviews Lisa had scheduled for them, but as the saying went, there really was no place like home. It seemed they both had been asked every personal question imaginable, and the entire trip had worn Charlotte completely out. Not to mention, it was the first time in a while that she'd gone to New York and hadn't gotten a chance to spend any real time on Fifth Avenue, her absolute favorite place to shop. There was nothing in her surrounding area that even slightly compared to Bergdorf's, but in all honesty, shopping had been the least of what had been on her mind. Partly because she still worried about more fallout from Reverend Tolson's announcement, and primarily because she worried about David and the fact that he just might win his case.

Before she and Curtis had left for one of the radio stations yesterday morning, she had called Attorney Vellman's office to find out if he'd have some time to meet with them when they returned, and his secretary had told her he had an opening this afternoon at 2:00 P.M. Right now, it was a couple of minutes before noon and Charlotte was glad they'd taken an early flight back to O'Hare, which was an hour from where they lived.

"It's so good to see both of you back here safe and sound," Tracy said hugging both of them. "Is there anything I can get for you?"

Charlotte walked into the kitchen and dropped her purse on the counter. "No, I think we're fine, and it's good to see you, too, Tracy."

Curtis followed behind them. "Just seeing your friendly face is more than enough and thank you for taking care of some of our errands while we were gone."

"I was glad to do it, and I'm so sorry about what that Reverend Tolson did to you on television. Only an evil, heartless man would do something like that, and no good is going to come to him. No good at all, I tell you."

"Well, what's done is done," Curtis told her. "And what we have to do now is move on."

"I'm sorry I missed service on Sunday, but you know I was out of town seeing my best friend. I wish I could have been here, but how did everything turn out?"

"Very well. The majority of the members were there, and I owe them everything."

"That's good. Very good to hear, and maybe things will be back to normal really soon."

"I hope so."

"Wait a minute," Curtis said quickly, turning up the television.

Tracy sucked in air and covered her mouth all at the same time, and Charlotte's eyes bugged. The noon news was on and one of the young reporters was standing next to Tabitha in front of her house—which had been vandalized from top to bottom. The reporter narrated the scene as the camera showed up-close and very detailed footage of the entire mess: a huge, broken picture window, a couple of other smaller windows that had been cracked, and the word *whore*, which had been spray-painted across multiple bricks at least ten different times. Even the drive-way displayed a good number of obscenities, and the garage read, "Whores aren't welcome in Mitchell."

This was definitely the work of Dooney.

"Ms. Charles, do you have any idea who would have done something like this to you?" the reporter asked.

Tabitha gave him a cynical look. "Did you see *Live with Michael Price* two nights ago?"

"As a matter of fact, I did."

"Then you already have your answer. The good Reverend and Mrs. Black are as guilty as sin, and as far as I'm concerned they should be locked up immediately. These people have done noth-ing but cause my daughter and me a ton of heartache, and I say enough is enough."

"Do you know if they were in town last night when this hap-pened?"

"No. I don't. But I'll put every penny I have on the fact that they paid someone to handle this for them. Wealthy people do this sort of thing whenever they feel like it, and unfortunately, they usually get away with it. Not to mention, they were defi-nitely in town Friday night when my tires were slit and the glass on my front door was damaged."

"Oh my God," Curtis said. "She's blaming us for what hap-pened."

"But you were in New York," Tracy explained.

"Yeah," Charlotte said. "But just the fact that she's planting such incriminating ideas in everyone's head is enough to make people question our innocence. It's enough to get rumors started, and it certainly isn't going to help anything."

"Charlotte is right. Because by this evening, every news chan-nel in the country will be airing Tabitha's interview. They'll be showing her house over and over again, even if only for shock value."

"Isn't there anything you can do?" Tracy asked.

"I don't know. But I will say that while Tabitha is wrong for accusing us of something we didn't do, I'm now wondering if she really was telling the truth when she called the other night, saying that someone slashed her tires and that they'd also broken the glass window near the door of her house. Plus, who in the world hates her this much?"

Charlotte wished they could talk about something else, but said, "With Tabitha, there's no telling how many enemies she's made and how many of them are out to get her."

"Still," Curtis continued, "it's strange, and I can't help but worry about Curtina's well-being because what if she'd been near all that glass when it was broken?"

Charlotte despised Tabitha, but she certainly didn't want any harm to come to Curtina. She'd wanted Dooney to cause enough damage, the kind that would make Tabitha sit up and take notice, but it had never been her intention to hurt Curtis's little girl—not when she sort of felt sorry for Curtina. Charlotte had tried to rid herself of any and all sympathy for a child Curtis had conceived with another woman, but she hadn't been able to do so, not since that day she'd seen Tabitha and Curtina in Macy's and Curtina had smiled so joyously at her—the day Charlotte's sympathy for her had come into play for the very first time. Charlotte had even wanted to smile back at the child but her bitterness toward Tabitha had prevented her from doing it.

Nonetheless, she would never let on to Curtis any of what she was thinking because she still wanted Tabitha out of their lives. For good. Although she did have to admit that Tabitha's public accusations made her nervous, and she hoped the police weren't planning to make anything of them. She also wondered why Dooney had decided to strike last night and not on Monday night the way he'd planned.

Curtis called Lisa to let her know about what they'd just seen on the news and Charlotte called her parents so she could speak to Matthew. She and Curtis hadn't spoken to him since yesterday, and he still hadn't sounded too happy with them.

"Hey, Mom," Charlotte said.

"Hi, sweetie. Are you back?" her mother said.

"Yes, we just got home a little bit ago."

"Wonderful."

"How's Matthew doing?"

"He talks to us just fine, but he's also been calling his father from his cell phone."

"What about?"

"I couldn't hear everything, but pretty much he keeps saying he wants to spend every weekend with him, and that he doesn't understand why you won't let him. He also told David that he's been reading some Internet websites, and that if David was to start paying you child support, you would have to let them be together."

Charlotte wanted to burst into tears. "I'm so tired of this, Mom."

"I know. And, honey, there's something else I need to say."

Noreen paused and then continued. "Maybe you should just try to go along with what David wants for now, because I just don't think it's a good idea for all of you to be battling out Matthew's fate in court. I know how strongly you feel about this, but in the end, Matthew is going to be the one who ends up hurt."

"But what if David tries to take him from us? What if he tries to convince Matthew that life with him could be so much better? Which wouldn't be hard to do right now, because Matthew is so upset with us. Curtis and I have disappointed him so many times, and all I keep playing over and over in my head is what Matthew said on Saturday about wanting to go live with David. The look on his face was so serious, and he was so angry."

"I understand that, but if you fight David on this, I have to tell you, I'm not sure what's going to happen. You and I just talked a few days ago about the fact that there are already so many strikes against you, like, for example, you not telling David until now that he had a son. And now with this other scandal, I just don't know what a judge might think. It's hard to say how he or she might rule, but what you have to ask yourself is how you would decide if you were the deciding judge. What would you do if you saw a child in Matthew's position and the parents he lived with had such a turbulent history? And, honey, please, please don't think I'm trying to criticize you or that I'm not on your side, because I am. But I just want you to do what's best for all of you. I want you to do what's best for Matthew."

"So you think I should let David see him whenever he wants?"

"Well, all he wanted was weekends anyway, right?"

"He also wants him on holidays and the entire summer."

"But maybe if you really try to talk to him again, you can work out something that will allow him to have certain days, and you and Curtis can have the others."

"I don't know."

"You have to try. It's your decision, but your father and I talked about this a lot on Sunday after Matthew went to bed, and we both think this is best."

"I'll talk to Curtis. And if he agrees, maybe I'll call David."

"Good. I'll get Matthew, and you take care of yourself, honey. Love you."

"I love you, too, Mom."

Charlotte waited for him to come to the phone and heard Curtis still talking to Lisa.

"Hello?" Matthew said.

"Hi, sweetie. How are you?"

"Okay."

"Are you ready to come home?"

"No."

"Well, you know you have to get back to school, right?"

Charlotte waited for him to respond but he didn't.

"The sooner you go back, the easier it will be and the quicker everyone will forget all this craziness."

Matthew still didn't say anything. Didn't make a sound.

"Honey, I'm so sorry about everything we've put you through."

"Mom, can I go now?"

He spoke with much irritation and this saddened Charlotte.

"Matthew, I really want to talk to you."

"I don't feel well."

"Why?"

"Because everything is all messed up."

"I know it seems that way, but things won't always be like this."

Charlotte waited for him to speak, but he fell silent again.

"Is being with David every single weekend really that important to you?"

"It really is, Mom. He's my father."

"Okay, fine. But let me talk to your dad first. And then I'll try to call David."

"You mean it?"

Charlotte wanted to scream the word *no*, but she said, "Yes. If it'll make you happy."

"It will. It really, really will."

Charlotte was glad he was now sounding more chipper, but she couldn't have felt more miserable. Although she couldn't deny what Matthew had just told her. David was his father. She would have done anything she could to change that particular fact, but she knew it wasn't possible.

She knew that she had no choice but to do what Matthew and David wanted, and that her mother had been right when she'd said a court struggle would mainly hurt Matthew. Something she certainly didn't want.

Not under any circumstances.

Chapter 28

What a day this had turned out to be. First Charlotte and Curtis had gone to see Attorney Vellman to see what he thought about their case, but they actually hadn't sat with him for more than a half hour because Curtis had agreed with Charlotte's mother. He, too, felt it might be best to try to settle things with David out of court and on a more personal basis. Attorney Vellman had told them he was all for having them do that, and if they could come to some sort of agreement, he'd work with David's attorney to draw up the paperwork, outlining the details.

However, the downside of what Attorney Vellman had told them was that if for some reason David wasn't willing to cooperate, they were going to be in for a tough fight. Partly because the DNA testing for Curtis and Matthew had been performed six years ago and Charlotte had never told David, partly because her daughter had fallen to her death in their household and she and Curtis were with her when it happened, and partly because there was a chance Matthew might tell a judge and medical experts that he wanted to be with David—thus leaving a judge to believe Matthew wasn't happy in his current household. Attorney Vellman had also made it clear that David's attorney was going to use all of this along with the Tabitha Charles scandal to discredit her as Matthew's mother and Curtis as his stepfather. David's attorney would use everything he could find, but at least the good news was that Attorney Vellman was going to do the same thing when it came to David's personal life. He'd promised them he would dig as deep as he had to if it became necessary.

But now, of all the things that could have possibly happened, they were sitting face-to-face with two of Mitchell's finest. In their family room. In the privacy of their own home. And all Charlotte could think was how happy she was that Matthew had begged to stay with her parents for a few more days.

The six-foot-two-or-more detective flipped over his notepad to a new page. "So can you tell us where you were last night around midnight?"

"Still in New York," Curtis answered. "And we didn't fly home until this morning. You can check our itinerary, which I have in my briefcase, and you can also check with the airline."

"When was the last time you spoke to Ms. Charles?"

"Five nights ago. First, when she mysteriously showed up at the restaurant where my family and I were eating, and then she called very late, saying someone had cut her tires and then broken the glass window in her front door."

"She mentioned that, and according to her, both of you were behind that as well."

"This is ridiculous," Charlotte said, and then regretted it because now the second detective, who was browsing the photos on the fireplace mantel, turned to look at her and the questioning detective stared at her as well.

"So, Mrs. Black, when was the last time *you* spoke to her?"

"Friday afternoon, when she just so happened to show up at Macy's department store at the same time I was there."

"And you were talking to her because . . . ?"

"She started harassing me. And this wasn't the first time we've been in the same place because about a week ago, she showed up at the salon I've gone to for years. She'd never been there before, so what she's doing is stalking us."

"Was there a confrontation? Did she speak to you directly?"

"No," Charlotte lied and already felt as though she was digging a hole for herself.

"Is there a reason you haven't reported any of this, Reverend Black?"

"Yes. Because we didn't want my connection to Ms. Charles to become public knowledge. Of course, now, after this weekend, none of that matters anymore."

"Has she showed up other places?"

"The church. She joined a few Sundays ago, and she ended up at a gas station I was at."

"Did she say anything to you?"

"Yes, she apologized for trying to come on to me and pleaded with me not to stop coming by to see my daughter."

"That was it?"

"Pretty much, and then I left."

"We found a report that was filed by one of our officers, and we see that someone recently threw a rock through one of your windows."

"Yes—" he said, and then Charlotte interrupted him.

"Someone could've gotten hurt. Our son could've been standing right where it happened, so if anything, Tabitha is the one who needs to be questioned."

"Well, in order for that to have happened, you would have had to tell us about her and why you thought she had something to do with it."

Charlotte saw the silent detective glance at her—the one who was no longer looking at the photos and was now standing a few feet away, stretching his neck and looking into various rooms of the house. She didn't like him, and she could tell he was purposely sticking his nose where it didn't belong, trying to make them uneasy. What he should have been doing was worrying about the five o'clock shadow he was wearing, the one that definitely didn't become him.

"Reverend Black," the first detective continued. "Do you also think Ms. Charles was responsible for the rock incident?"

"It's possible, but there's no way to know for sure. We didn't see the vehicle well enough before it sped off."

"Well, getting back to the reason we're here this afternoon. Is it my understanding that neither of you knew anything about what happened last night at Ms. Charles's residence?"

"That's right," Curtis confirmed.

"We knew nothing about it at all," Charlotte added. "Not until we arrived home and saw the midday news."

The detective closed his notepad and slipped his pen down the inside pocket of his blazer. Then he gave Curtis one of his cards. "We'll be going forward with the rest of our investigation, but we may have more questions at a later date. Also, if either of you thinks of anything else, please don't hesitate to give us a call."

"We will," Curtis said.

Charlotte and Curtis escorted both men to the door, and Mr. Five-O'clock-Shadow said with no emotion, "You folks have a real nice evening."

When they were gone, Charlotte and Curtis returned to the family room and Curtis flipped on the television.

"I really don't like the fact that the police were just here," he said.

"Neither do I, and we owe every bit of this to Tabitha. That woman will stop at nothing when it comes to trying to ruin us, and she'll never be over you."

"It's been one thing after another, and all I can hope is that those detectives don't think we were involved in some kind of criminal activity. I've done a lot of things, but destroying people's property is not something I would even consider doing. Not to anyone I can think of."

"I'm not going to worry about it because in the end, everyone will realize that Tabitha is only doing this because you've cut her off. She's telling one lie after another, and eventually all of her lies are going to be exposed."

"That may be true, but it's like you said earlier, when people hear negative claims like the ones Tabitha is making, they'll definitely question whether we're innocent or guilty."

"But not forever. Not once the truth comes out."

Curtis didn't say anything else, so Charlotte said, "I'm going upstairs to change into something more comfortable and when I come back down I'll warm up some dinner. I think Tracy made some sort of potato soufflé and baked some chicken."

"Well, I'm too tired to move, so I'll be here."

As soon as Charlotte went upstairs she closed the bedroom door and called Dooney.

"What's up?" he answered.

"Where are you?" she whispered.

"Just comin' back from gettin' a little somethin'-somethin' to eat."

"Did you see the news today?"

"Yeah, I saw it. And just before I ran out, I saw it again on one of those national cable channels."

"Well, worse than that, two detectives just left here a little while ago."

"Five-O? For what?"

"They were interrogating us. Didn't you hear Tabitha tell that reporter that we were behind what happened?"

"So what? She can't prove one thing."

"I don't care. I think you may have gone a little too far."

"Look, Cuz, it's like I told you before. If you want that trick outta here, it's gonna take a lot more than just playin' a few head games with her."

"I hear what you're saying, but I don't think I can take any more chances. And I don't want you taking any more chances either because they're definitely going to be watching Tabitha's house from now on. Especially since there were two episodes in one week. And hey, why'd you end up going over there last night and not on Monday? Did something happen?"

"She had company. There were lights on in the house and a car was in her driveway until well after midnight, so I figured I should wait."

"You did the right thing. But like I said, we can't take any more chances, so let's just end this while we're ahead."

"So that's it? You just gonna keep lettin' her treat you any way she wants? You just gonna let her go scot-free with no repercussions?"

"For now. But I'll call you if anything changes, and I think it would be best if you leave here as soon as you can get your things together."

"Whatever you say. But if you do call me, you'll have to call Mom's number because I'm ditchin' this c-phone in the river as soon as I get back to the city."

"Good. And, Dooney, hey. Thank you."

He laughed. "You're welcome, but it's not like I really did anything. To be honest, I feel like I robbed you or somethin'."

"You put your freedom on the line for me, and I won't ever forget that."

"It was nothin'."

"You take care of yourself, Cousin. I mean that."

"You, too."

Charlotte set her phone down on the bed, and wondered if she'd done the right thing by sending Dooney back to Chicago. She certainly didn't want either of them getting caught, but what bothered her was the fact that after all that Dooney had done, Tabitha was still there. Living right there in the same city and only a few miles away.

Living far too close to her and Curtis.

Far too close for comfort.

Charlotte and Curtis had just finished eating dinner, and now she was waiting for David to answer his phone. She'd put off calling him for as long as she could, but she and Curtis had agreed she should speak to him tonight.

"Hello?"

"David, this is Charlotte."

"Uh-huh." His tone was definitely not a warm one.

"I've been doing a lot of soul searching, and I really want us to settle this situation regarding Matthew without having to go to court."

"I'm listening."

"I was thinking that maybe we could figure out which weekends he can be with you, which holidays, and then instead of him being with you the entire summer, maybe he could be here with us for at least a couple of those weeks, too. That way we all get to spend quality time with him."

"You know, Charlotte, maybe I didn't make myself clear."

"I don't get what you mean."

"My time with Matthew isn't negotiable. I told you I want every weekend, every holiday, and the entire summer, and I'm not accepting anything less than that."

"Why are you being so unreasonable about this?"

"I'm not. He's my son, and I have every right in the world to see him on a regular basis."

"But what about Curtis and me? What about our relationship with Matthew?"

"That's not my problem. You deliberately kept him from me, and every time I think about that, I get angry all over again."

"I'm sorry, David. But I really thought I was doing the right thing."

"I'm sure you did, and that's why *I* did the right thing this morning."

"Which is what?"

"I drove over to Mitchell and met with my attorney. I decided to find representation there because I want someone who's familiar with the county Matthew lives in and someone who's familiar with that particular court system."

"I can't believe you're really going to hurt Matthew this way."

"How am I going to hurt him, Charlotte, when he's been call-ing me every day, wanting to know if I would come pick him up from his grandparents'?"

Charlotte couldn't remember feeling more defeated, and she didn't know what else she could say.

But David continued, "You have no idea how badly I wanted to, and the only reason I didn't was because I figured it was best to handle all of this in a proper way."

"So you're really taking us to court?"

"Yes. And just so you know, my attorney filed the papers this afternoon and he's requested a speedy hearing date."

"Based on what?"

"Everything. You, your history, and the type of man you've had Matthew calling Daddy all these years. I thought Curtis was a pretty good guy, but now I know differently, and it's time Mat-thew had a more positive male figure in his life."

"No matter what you think, Curtis has been the best father to Matthew, and Matthew means everything to him."

"That's your opinion."

"It's the truth."

"Look, I have to go."

"You are so, so wrong for doing this, David."

"No, actually this is the best decision I've made in a long time. Now you take care."

Charlotte hung up the phone and told Curtis everything David had said.

"It sounds like his mind is completely made up, so what we have to do now is call Attorney Vellman and then go from there," Curtis said. "We'll call him first thing in the morning."

"All of this really scares me, but what I mostly don't under-stand is why Matthew seems to be so taken with a man he just met. He's acting as if he's known David since birth."

"I've thought about that, too, but I guess every son wants a father. Matthew's had me for a long time, and I don't think he loves me any less, but I'm sure he's found a certain amount of pride in getting to know his biological father. Plus, he's only thirteen and the newness of the situation hasn't worn off yet. And it probably won't for a while, not until David has to do more than just have fun with him. Because believe me, the first time he has to punish Matthew or tell him he can't do something he wants to do, I think we'll see a whole change in Matthew's attitude. He'll finally start to see David as a real parent and not just as some new playmate he can have hours and hours of social time with."

"Maybe. But that still doesn't change the fact that by then, David might already have custody."

Curtis drew Charlotte closer to him and placed both his arms around her. "If he does, then, baby, we'll just have to deal with it. We'll deal with it the same as we've dealt with every other obstacle we've had to overcome. And who's to say David is going to win anyway? Especially since you and I are going to pray that God favors us instead."

Charlotte rested her head against Curtis's chest and closed her eyes. She was thankful for the way he was trying to encourage her, and she truly did want to believe in the power of prayer, but still, she had to be realistic about all of this.

The reason: she knew it was going to take an absolute miracle for this to turn out the way she wanted it to.

Chapter 29

A men," Curtis said after finishing his prayer, the one he always prayed in private, just before going into the sanctuary to deliver his sermon. He was ready and admittedly feeling much better today than he had last Sunday, the day he'd had to face his congregation and give them that dreaded confession. And he was glad he had because only a few minutes ago, Elder Jamison had stopped in to say that the church was packed this morning. There wasn't one empty seat on any pew, and they'd even had to line up chairs in the vestibule as well as down one of the aisles, just so they could accommodate everyone in attendance.

This, of course, was a good thing because it meant all of Curtis's members had decided not to leave him. They'd heard the worst of the worst, yet still, they'd decided to stand by him, and he was thankful for it.

Curtis heard a knock at his door and looked up. He was sure it was Elder Jamison and Elder Dixon coming to get him, so without giving any real thought to it, he said, "Come in," and then looked back down toward his desk.

But when he glanced up again, he swallowed a lump in his throat.

It was Tabitha and Curtina.

"What are you doing here?"

"Come on now, Curtis. My daughter's father is the senior pastor of this church, and she and I are members here, remember?"

"Tabitha, you need to go. You need to leave my office now."

"Why? Because I'm willing to bet you don't treat any of your other parishioners this way."

"If you don't leave, I'm calling the police."

"Go right ahead, because I'm not doing anything wrong. All I'm doing is having a nice conversation with the father of my child and the head of the church I belong to."

Curtis picked up the phone.

"Don't even waste your time, because your daughter and I are out of here. We're staying for the service, because I wouldn't have missed today's service for anything, but after that, I'm making sure you don't ever see Curtina again. Oh, and one other thing, I'm contesting that agreement you and your wife forced me to sign, so that I can get my child support increased. You make far too much money to just be paying me fifteen hundred a month and I never should have agreed to that."

Curtis said nothing and Tabitha finally walked out into the hallway.

But now he replayed certain words such as "I wouldn't have missed today's service for anything" and every one of those words made him nervous. They worried him, but at this point, he didn't see how he could do anything about it. He would warn Elder Jamison and Elder Dixon, but outside of that, he would try to prepare himself for whatever was coming.

Janine, Carl, and Tracy were sitting next to Charlotte, in that order, and Charlotte was happy they'd all been able to make it to service this morning. She was glad to have their support and actually, she couldn't get over just how full the church was, not to mention there were quite a few faces in the crowd she didn't recognize. Although the more she thought about it, the more she realized a lot of these "visitors" were probably only here hoping they might be fortunate enough to witness some good old-fashioned drama. They'd seen all the news coverage and since the Tabitha saga was definitely the most interesting news Mitchell residents had ever experienced locally, Charlotte was sure they couldn't get enough of it.

Curtis walked into the pulpit, set down his Bible and notes, and grasped both sides of the podium. But before he could speak, Reverend Tolson walked inside the door at the back of the church and down the center aisle.

Charlotte and Janine frowned in confusion and the rest of the congregation spoke in loud whispers, but that didn't stop Reverend Tolson from stepping up on the platform and removing the cordless microphone from its holder.

Charlotte looked at Curtis and while he looked back at her, he was obviously too shocked to do anything and just stood there. But each of the male elders stood up and gradually moved toward Reverend Tolson.

"I'm not here to cause any trouble," Reverend Tolson said. "I just came here to tell each of you good people that you don't have to put up with all of this deceit. You no longer have to believe all of Pastor Black's lies, and if you'll just give me a chance, I can be the type of pastor you can trust. As a matter of fact, that's exactly the kind of pastor I was to all of you the entire time Pastor Black here was out on the road, living in total sin. He was out there trying to serve two masters, God and Satan, and as far as I'm concerned he slapped all of you right in the face. He doesn't care about any of you and because he founded this church, you can't even get rid of him the way his two Chicago congregations did."

"Okay, that's enough," Elder Jamison said matter-of-factly.

"Either you leave this church or—" Elder Dixon started, but there was an interruption.

Reverend Tolson's wife, Vivian, was headed toward the front of the church with two slightly blackened eyes and two men in blue behind her. She said, "My husband is the one in the dark gray suit with pinstripes. He's the one who beat me this way, and he's also the one who threw a rock through Reverend and Mrs. Black's house window, and here's a copy of the agreement for the car he rented on the night he did it."

There were whispers and gasps and Charlotte was even more stunned than she had been a few minutes earlier.

"Are you John Tolson?" one of the officers asked.

"Yes, I am, but you've got the wrong man. My wife is sick, and she's flat-out lying to you about everything."

"Please place both your hands on your head and slowly face the other direction," the officer instructed.

"For what? I haven't done anything."

"I'll ask you again. Please place your hands on top of your head and slowly turn the other way."

This time, Reverend Tolson did what he'd been asked and the officer pulled one of his arms toward his back, handcuffed his wrist, and then handcuffed the other. At the same time, the other officer read Reverend Tolson his rights.

But when they prepared to escort him out, Vivian said, "Officers, I know you're not required to do this, but if you don't mind, please don't take him until I've had my say."

The first officer nodded and the three of them, both officers and Reverend Tolson, stood where they were. Charlotte and Curtis locked eyes again, and she could tell he was just as curious as she was. Charlotte couldn't imagine what Vivian was about to say but she was glad Matthew wasn't here to hear whatever it was. He'd begged to stay the rest of the week at her parents and then yesterday, he'd pleaded with her to let him spend today with David, and while she hadn't been happy about him doing that, she'd told him he could. He wouldn't be home until this evening.

"First, Pastor and Sister Black, I just want to say how truly sorry I am for all of this. Sister Black, I tried my best to apologize to you that day I saw you at the mall, but I just didn't have the courage to tell you why. I didn't have the courage because for years, John has beaten every ounce of courage completely out of me, but after last night, I decided I wasn't going to take his abuse anymore. I decided that I wasn't going to let him get away with what he was planning to do this morning," she said, and Reverend Tolson charged toward her.

But the officers snatched him back.

"Ever since he did that horrible interview last weekend, he's been threatening to come before the congregation so that he could try to convince all of you here to leave Deliverance Outreach and go with him. He's wanted his own church for years, and his plan was to try to talk all of you into helping him start one. He's even been looking at possible sites and checking rental costs . . . but that's nothing compared to the filthy and sinful personal life he's been leading. You see, while my husband couldn't wait to tell you everything he could about Pastor Black, he had no idea that I've been watching his every move. He's always thought I was too dumb and too naive to pay any real attention to anything he did, but he was wrong. He had no idea that I would ever tell anyone that he's HIV positive. And so am I."

Now people spoke loudly and quickly, including Anise and Aunt Emma, and there was no way to tell who was saying what.

"Please, please," Vivian said. "I promise I'll only take a few more minutes of your time."

When everyone settled down, she continued.

"It's true, and the sad part is that he's been having an affair with you," she said, pointing toward the back of the church. Charlotte turned around to see who Vivian was referring to. "Yes, you, Tabitha. You've been seeing my husband for over three months now, and I've read just about every e-mail and text message you've sent him because John thought I was too stupid and too afraid of him to ever read them, and he never bothered deleting them. But as you can see, he was wrong about that, too."

Charlotte hadn't even known Tabitha was there and now everyone was staring at her in disgust.

"So if I were you," Vivian kept on her monologue, "I would rush to the nearest medical facility I could find to get tested because chances are you're HIV positive, too."

"Oh, my God," a woman sitting next to Tabitha said. "You touched my arm when you first sat down. Oh, Lord have mercy, why did you have to sit next to me?" the woman yelled and hurried out of the pew. Then another woman who was sitting on the other side of Tabitha quickly stood up and stepped out into the aisle. She didn't say anything, but she looked just as terrified as the first woman.

"And then, as much as I hate to tell you this, Pastor and Sister Black, you need to have a nice long talk with your housekeeper because she's the one who's been informing Tabitha of all your whereabouts," Vivian said, looking at Tracy. "She told Tabitha every time either of you had certain appointments or pretty much when you went anywhere and, Sister Black, that's how John was able to send you those anonymous e-mail messages with information about Pastor."

All eyes locked on Tracy, and Charlotte could see Tracy's body shaking nervously. Charlotte stared at her, but when Tracy refused to look her way, Charlotte turned her attention to Curtis, whose face showed great pain. Charlotte didn't want to believe what Vivian had just told them, but it certainly would explain how Tabitha had been able to follow them so closely. Still, though, what Vivian hadn't explained was why Tracy would betray them this way. She'd been with them for years, and Charlotte and Curtis treated her like family, so it didn't make any sense. It was so not like her to do such an evil thing, and Charlotte couldn't help wondering what her excuse was going to be.

"I'm sure by now all of you are wondering why I chose to

do this here when I simply could have gone to Pastor and Sister Black behind closed doors. Well, the reason I didn't is because I wanted my husband to know what it feels like to be exposed publicly, the same as he tried to nationally expose some of Pastor Black's mistakes on television. And, most important, I wanted all of you to hear everything I had to say from my own mouth because it's so easy for people to hear one thing, get it twisted, and then go and repeat something totally different."

"Amen," someone agreed.

"You hang in there, Sister Tolson," another said.

"I will. And I want you to know how much I appreciate the wonderful way you've all treated me the entire time I've been here. You're all good people and no matter what mistakes Pastor Black has made, I hope you'll do what Jesus has done for each and every one of us too many times to count. I hope you'll forgive, forget, and go on with life. I hope you'll continue to love Pastor and Sister Black the same as always. Finally, I just want to ask that you keep me in your prayers because I'll certainly be doing the same for all of you. May God bless you and keep you always."

Vivian passed Curtis the microphone, hugged him, went over and hugged Charlotte, and then hugged a slew of people on her way out. She did this in the midst of much praise, a standing ovation, and applause.

Once Vivian was no longer in sight, the arresting officers escorted Reverend Tolson out of the sanctuary and out of the building.

Then Tabitha gathered up Curtina's carrier and left behind them.

And the congregation applauded again.

Chapter 30

Tracy, why in the world would you do something like this?"
Curtis asked, and he could tell Charlotte, Janine, and Carl
were just as anxious as he was to hear her answer. They were all
gathered in the kitchen, not saying a word.

It was the question of the decade and Curtis was hoping that
somehow, maybe some way, Vivian had made a mistake. He was
hoping that maybe Vivian had somehow gotten Tracy mixed up
with someone else. Hoping the woman he and Charlotte had welcomed into their household, the woman they had trusted with
their children, would never consider betraying them in such a
harsh way.

"Mr. Curtis . . . I'm . . . so . . . sorry . . . Ms. Charlotte . . . I'm . . . ,"
she said and sobbed uncontrollably.

"After all we've done for you," Curtis told her.

"We've always considered you as part of our family," Charlotte
added.

"I . . . know . . . and . . . I'm . . . sorry. But . . . that . . . woman . . .
made . . . me."

"Made you how?" Charlotte wanted to know.

Tracy sniffled multiple times, and Janine passed her a couple
of tissues from her purse. Carl didn't move.

"She was . . . blackmailing me. She was going to . . . turn me in," she said, crying loudly.

"What do you mean?" Curtis asked.

"I'm not supposed to be here. I'm not legal."

Charlotte folded her arms. "Are you saying you're not a citizen here?"

"I'm not. And I'm so sorry for not telling you and Mr. Curtis."

"But why aren't you?"

"I didn't pass the test."

"How many times have you taken it?" Curtis asked.

"Just once."

"When was that? And why didn't you keep trying?" Charlotte said.

Tracy burst into tears all over again. "I don't know, I don't know, I don't know."

Curtis knew he should have been beyond outrage at Tracy, but he felt sorry for her. He wasn't happy about what she'd done, but he couldn't imagine what life must have been like for her, being a single woman and living here as an illegal alien. "Tracy, why didn't you just tell us? Why didn't you just come to Charlotte, me, or anybody for that matter so we could help you?"

"I was ashamed, and I was afraid that if you found out, you would fire me. Ms. Charlotte had already fired me that time I didn't tell her about some things I had seen little Marissa do, so I was scared to say anything. I just hoped and prayed that no one would ever find out."

"But how have you been getting by?" Janine asked. "Because there are so many things in America you can't do if you're not a citizen."

"I have friends who are citizens, and they've helped me a lot."

For the next thirty seconds no one said a word, and then Curtis asked, "So how exactly did Tabitha start contacting you?"

"About a month ago. Somehow she got my phone number, and she called me. She told me that she had a friend that worked for the Immigration and Naturalization Service and that she knew I wasn't legal."

Curtis knew Charlotte was upset with Tracy, but he could also tell that Charlotte was even more incensed by the way Tabitha had used Tracy the way she had.

"She told me that if I didn't call her every day with the information she wanted, she would report me to the authorities. And I did it because I didn't know what else to do."

Curtis rested his hand on Tracy's. "I'm sorry that you even had to become involved in this whole Tabitha matter."

Curtis waited for Charlotte to make her offer of sympathy as well, but instead, she looked away from Curtis and Tracy and went over to the refrigerator and pulled out a bottle of water.

"Janine. Carl. Can I get you anything?"

"I'll take some water, too," Carl said.

Janine shook her head. "No, I'm fine."

"Please, Ms. Charlotte," Tracy said, pleading. "Please let me make this up to you. Let me make this up to you and Mr. Curtis."

"I don't know, Tracy. I just don't know if we can ever trust you again, because you should have come to us right away. You should have come to us as soon as Tabitha contacted you."

Tracy dropped her head with sadness, and Curtis knew she was worried about losing her job. She was worried that they no longer wanted her working for them, that she would definitely be turned in, and that she would ultimately be deported. He felt bad for her and deep down, no matter what Charlotte had just said, he knew Charlotte felt at least somewhat the same way. Charlotte felt deceived, but he knew she cared about Tracy.

"This is all a lot for us to digest," he finally said. "Especially since we have so many other problems going on right now. So if you'll just give us some time, Charlotte and I will talk about this and then make a decision."

"I understand," she said, tears rolling down her cheeks.

"We do love you, Tracy," Charlotte admitted. "But you've really disappointed us. You've really hurt us in a way we weren't expecting."

"Yes. And until the day I die, I'll be sorry for what I've done to you. I'll never forgive myself."

Curtis wanted to believe her and for the most part he did, but, like Charlotte, he wasn't sure they could keep her on. Not with the way she'd so quickly allowed fear to blind her judgment. If only she'd come to them at the very beginning, they could have done something about it. They could have helped her, and they would have known just how far Tabitha was willing to go.

Right after Tracy left, Curtis, Charlotte, Janine, and Carl went out to dinner, and now Curtis and Charlotte were back home. Curtis was trying his best to relax but the more he did, the more he thought about Tabitha and the HIV announcement Vivian had made to the congregation. He worried about Tabitha's well-being, only because she was the mother of his child, and he wanted to call her to see if she had in fact been sleeping with Tolson. He couldn't imagine that Vivian would have lied about any of what she'd said, but still, he was hoping, for his daughter's sake, that Tabitha hadn't contracted such a deadly virus.

"I need to call her," he said to Charlotte.

"Call who?"

"Tabitha."

Charlotte squinted her eyes. "For what?"

"To see if it's true."

"What? Whether she was having an affair with Reverend Tolson? Whether she was sleeping with another woman's husband? Of course she was. She slept with you, didn't she? So what's to keep her from sleeping with every other married man who will have her?"

"I'm worried about Curtina. I mean, I know you can't get HIV just from having someone touch you, but let's just say Tabitha accidentally cut herself and Curtina had some little scratch and the blood accidentally got on her. I know that may never happen, but it is possible. Especially if you don't know you're infected."

Charlotte looked away from him and flipped the page of today's church bulletin.

"Baby, I know you don't want me talking to her, but please. Just this once. Because if she slept with him she needs to get tested right away."

This time Charlotte turned to the back of the bulletin.

"Baby, try to understand what I'm saying. This isn't about Tabitha or me. It's about Curtina."

"Fine."

Curtis pulled out his cell and dialed the number.

"Hello?" she answered.

"Tabitha?"

"Oh God, Curtis," she said, sniffling. "What am I going to do?"

Curtis sighed because he now had the answer to his question. Tabitha had definitely slept with Tolson and there was a chance she'd been infected by him.

"This is bad," he said.

"I didn't know," she screamed hysterically. "I didn't know he had HIV. How could he do this to me?"

Curtis heard Curtina crying in the background and his heart ached for her. He hadn't held her in days, and his separation from her was nothing less than complete torture.

"Tabitha, you've got to try to calm down. I know it's hard, but you're going to have to deal with this, and you're going to have to stay strong for Curtina."

"I don't know if I can. I just don't know how to be strong when I might have . . . oh my God, Curtis . . ." Her voice trailed off and she cried the way most people did when their mother or child had passed away.

When she settled down some, Curtis said, "Is anyone there with you?"

"Yes, a friend of mine. But do you think you could come by? Just for a few minutes?"

"No. I'm sorry," he said and saw Charlotte staring at him.

"I'm sorry for all the problems I've caused," Tabitha said.

"The past is the past, and I hope we can let it stay there. And what you need to do is get tested as soon as possible," he said.

"I am. First thing tomorrow morning."

"You take care, and let me know when you have the results."

"I will. And, Curtis, no matter what you think, I was only with John because I couldn't be with you and because I wanted to get back at you. But I still love you."

"Like I said, let me know when you have the results," Curtis repeated and said good-bye because while he didn't want to keep secrets from Charlotte, he just didn't see where it was worth letting her know that Tabitha was still insisting on how she felt about him.

Which to him was very sad. Sad because her thoughts should have been focused on her possible infection and the hope that she didn't have it. Of course, there was a chance she hadn't contracted anything, but still this was very serious. More serious than Curtis wanted to imagine.

It had been a couple of hours since Curtis had phoned Tabitha, but Charlotte was still sitting there thinking about it. Of course, she didn't like Tabitha, actually couldn't stand her, but she would never wish that horrible virus on anyone. Worse, she would never wish this sort of situation on a child because every child needed and deserved to have a healthy mother.

When the phone rang, Charlotte looked at the screen and hesitated. It was someone calling from the local newspaper, and she wondered what they wanted now. But against her better judgment, she answered.

"Hello?"

"Mrs. Black," a young man said.

"Yes?"

"My name is Byron Hunter, and I was hoping to talk to you about the story we're running tomorrow in the *Mitchell Tribune*."

"Well, if it's about my husband and everything you and the rest of the media have been publishing, then there's nothing else we can add."

"Well, actually, Mrs. Black, part of the story is about what Reverend Tolson's wife announced in church today. You know, about them having HIV and that Ms. Charles may have it, too. But what I'm contacting you about is in regard to the court documents that were filed a few days ago by a man named David Miller who claims to be your son's father and who is now suing for full custody."

Charlotte wondered how much more public embarrassment she and Curtis would actually be able to handle. In his sermons, Curtis regularly quoted the scripture "Weeping may endure for a night, but joy cometh in the morning," but as far as Charlotte was concerned, she didn't see how they'd possibly be able to experience any real joy ever again.

"Mrs. Black, are you still there?"

"Yes."

"Do you have any comments?"

"No. And I'd really appreciate it if all of you, every single one of you at that newspaper, would leave us alone. Now is that too much to ask?"

"Mrs. Black, I'm only trying to do my job."

"Really? Well, that may be true, but for this article, you'll be doing it without me," she said and hung up.

But as soon as she did, it rang again, and this time it was a national tabloid. She wanted to tell them the same thing she'd told Byron, but Curtis had told her to let the call go to voice mail. So she waited and then picked up the phone again to see if they'd left a message. Of course they had.

"Hello, my name is Shelia Tanner, calling from the *Quest*

Weekly, and I'm calling for Reverend or Mrs. Black or both of you, if you'd be willing to speak to me. It's our understanding that Reverend John Tolson infected both his wife and Ms. Tabitha Charles with HIV, that Ms. Charles infected Reverend Black and that Reverend Black infected his wife. We're trying to confirm every piece of information our sources have given us, but we'd also like to hear from you. We'd like to hear your side of the story and what your feelings are in general."

Charlotte heard the woman rattling off her phone numbers and e-mail address, but Charlotte hung up before she'd finished. Petty rumors were now turning into hideous lies, but what worried her most was that these lies might really hurt them in court.

She worried that there really was a chance they could lose Matthew.

Chapter 31

The phone was still ringing nonstop and Charlotte wondered when any of this was ever going to cease. It seemed that every media outlet in the country was now aware of David's custody filing and the HIV scenario, and they were shamelessly trying to get Charlotte and Curtis to comment. But Lisa had advised them against speaking with anyone until she was able to schedule a formal, exclusive interview. She was also preparing another press statement to send out over the wire, so hopefully this would answer most of the media's questions.

But even with the circus of reporters working so hard to contact them, none of that compared to the court papers that had been served to Charlotte this morning. The documents clearly outlined everything David was asking for and the hearing date was less than two weeks away. Charlotte had been hoping she'd have a chance to speak to David when he'd brought Matthew home last night, but once David had waited to make sure Matthew was in the house safely, he'd backed out of the driveway and left. She'd debated whether she should try to reason with him one last time, but she'd decided it probably wasn't going to make any difference. It was also why she'd decided to swallow every ounce of pride she had and was now preparing to call her cousin Anise. She hadn't wanted to, not with the awful terms she and Anise had been on for more than six years, but she didn't see where she had any other choice. There was no choice—no choice except to try and get Anise to talk some sense into David before it was too late.

Charlotte took a deep breath and dialed Anise's number.

She picked up after the third ring. "Hello?"

"Anise?"

"It's about time you called me back."

"What do you mean? I didn't even know you called."

"I've tried you at least five times, both on your home phone and your cell and mostly my calls went straight to voice mail. Actually, I just tried Curtis's cell about an hour ago, but he didn't answer either."

"We've been getting tons of calls all day, so we finally just stopped checking the caller ID altogether. And then Curtis has been on the phone with his publicist and Elder Jamison, so he probably just didn't answer."

"Well, I was calling because I received a phone call from David's mother this morning, and she wants to talk to you."

"About what?"

"David. And while she told me a few of the details, I think it will be best if you speak to her directly."

"Anise, why can't you just tell me?"

"Look, if you want the number, then I'll give it to you."

"My God, girl, what is it going to take for you to stop being so hateful toward me? Yes, I made a mistake, but I've apologized how many times?"

"The only reason I'm calling you is because I care about Matthew, and I would never allow anyone to hurt him. So do you want the number or not?"

Charlotte couldn't imagine what David's mother could possibly need to speak to her about, but figured it couldn't hurt anything. "What is it?"

Anise recited the number and Charlotte wrote it down.

"Before you go," Charlotte said, "do you have a few more minutes? Because I was calling to ask you a favor."

"What is it?"

"I need you to talk to David about this custody case he just started. Because even though he won't listen to me, maybe you can get him to see how damaging all of this is going to be for Matthew."

"Look, why don't you just call David's mother. Okay?"

"You know what, Anise? Just forget it."

Charlotte hung up and tried calming her nerves. She'd been hoping Anise might be mature enough to put aside their differences, even if only for Matthew's sake, however, she could tell it wasn't going to happen.

Although the one thing Charlotte had to admit was that if Anise had put forth the effort to call her at all, she really did think it was important for her to speak to David's mother. So she went down to the family room and told Curtis about it.

"That's strange," he said. "But if she wants you to call her then it must be for a good reason."

"Maybe, but if she's going to try to defend her son, then I don't wanna hear it. I don't wanna hear anything about David and how he has rights when it comes to Matthew."

"I still think you should call."

"I guess," she said, picking up the phone.

When she'd finished dialing, she walked over to the window.

"Hello?" the woman answered

"Mrs. Miller."

"Yes."

"This is Charlotte Black, Anise's cousin."

"Yes. How are you?"

"I'm well. And you?"

"Fine."

"You wanted to speak to me?"

"Yes. I'm sure you're a little shocked about that, but after seeing all the news coverage about David filing for custody of his son, my husband and I decided we needed to get in touch with you right away."

"Is there some sort of problem?"

"Well, the thing is, Charlotte, David has known for years that he can't have children, but he's always been in denial."

"I don't understand."

"He was injured as a small boy, and the doctor told us back then that his chances of having a child were next to none. But he's always wanted children and refused to believe any medical opinions."

"Did Anise know that?"

"No. Not until I called her this morning. I always wanted to tell her, especially when they were married, but I knew my son would hate me for it and that he would feel it wasn't my business."

"What I remember is him being angry at Anise because she didn't want children."

"Yes, because he always believed that if she had stopped taking birth control pills, they could have had as many children as he wanted. Then, of course, they split up and he remarried. But eventually, he divorced his second wife, too. David doesn't have much to do with his father and me, but his second wife told me that after they'd tried for more than a year to get pregnant and nothing happened, he blamed her for everything. He told her it was all her fault, and the next thing she knew, he was serving her with divorce papers."

"I had no idea."

"But worse than that, there's another reason David wants a child so badly."

"Which is?"

"My father passed about five years ago, but before he died, he and my mother revised their will. So when my mother passed last year, David learned that they'd left him a sizable trust fund. But until now he's only had access to twenty-five percent of it. And the only way he can get another twenty-five percent is if he has children. And then the other fifty percent is to be divided among David's children in two installments. When they turn eighteen and then again when they either graduate from a four-year college or turn twenty-five, whichever comes first. My parents were never happy about the way David treated my husband and me, so they decided they would leave half of what they would have given to David to their future great-grandchildren. Which is why having custody of a child would at least allow him to get the other part he has coming to him immediately, and we're talking easily another one hundred fifty thousand dollars."

Charlotte heard what Mrs. Miller was saying but none of it made any sense. She had no problem believing that there was a trust fund and that David was looking to cash in on it, but what she didn't believe was that David couldn't have children. Because regardless of what his mother thought, Charlotte knew for sure that David was Matthew's father because they had proof that Curtis wasn't. The DNA test Curtis had taken had confirmed everything and Charlotte certainly hadn't slept with anyone else around the time Matthew had been conceived.

"This is a lot," Charlotte finally said, but didn't bother telling her what she was thinking.

"I'm sure it is. And while I hate having to go behind my son's back, telling you all of this, I couldn't just sit back and let him claim a child that might not be his. I wanted to let you know so that you can, at the very least, have a paternity test done. It may turn out that David is the father, but I figured you'd want to find out for sure."

"I appreciate your concern."

"I'm sorry for any problems this may cause, but, as I said, my husband and I felt an obligation to tell you."

"Thank you again."

"You take care now."

Charlotte turned toward Curtis.

"So what did she say?"

"You won't even believe it. She said that David can't have

children and that he wants custody because of some trust fund stipulation."

"Can't have children?"

"That's what she said."

"But how can that be?"

"I don't know."

Curtis frowned. "So what his mother is saying is that she doesn't think David is Matthew's father?"

"No. She doesn't."

"Then if he's not, who is?"

"He has to be because you were already tested."

"Exactly. So if I'm not and David might not be, then I ask you again, who is?"

"Wait a minute, Curtis. What are you trying to say?"

"I don't know. You tell me."

"Tell you what?"

"Well, if I'm not Matthew's father and let's just say David isn't either, then it has to be someone else."

"What?!"

"I'm just trying to figure this all out."

"I was only with you and David, Curtis. Period."

Charlotte spoke confidently, but she also thought back as far as she could, trying to remember if maybe she had slept with someone else, even if only for one night. But she couldn't. She had no recollection of sleeping with any other man during that time and she resented what Curtis was trying to insinuate.

"You can think whatever you want," she said. "Because regardless of what David's mother or anyone else has to say, David has to be Matthew's father. I wish he wasn't, but he is."

"I hope you're right."

"I am," Charlotte said.

She hoped she was telling the truth.

Epilogue

ONE YEAR LATER

Charlotte beamed with great joy as she watched Curtis and Matthew, smiling and posing for the photo she was about to take of them, something Curtis seemed to ask her to do a lot as of late. Something he'd been asking her to do on a regular basis, ever since he'd learned that Matthew was his child. His biological son.

It had come as a shock to all of them, but after David's mother had called with such astonishing news, Charlotte had done what Mrs. Miller had suggested. She and Curtis had gone to court on the day of the hearing and Charlotte had asked Attorney Vellman to request that a paternity test be taken—which hadn't been a problem since the judge had been quick to say that if he'd been David, he would have already insisted on that anyway. Especially after being told about a child thirteen years after the fact. Of course, David had become outraged, but the case had been continued and as it had turned out, there was no way David could have been Matthew's father. The normal DNA testing had been administered, but what they'd also learned was that David had the rarest blood type of all, AB negative, and Matthew was O positive. Meaning any offspring of David's would have had to fall into the A or B category and there was no possible way he could have an O child.

But still, as far as David had been concerned, those results had meant nothing, and it was only after two other tries with two other facilities and hearing the same outcome that he'd finally given up the fight. It was only after this that he'd relented and accepted the fact that Matthew wasn't his son. Although, for a while, this particular truth had caused major issues between Charlotte and Curtis because Curtis had been sure Charlotte had slept with another man and was refusing to admit it. But Charlotte had promised him she hadn't and had eventually convinced him to be tested again. Curtis had thought it was a total waste of time but when she'd printed out an article about a well-known, celebrity hairstylist by the name of Andre Chreky and how it had taken a two-year legal battle and hundreds of thousands of dollars to prove he wasn't the father of a certain child, Curtis began to listen. Andre had been wrongly accused and the reason it had taken him such a long time to prove he wasn't the father was that one of the largest paternity labs in the country had made an error and no one had wanted to believe this could happen.

But it had. And it was the reason Curtis had decided that maybe it was worth being retested and why the DNA lab in question was currently under state investigation. It was the reason Charlotte and Curtis could now say they had a child together, one that truly belonged to both of them, genetically.

Best of all, Matthew had finally forgotten about David, the man he'd known as his father for a short while, had become fascinated with, and had wanted to see on a regular basis. As soon as he'd discovered Curtis was his natural father, however, he'd apologized to Curtis many times over, and now he and Curtis were closer than they had been originally. They were together all the time and neither of them seemed to want to do much of anything without the other. It was almost as if their being together gave them both a certain sense of security. They had always thought the world of each other but now they seemed to treasure their father-son relationship even more and Charlotte couldn't be happier.

"Now, Mom, you take one with Curtina," Matthew said, stepping across the family room and reaching for the digital camera."

"Come on, sweetie," Charlotte said, and Curtina ran over to her.

Charlotte picked her up and Matthew positioned the camera in front of his face. "Smile, Curtina."

When she did, he pressed the button and then looked at the screen. "That was a good one. Now, Mom, you take one of Dad, Curtina, and me."

"Okay," she said, and Matthew passed the camera to her.

"Smile," she said, and this time Curtina giggled loudly and they all laughed with her.

"Come on, Curtina," Matthew said. "Let's you and me go get some ice cream."

"Yeaaahhh."

"I don't think there's any in there," Charlotte told him.

"Yes, there is. Justine bought two gallons of it yesterday," he said, referring to the new housekeeper.

When they left the room, Curtis looked at Charlotte and said, "Thank you."

"For what?"

"For accepting my little girl. Because I know it was the hardest thing you've ever had to do."

"Sometimes it's still hard, but when Matthew told me how wrong I was for not allowing you or him to see her, it was a wake-up call. I felt so ashamed when he reminded me that you could have treated him the same way when you thought he was David's son, so how could I be so mean when it came to Curtina."

"This has been a rough couple of years for all of us, and I'm just glad we're still together."

"So am I. But I'll be honest with you, Curtis. I still can't promise you that I'll ever be able to be a mother to Curtina. I mean, I'm sorry that she might lose her real mother one day, and that you feel it would be your responsibility to take her in, but I just don't know if I could ever commit to having her here on a full-time basis."

Curtis didn't say anything and Charlotte knew it was because he was worried about Curtina's future. He worried because Tabitha had indeed contracted HIV from Reverend Tolson, and she was already having to take medication for it. There was no guarantee that she would get full-blown AIDS, because nowadays so many people were able to live normal lives, but Charlotte knew Tabitha had reason to be concerned. Especially since they'd learned from Vivian that she, too, was having to take medication and that Reverend Tolson was dying. All of which Curtis had told Tabitha about. Of course, Vivian was no longer married to Reverend Tolson and hadn't spoken to him directly, but she'd heard from her ex–in-laws that he'd now been given only a few months to live.

"I'm sorry," Charlotte continued and walked over to the row of windows facing the backyard. "I just don't know."

Curtis walked up behind her and wrapped his arms around her waist. "I understand. I know it would be a huge step to have to take, and we'll worry about that only if it becomes necessary."

"It's not because I don't love you or because I don't care about Curtina, because I do, but I still have such angry feelings toward Tabitha. And as much as I hate to say this, whenever I see Curtina, it makes me think about the affair you had with her mother."

"I'm sure it does, but maybe it'll get better with time. Especially since Tabitha now realizes that you're the only woman for me and that I have no interest in being with her."

"I hope that's true, and I will say that I'm glad she's finally stopped harassing us."

Curtis squeezed Charlotte tightly and rested the side of his face against hers. "I love you so much."

"I love you, too. I'll love you for the rest of my life."

"And I'll love you for the rest of mine," he said, and Charlotte knew he meant every word. She knew, for the first time since they'd gotten married, that only death would separate them.

And she couldn't remember ever feeling more sure about anything.